"Not  friend I had no intention of seducing you," Alex said with just the hint of a smile.

The noise she made was part gasp, part choke, and he hoped she wouldn't bolt and flee. He'd taken the precaution of standing between her and the door, but there was little else he could do if she chose to leave.

But instead she looked up at him, her eyes glittering with mischief. "Tell me, Alex, do all Englishmen provide such assurances before going out with a woman for the first time?" It was all he could do not to lean down and kiss her right then.

He didn't, though. "I don't know about other men, but I've never said anything like that before." He stroked the hair lying across her shoulder. "What I said was it would be a seduction only if I corrupted you into doing something you didn't want to do."

She laughed with him for a moment, then felt her heart race as his expression grew more serious. Cupping her chin in his hand, he murmured, very close to her lips, "I won't seduce you, Jacqueline. Anything we do, we do together. . . ."

WHAT ARE *LOVESWEPT* ROMANCES?

They are stories of true romance and touching emotion. We believe those two very important ingredients are constants in our highly sensual and very believable stories in the LOVE-SWEPT line. Our goal is to give you, the reader, stories of consistently high quality that may sometimes make you laugh, sometimes make you cry, but are always fresh and creative and contain many delightful surprises within their pages.

Most romance fans read an enormous number of books. Those they truly love, they keep. Others may be traded with friends and soon forgotten. We hope that each LOVESWEPT romance will be a treasure—a "keeper." We will always try to publish

LOVE STORIES YOU'LL NEVER FORGET
BY AUTHORS YOU'LL ALWAYS REMEMBER

The Editors

Loveswept ® 729

STALKING THE GIANT

VICTORIA LEIGH

BANTAM BOOKS
NEW YORK · TORONTO · LONDON · SYDNEY · AUCKLAND

STALKING THE GIANT

A Bantam Book / February 1995

If you would be interested in receiving protective vinyl covers for your
Loveswept books, please write to this address for information:

> Loveswept
> Bantam Books
> P.O. Box 985
> Hicksville, NY 11802

> ISBN 0-553-44449-2

Published simultaneously in the United States and Canada

Bantam Books are published by Bantam Books, a division of Bantam Dou-
bleday Dell Publishing Group, Inc. Its trademark, consisting of the words
"Bantam Books" and the portrayal of a rooster, is Registered in U.S. Patent
and Trademark Office and in other countries. Marca Registrada. Bantam
Books, 1540 Broadway, New York, New York 10036.

PRINTED IN THE UNITED STATES OF AMERICA

OPM   0 9 8 7 6 5 4 3 2 1

AUTHOR'S NOTE

Into the life of every author there comes a challenge that can't be ignored. In my case it was more of a dare.

Imagine, if you will, a small group of friends gathered around the dining room table. Postdinner conversation ranges from who gets the last crumbs of the chocolate soufflé cake to the call from my editor that afternoon. Among other things she'd asked if I was interested in writing a Treasured Tale for Loveswept, and if so, what?

The suggestions from my guests verged on the absurd —I'd been prepared for that—but when "Jack and the Beanstalk" was mentioned, I was appalled. Wasn't that the story where Jack got ripped off in a cow-for-beans trade? Didn't he climb the beanstalk to steal gold and assorted treasures from the giant? Doesn't the giant have this penchant for eating little boys—whom, by the way, he can smell a mile off? And, in the end, wasn't there something about Jack and his mom chopping down the beanstalk and killing the giant so they could live happily ever after on his riches?

Where, I asked, was the romance in any of that?

My guests shrugged and pointed out that I was the

writer. "You figure it out," they dared, then went back to fighting over the crumbs as I picked up the telephone and boldly dialed my editor. "Jack and the Beanstalk," I told her, had definite romantic possibilities.

I hope you think so too.

Victoria Leigh

PROLOGUE

"You can't sell that, Jack. Grandma gave it to you."

"It's a piece of junk, Mom," Jacqueline Sommers said, one arm hooked through a rung in the ladder as she reached for the eighteenth-century porcelain cow that grazed on the top shelf of the built-in bookcase. "Even Grandma said so."

"But it's an antique, darling, a family heirloom."

Jack's fingers closed around the cow in question. "*Old* junk, then." She headed down the ladder, her feet passing where her mother gripped the metal rail. Only when Jack was safely on the ground again did Eleanor Sommers loosen her hold and step back. Leaning back against the ladder, Jack raised the porcelain figurine to eye level.

Her mother smoothed an imaginary wrinkle from her close-fitting wool jacket and narrowed her gaze on the black-and-white object. "I don't think I've ever looked at it up close before." Laughter was in her eyes as she met Jack's gaze. "It's really quite ugly, isn't it?"

Jack nodded, a delighted grin splitting her lips as waves of black hair drifted across her shoulders with the movement of her head. "Ugly, but not entirely useless.

According to the appraiser who went through Grandma's things before she died, I should be able to get five hundred dollars for it."

Eleanor looked doubtful. "Even so, Jack, I can't think what's got into you. You're always the one who won't let me throw away things because of their sentimental value."

"I need the cash to buy that stock Tony told me about. This"—she waggled the cow in her fist—"will get an owner who appreciates it, and I'll get rid of a dust collector." She blew on it, raising a layer of dust that had the older woman fanning the air in front of her face.

"But, darling, that cow was given to your grandmother by Seymour Jenkins. He played an important part in her life."

Jack threw back her head and hooted. "The only thing noteworthy about Seymour Jenkins is that Grandma had the good taste *not* to marry him." She bent over to brush at a slash of dirt on her jeans, which had been clean before the tussle she'd had getting the ladder up from the basement storage room. The smudge stayed where it was, and Jack resignedly wiped her palm on her thigh-length sweater, which had been through the same treatment.

"But if Seymour hadn't pestered her so much, she wouldn't have run away to New York, where she met Adrian Sommers, and then where would we all be?" Eleanor took the cow out of Jack's hand and perched on the edge of the huge leather sofa that dominated the loft's living space. "We should be grateful Seymour was such a . . ." She looked up at Jack as though unsure how to finish that thought.

"Slug?" Jack supplied, her blue eyes twinkling below the fringe of bangs.

"Precisely." Eleanor smiled, absently caressing the cow's smooth flanks. "Which is why I wouldn't think you'd want to sell this. Think of what memories it holds."

"The prayer rug holds all the memories I need of Grandma," Jack said, glancing at the jewel-toned carpet that she'd nailed to the wall above the fireplace. "When I look at it, I remember when I was a little girl. I'd sit on it in front of Grandma's fireplace and pretend it was a magic carpet come to fly me away to an adventure in a far-off land." The familiar warmth of those memories brought a smile to her lips. "There were times when Grandma would pretend with me. She'd sit on the floor with her arms around me, and we'd zoom over pyramids and oceans together. She had a fabulous imagination."

"You'd come home from seeing her so full of dreams and fantasies that I worried you'd ever get a firm grip on reality." Eleanor cocked her head curiously. "I've always been surprised you don't travel or do something really exciting with your vacations. As pretty as northern California is, it's not the pyramids."

"No, it isn't," Jack agreed, shutting her eyes for a moment to savor that last wisp of memory. The wild fantasies of her childhood had evolved over the years into gentle daydreams, the pyramids scoring less mileage than visions of a life that was almost inexplicably different from the one she was living. The disparities between fantasy and reality were best described, she'd decided one day, as snatches of pure joy, whereas now she settled for simple happiness.

The gap between the two filled her with a disquiet that grew stronger every year, frustrating Jack because she didn't know how to breach it. She couldn't even talk about it, lest it sound as though she was dissatisfied with a life that was, for all intents and purposes, exactly what she'd chosen for herself. Hers was a good life, she reminded herself. Living in northern California among family and friends, she had a job she enjoyed and enough surprises to keep things interesting. Still, there was something missing. . . .

Her eyes flew open as the familiar frustration welled inside, but with the ease of many years' practice, Jack ignored it and gave her mother a look that was meant to show how little the pyramids counted in the scheme of things. "When I'm ready to travel and have adventures, I'll do it. For now I'm trying to be sensible and build a secure life for myself."

"You're twenty-six, not fifty-six," Eleanor said. "Besides, taking risks on the stock market doesn't sound sensible to me."

Jack threw herself sideways onto one of the overstuffed chairs that were scattered throughout the room and turned her face to her mother. "That's why I'm going to sell the cow. Risking my savings is out of the question, but Tony is absolutely convinced this stock in Legume Limited will win big-time." Pillowing her head in her arms, she swung her legs over the arm of the chair. "If he's right and I don't buy in, he'll never let me forget about it."

"Your brother doesn't let anyone forget lost chances," Eleanor said wryly. "I'm still hearing about the biotech stock that quadrupled the week after he tried to get us to buy it."

Jack grinned. "Thank goodness he's had his share of losers. Otherwise he'd be unbearable."

Eleanor leaned forward to set the cow carefully on the coffee table. "If Tony's right this time and you make a little bit, I suppose you'll do something sensible with the profits?"

"Don't count your eggs before they hatch. That's my motto. I'll worry about what I'll do with the money if and when the stock pays."

Eleanor sighed, lifting a hand to smooth her hair,

which matched Jack's in color if not in length. With not a single gray hair to mar the sheen, she wore it short and styled carefully to frame a face that was smooth and nearly unlined, leaving one to guess her age from hints of character rather than any obvious wear and tear. Her gaze swept across the room to the prayer rug, then back to her daughter. "You should do something exciting with it, something you wouldn't do otherwise. I think Grandma would be very disappointed if you didn't."

Jack laughed. "I get enough excitement at work, Mom. Anyone who spends most of their waking hours riding herd on hormone-crazed teenagers doesn't need any extracurricular thrills. Did I tell you about the kid who swallowed his clarinet reed on a bet, then changed his mind before it got all the way down? I thought he'd never cough that thing back up, but all of a sudden—"

"Don't be disgusting, Jack," Eleanor interrupted with a grimace of distaste.

Unchastened, Jack slouched deeper into the cushions. "If it really bothers you, I won't sell the cow. But you'll have to explain to Tony why I'm not investing in that stock. After two days on the road chaperoning the band, I don't have the energy to fend him off."

"I'm sure your father will lend you the money—"

"I won't borrow from Dad," Jack cut in. "Not for an investment that might not pay out."

"You've always been a stubborn child." Eleanor got to her feet and walked to the kitchen counter, where she'd left her things.

Jack let her get as far as pulling on her gloves before speaking. "If you won't let me sell the cow, you'll have to take it home and dust it yourself. I don't want it."

Her mother stood quite still, a horrified look on her face as her gaze slid between her daughter and the cow.

"Don't be silly, Jacqueline. I wouldn't have that thing in my house if it was the only heirloom left of the batch."

And that was the end of the eighteenth-century porcelain cow, an unrevered heirloom sacrificed on the altar of chance.

Jack wasn't unduly upset the following week when Tony's surefire tip fizzled and took a nose dive into the deep end. She chalked up the cow as good riddance and the stock-market adventure as experience and went on with her life much as before.

The stock, not quite worth the imitation parchment it was recorded on, sat quietly in a drawer, drawing no attention to itself, until one day nearly two years later when, quietly, it began to grow. . . .

ONE

Her scent was light and elusive, rainbows and lilacs, filtering into his awareness with the delicacy of a summer's rain. Alex looked up from the race card and glanced around him, the fragrance quickly becoming a memory as he studied the shifting crowd.

Where was she?

Beneath a timid English sun race-goers both familiar and unknown to him drifted past, their attention on the horses circling the parade ring. Realizing his eyes were useless when he didn't have a clue what the woman looked like, he shut them and inhaled deeply, but the ordinary smells of horses and turf were all that registered.

It was gone now, the scent. As was the woman. There was no doubt in his mind that she'd been very near, passing within inches of where he stood. He knew the source of the fragrance was a woman, just as he knew she would be as subtle and fascinating as the perfume she wore.

Folding his race card, Alex slipped it into his pocket and headed toward the bar, where he'd arranged to meet some friends.

The scent was gone, but the memory lingered.

He'd know her if they chanced to cross paths again.

＊＊＊＊＊＊＊＊＊＊＊＊＊＊＊

Jack finished her reconnaissance of the racecourse's public areas, then watched the afternoon's first race from the stands before heading back to meet up with her old college friend, Hillary Goodwyn, in the saddling enclosure. Eight horses in various stages of preparation were there, and her gaze flitted from group to group until she found the one surrounding Golden Legs.

Hillary saw her at the same moment and signaled to Jack to join them. Jack crossed to the far side of the enclosure and watched with excitement as the number cloth and saddle were lifted in turn onto the horse's sleek back. Tucking her hands into the pockets of the tweed jacket she'd bought three days earlier in Stratford-on-Avon, she tried to keep her enthusiasm under a modicum of control.

It couldn't be done.

"I was looking at the map earlier," she said to Hillary without taking her eyes from the prerace tableau unfolding step by ritualistic step.

"So what else is new?" Hillary slid her gaze from where her husband, Bobby, was checking the horse's saddle to Jack's animated face. "You've looked at the map of England more in the past week than I have in the seven years I've lived here."

Jack ignored the friendly jibe and said, "Stonehenge is on our way home. Think we'll have time to stop?"

"It's at least thirty miles out of our way," Hillary said. When Jack didn't comment, she added, "You keep forgetting that those harmless-looking little lines on the map are narrow, twisting roads, which quadruple your travel time and leave you frazzled when it's done. This isn't like the States where sixty miles means sixty minutes."

"Does that mean no?" Jack asked, inserting a

wounded note into her tone in hopes Hillary would relent.

She didn't. "There will always be an England, Jack. And if not always, I think we can count on it lasting the few weeks of your vacation. I'll take you to Stonehenge another day."

"If you'd let me drive, you wouldn't have to traipse around with me," Jack grumbled.

"I *did* let you drive, remember?" Hillary shuddered and turned back to the horse. "The experience took ten years off my life, which I suppose is better than what can be said for that pheasant."

"I didn't hit it," Jack protested.

"No, but you probably scared it to death." Hillary ran her fingers through her short, curly hair and shuddered again. "What with the squeal of brakes and the way you were swerving all over the road, I'd be surprised if it didn't drop dead of a heart attack behind the hedgerow."

"I was trying not to hit it," Jack said. "You said it was illegal—"

Hillary groaned. "I *said* it was illegal to hit a pheasant with a vehicle, then pick it up and take it home."

"But what about the next guy who comes along? Can he pick it up?"

"Of course. He didn't hit it."

Jack grinned. "I love English law."

"You shouldn't. They have a traffic ticket specifically for, and I quote, 'driving very, very badly.'" Hillary grinned back at her. "I think they lock you in the Tower for that one."

"They have to catch me first," Jack said, falling into step beside Hillary as the horse cum entourage moved from saddling enclosure to parade ring. She took care to stay well behind the elegant four-legged creature, who looked more ready for a nap than a race. In contrast to the horse, Jack fairly sizzled with excitement, her eyes wide and bright and missing nothing of what was happening around her.

England might very well be there forever, but her vacation wouldn't. She had to make every second count.

"I'm going over to check out the bookies," Jack said. "I've got five pounds burning a hole in my pocket. Want to come?"

Hillary shook her head. "I promised Laura Beckett, the jockey's wife, that I'd hold her hand during the race. She still gets the jitters every time she thinks about how Sam came off last week at Cheltenham."

"I thought you told me jockeys never fall off."

"You're right, they don't," Hillary agreed with a laugh. "The horse falls, and the jockey just follows it down. Laura merely wants company in case Golden Legs takes Sam closer to the turf than necessary."

"Is that likely to happen?" Jack asked, reflecting on the five pounds and if perhaps she should rethink the investment.

"You mean, will Golden Legs fall? I doubt it." Hillary looked across the grass to where the horse under discussion was drifting into place in the parade ring. "On the other hand, loyalty prevents me from making a more positive endorsement of the horse's overall chances."

Jack thought the horse was more likely to rock Beckett to sleep long before the race was over, but she restrained herself from saying as much. Telling Hillary she'd meet up with her later, she veered off from the parade ring and headed to the rails, where the bookies set up shop.

There was nothing in the rule book that said she had to put the entire five pounds on one horse, Jack mused.

There was also nothing that said she had to bet on a horse that looked ready for a good, long sleep.

❧————————❧

"Golden Legs always looks like that before a race," Bobby said to Alex Hastings without taking his eyes off the horse, which was slogging around the parade ring. "If you'll remember, he looked worse before the Marigold Cup in October and still came in five lengths ahead of the favorite."

"He looked the same for his last two races and didn't even show," Alex said, turning slightly to keep his horse in sight.

"A seven-year-old with his record should be nearing his prime, not past it." Bobby, Golden Legs' trainer, sighed and shook his head. "I'm hoping six weeks without a race will have made a difference."

"If he loses again, I'll have to consider selling," Alex said, and knew it was only because Bobby had come to know him well that he didn't look surprised. Upset, perhaps, but not surprised. "Every lost race decreases his eventual value at stud, and there's no sense in racing him if he's not going to win."

"He might just be in a slump," Bobby argued. "I'd hate to see you part with a good animal prematurely."

"He's been a good investment until recently. I'd have to be greedy or stupid to hold on to him through a downslide you can't guarantee won't stop."

"If I knew what was wrong with him, I could fix it. That's the only guarantee I can give you."

"I never thought otherwise," Alex said calmly, not allowing Bobby's distress to sway the necessity for a cold, rational decision. "I bought Golden Legs because he showed enormous promise as a three-year-old. Any profits I've made will evaporate if he continues to lose. This race will likely decide things for me one way or the other." Alex slid his gaze from the less than euphoric chestnut to the lanky blond trainer who stood next to him on the grassy part of the ring. Bobby Goodwyn's reputation as a jump-race trainer had grown considerably over the past several years, with Golden Legs sending Bobby's star even higher. Alex had sent his horse to Bobby partly because of that reputation and partly because Goodwyn's stables were near enough to his estate that Alex could easily keep tabs on the expensive piece of horseflesh.

It was his custom to maintain a close watch on all of his investments. Golden Legs was no different from a block of flats, or a shopping complex, or any other project Alex became involved in. No different, except that the horse was his only investment that ate carrots.

And, like any other investment, Golden Legs was of value only as long as the ratio of earnings to investment continued to be favorable.

Sam Beckett, the jockey who rode most of Bobby's horses, joined them in the parade ring, and Alex listened as Bobby gave the young man his riding instructions. After a few moments they all walked over to where the head traveling lad stood with Golden Legs. Sam stood at Golden Legs' head for a pep talk, which consisted of Sam telling the horse he would appreciate winning because the money was better that way, and besides, it was a lot of fun. Golden Legs nuzzled Sam's ear, then snorted and shook his head as though disagreeing.

Alex didn't think much of Golden Legs' level of enthusiasm.

The signal was given for the jockeys to mount, and Bobby gave him a leg-up into the saddle. Beckett, Champion Jockey a few seasons past and still in the top ten, saluted Alex and Bobby with his riding crop, grinned confidently, and patted Golden Legs on the neck as they moved away toward the track. Brightly patterned shirts and hats bobbled off in an uneven line, Alex's colors of purple-and-yellow checks trailing pink-and-white stripes.

"After the last race when the Stewards hauled us up for an enquiry," Bobby said, "I've thought and done everything I know how to do to get Golden Legs back up to snuff."

The Stewards—horse racing's trustees of fair and honest play—had, quite naturally, seen the change from winning to a streak of losses as abnormal and had acted on it by calling in trainer and jockey. Both men had been cleared, but the formality of the enquiry had impressed on everyone the need to discover a reason for Golden Legs' abrupt change in status.

Alex knew Bobby's efforts had been almost superhuman. Everything from Golden Legs' diet to his daily routine had been scrutinized and compared to when the horse was winning. The lad who took care of him was put under the same microscope, and even the box where the horse was customarily kept had been gone over with a fine-tooth comb.

Nothing had changed, and nothing gave any hint as to the horse's behavior.

Alex said, "I know the Stewards grilled Beckett pretty thoroughly, but have you given any thought . . ."

Bobby bristled at the suggestion of any deliberate wrongdoing by the jockey, but his answer showed he'd not left even that stone unturned. "Putting aside the fact he only has a chance at making Champion Jockey again by riding winners, I still talked with him. As far as I can tell, he's as honest now as he always was. In his entire career Sam's never been accused of holding a horse back."

"Then that's that. We'll just have to leave it up to Golden Legs." Alex turned to Bobby and said, "If you'll excuse me, I'll watch the race from the stands. There's someone I need to speak to."

"I'll meet you afterward," he agreed, then added, "and don't forget you're coming for drinks tonight. Hillary made me promise I'd remind you."

Alex kept his reservations about the invitation to himself and said he'd be there. As he walked across the grass toward the stands where he'd seen Charles Stevens in the company of a woman he hadn't expected to meet at the races, he wished he'd known Bobby's American wife had a houseguest before accepting the invitation in the first place. Although Bobby himself hadn't said anything about the young woman staying with them, Alex had learned from his own housekeeper that she was Hillary's roommate from college, single and pretty.

In other words, available. Alex wouldn't have minded except Hillary wasn't yet thirty years old, so any roommate would likely be as young. He hoped Hillary wouldn't be too disappointed when he left their place without making any plans to see her guest again.

He preferred his women older, closer to his own forty years. They tended to have fewer illusions by that age, and certainly no expectations beyond a pleasant, no-strings affair.

From the gate leading to the stands he scanned the crowd. Alex stood taller than most men, and his height made the job easy. He spotted Charles and the svelte brunette walking toward the stairs that led to the private boxes. Checking over his shoulder that the horses down on the track were still a fair distance from the starting line, he went to intercept the couple.

Before he reached them, Charles glanced his way and smiled in recognition. Leaving the woman at the bottom of the stairs, he came to meet Alex. They shook hands, Charles's blue eyes twinkling in a slightly rounded face that exuded charm and unfailing geniality. "I saw you earlier, but thought I'd wait to catch you when you came out of the winner's circle."

"Golden Legs will more likely go to sleep before the tapes go up, if his behavior in the parade ring is anything to go by," Alex said.

Charles grinned. "Racehorse owners are supposed to be in it for the thrills, not profit and loss."

"I should have sold him to you last year when you were on your knees, begging me for him." Last year Golden Legs had been a solid-gold investment Alex wouldn't have dreamed of parting with, on top of which there was nothing in the horse's heredity or form that could have predicted his fall from glory. Timing, Alex reminded himself ruefully, was everything.

"You would have missed winning the Marigold Cup."

"Training fees and such have taken care of the purse from that race," Alex returned, "and these last three losses haven't done his overall value any good."

The brunette sauntered over then, and conversation skidded to a halt as she slid her hand into the crook of Charles's arm, her red lacquered nails splayed artistically against the soft navy wool of his sport coat. Almost of a height, the couple turned together to look up at Alex, who at six feet four inches towered over them.

Alex kept his expression bland as he said a polite hello to the woman who had been his lover years earlier, long before she'd stopped bothering with discretion and fidelity. "I've never seen you at the races, Anita."

She lifted a delicate shoulder in a shrug, a practiced gesture that he recognized as just one of many mannerisms she employed to attract the male eye. "Charles has a horse in the fifth race," she said. "I naturally wanted to be with him."

"Naturally," Alex murmured. Being photographed with Charles in the winner's circle was likely closer to the truth. If Anita's public relations manager achieved the desired results, the blurb beneath the picture would read something like "Anita Carroll, proprietor of one of London's hottest nightclubs . . ." Publicity was free advertising, and she never quit angling for more.

Alex didn't worry that Charles imagined Anita's motives were anything more than self-serving. Like himself, his friend was too jaded to be blindsided by a woman of Anita's much-rehearsed charms. Alex looked down at the impractical high heels she wore and couldn't help the grin that tugged at his mouth. The winner's circle would be a challenge on those stilts.

"That's the MacLear Cup, isn't it?" he asked Charles. It was the big race of the day, heavier in prestige than prize money. The sponsor was a pharmaceutical company that several years earlier had been coerced by a race-mad director to put up the purse in return for publicity. Winning the MacLear Cup would pave the way for the bigger races of the season.

Charles nodded enthusiastically. "I went to watch them unload Starfire. He looks ready to jump out of his skin."

Alex murmured a few words of good luck before turning back to Anita. "Be sure to give Starfire a nice congratulatory pat or kiss," he said to her. "It makes for a good picture. 'Owner's Companion Praising Horse.' You know the pitch."

She looked at him from under long, mascaraed lashes, her expression calculating. "Thank you, Alex. It's always nice to get advice from old . . . friends."

"In case you're confused, Starfire is the horse, not the jockey. Do try to get it right." He watched impassively as a deep red flush blotched her skin.

"You're a bastard, Alex," she said without raising her voice.

He agreed, but that wasn't the point. "Just trying to be helpful, Anita. You're not exactly famous for your decorum."

"Charles, are you just going to stand there and let him speak to me like that?"

Charles brushed a hand across the thinning blond hair at his temple and shrugged, his good humor clearly unaffected. "I haven't heard anything I disagree with, pet. As I see it, you've spent years establishing a scandalous reputation. Alex is merely commenting on your success."

She dug her long nails into his arm, fine lines of anger bracketing her mouth. "If it bothers you—"

He quieted her with two fingers across her lips. "I didn't say it bothered me. You're here today for some free publicity. I agreed to escort you for my own reasons. Just don't ask me to play the white knight for you. If you can't handle Alex, you should avoid him." To Alex he said, "Was there something special you wanted to say to Anita? It's not like you to be boorish, at least not without a good reason."

Alex nodded and fixed his most intimidating gaze on the fuming woman. "I understand you've accepted an invitation to the Greshams' house party next weekend."

Anita looked at him warily. "What does that have to do with you?"

"Quite a bit actually. David Gresham is a business partner."

"I can't place the name," Charles said. "Which partner is this Gresham? You've half a dozen strewn out across various companies."

"The builder," Alex said. "They have a home near Tunbridge Wells."

"Of course," Charles said. "I remember you going to Scotland for the wedding a while back."

Alex hadn't taken his eyes off Anita, who didn't quite

manage to look as though she didn't know what he was getting at. "Yes, Charles, there was a wedding, and now Mrs. Gresham is six months' pregnant. She is also blissfully unaware of the, er, history between David and Anita."

"Awkward" was Charles's succinct comment.

Alex agreed. "Particularly if Anita makes an issue of it over the weekend. David seems to think she might." He glanced over his shoulder to find the horses had nearly reached the starting point. He refocused his gaze on Anita, in a hurry to finish his task. "David says you've been ducking his calls, and asked me to see what I could do about thwarting your plans."

"Missy invited me, not David," Anita said evenly. "And I've already told her I'll go."

"Missy invited you not knowing you're the woman who sent her black roses on her wedding day." Alex ignored Anita's start of surprise and said, "What's the matter, Anita? Still miffed because David dumped you?"

"He didn't dump me." She glared up at him, but the effort was wasted on Alex.

"So long as you change your mind about the weekend, I don't care what you believe. Just remember that the permit you need to expand your club is coming up for review next month. You know I'd hate to hear it had been turned down." He waited a moment for the threat to sink in, then added, "And don't bother the newlyweds in the future either. You'll find the club much easier to run without having inspectors crawling over it every few days."

Her brows arched in pretended disbelief, but the look in her eyes told him she knew she'd been outmaneuvered. "I'd forgotten how you like to throw your power around," she said.

"Only for good causes, naturally." Without so much as an acknowledgment of her acquiescence, he turned to

Charles and said, "Come down to the rails with me. We can watch Golden Legs plodding along from there."

Charles agreed, acting as though nothing untoward had taken place. Ignoring the fuse burning in the woman beside him, he said, "Go on up to the box, Anita, and pour the champagne. I'll be there before the strawberries drown."

When she didn't immediately let go of his arm, Charles's gaze slid from her face to her hand, then back again. "Anita, pet," he said, his voice soft and cautioning, "I'd hate for you to miss seeing my horse run, particularly after you've come all this way."

With an unladylike expletive and a final seething glance at Alex, she released Charles and began to climb the stairs, her back ramrod straight, her shoulders carrying her fury with no attempt to disguise it.

"You were damned rude to her, Alex. She'll be in a snit all afternoon." Charles laughed shortly, then turned and walked with Alex toward the track.

"I wouldn't have presumed to intrude on your afternoon, but I didn't want to have to go to her club to corner her." They stopped about twenty feet shy of the rails behind the crowd already lining the track. Alex raised the binoculars he wore around his neck and focused on the distant starting gate. The crowd shuffled noisily around them, the tension mounting as the jockeys began sorting the horses into position on the far side of the track.

"You think Anita would deliberately cause trouble?" Charles asked, the cynicism in his voice lending a rhetorical note to the query.

"With Missy pregnant, David doesn't want to take a chance of anything upsetting her." There was a fuss at the starting tapes as one of the horses refused to stay in line. Alex lowered the glasses, the corner of his mouth twitching in amusement. "If I'd known you were friendly with Anita, I'd have left it for you to sort it out."

"Today is strictly a one-off," Charles said. "If I hadn't been in need of a little camouflage to fend off my trainer's oversexed daughter, I would have told Anita to find some other chump and some other race."

"What's wrong with the daughter?" Alex asked.

"She's nineteen," Charles said with an exaggerated shiver. "Makes me feel like a lecher." The loudspeaker blurted out notice of the race's start, and both men gave their attention to the far side of the track as the tapes went up and twelve horses shot forward.

To his credit Golden Legs appeared not to mind as Beckett carved out a niche in the middle of the pack instead of in the back, where they'd started and finished in the last three. This race was just under two miles in all, a total of fourteen jumps and one and a half circuits around the track. It should have been a skate for Golden Legs, who, in top form, had taken on Cheltenham's longer and hillier course with a grace and vitality that lasted throughout.

Alex watched the far-off bits of the race through the field glasses, lowering them as the horses thundered past the stands. Nothing much happened in the first mile. No horses fell at a jump or lagged much behind the others. At the start of the second circuit, though, the jockeys shook up their mounts and began to sort themselves out, with the better horses pulling away from those who couldn't manage the pace.

Golden Legs managed to stay aloof, galloping in between the two groups with no apparent allegiance to either. Alex was easily able to keep the horse in view, a circumstance that didn't much please him. About two furlongs from the finish Beckett must have gotten through to the horse, because Golden Legs suddenly appeared to wake up. He took the second-to-last jump as though air were his natural habitat, then raced without a sign of exhaustion to the next, where the four leaders were already pitching themselves across. The lead horse landed badly, throwing his jockey and scrambling away without him. Through the field glasses Alex watched as Golden Legs neatly avoided tromping on the jockey, who'd curled into a ball to provide the smallest possible target for slicing hooves.

Fourth, with a shot at placing. Alex hadn't realized how much he wanted Golden Legs to come in among the first three until it looked as though it were possible. His fingers tightened around the twin barrels of the binoculars as Golden Legs surged ahead, Beckett lying as close to the animal's neck as possible to cut wind resistance. The crowd roared encouragement and disbelief as the air swirled with rainbows and lilacs. . . .

Alex dropped the glasses to his chest and pulled his focus to the people around him, his eyes flitting past the men to the few women, none of whom were that close, not really. Then, out of the corner of his eye, he caught a glimpse of black hair shimmering in the sunlight. He turned toward it, but the vision was already blocked by people taller than she. Frustrated, Alex took a step to follow when he felt a hand on his arm. Looking back over his shoulder, he found Charles peering at him.

"Not going to let me buy you a consolation drink?" Charles asked.

"Consolation?" Alex said, then for the first time connected the milling crowd to the race's end.

Charles looked at him curiously. "Golden Legs, I'm afraid, came in a close fourth. I thought the idea of coming to the rails was to watch."

His gaze scanning the crowd, Alex said, "I watched most of it, but something . . ." He hesitated, wondering if Charles had smelled the intriguing fragrance, knowing he hadn't because he wouldn't have watched the race's finish either. "Something distracted me. It's not important."

But it was. He wanted to find the woman, even though it was too late. Another glance told him as much, and he shook his head to clear it of unsettling illusions that shouldn't have been there in the first place. Rainbows and lilacs . . .

He smiled halfheartedly at Charles. "You can buy me that drink another time. Bobby's probably pulling out his hair by now. I told him earlier I'd have to sell soon if things didn't change."

"Ever think of changing trainers?" Charles asked.

It was a normal enough consideration, but Alex knew the problem didn't lie with the trainer. Bobby Goodwyn was one of the most honest men Alex had ever known, and a friend besides. He'd sell the horse rather than demonstrate a lack of faith by changing trainers.

"Bobby would be my choice if I bought any more horses—which I probably won't. It's easier to sleep nights not having to worry about investments that get colic, throw a shoe, or go into a sulk if their routine is upset."

"You'll make a lousy father someday," Charles said with a laugh, then walked away.

Alex hardly heard him. He was too busy searching the crowd again as he headed over to the unsaddling enclosure, hoping for a glimpse of hair so black and thick and long, he was certain he'd imagined it.

An illusion . . . like rainbows and lilacs, elusive in form and scent.

TWO

In her entire life, nothing had prepared Jack for her almost passionate love of all things English. From the moment she stepped off the plane, she knew this was the faraway place she'd glimpsed from her magic carpet.

The place of her dreams.

There were no pyramids or sphinxes, no noisy bullrings, and certainly no moody rivers that wound through dense jungles alive with parrots and deadly reptiles. Instead of the exotic fantasies of her childish imagination, Jack's dreams materialized in the reality of softly rolling hills, narrow winding roads, and quaint villages.

She was in love with England, and knew that the month-long vacation wouldn't be enough. Not even the long, dark nights and moist, chilly January days put her off. The countryside—particularly that around Cheltenham where Hillary lived—was charming and full of people who had turned their normal cool reserve into uninhibited welcome once they understood the joy she experienced just by being in such a wonderful place.

Unfortunately a month's worth of the dream was all she had coming to her. With the school at Walnut Pass on a full-year schedule, her vacation came in two bits of six weeks each, and she needed the two weeks after the trip to get organized for the next term. By March she'd be knee-deep in intermediate trombonists and beginning drummers. By March the money she'd gotten from the sale of the stock would be nearly gone.

She'd never imagined Seymour Jenkins's porcelain cow would yield the vacation of a lifetime. After two years in which she'd forgotten the existence of the shares, Tony had jolted her back to awareness—first a heads-up that the stock was recovering, and second, a month later, the urgent instruction to sell because the peak was likely to fall off. She'd sold, and when Hillary's letter had arrived that same day, she'd given in to her chum's much-repeated invitation to visit.

It was the least sensible thing she'd done in her life, and her mother had cheered her all the way down the ramp to the plane.

Propping her elbows on the top rail of the fence, Jack looked across the pasture to where Hillary's personal mount—a pearly-gray mare with dainty white socks on three feet—was nuzzling the ground in hopes of a tender new shoot of grass. It was too early in the year for spring's renewal to begin, but the brilliant sunshine of late afternoon slanted through the trees, fooling the mare into believing there was a chance of finding something fresh amid last summer's leftovers.

Jack lifted a hand to push the long, heavy hair from her face, her sigh of contentment mixing with the rustling leaves that clung, brown and shriveled, to the branches of the red beech overhead. After a week of dashing about in a frenzy of tourist-related activities, she and Hillary had elected to join Bobby at the races that day. They'd stayed only for the first three before accompanying Bobby's two runners back to the stables. Jack had enjoyed the hours at the track, but was equally content to be back at Hillary and Bobby's.

Stonehenge would have suited her, too, but, as Hillary had said, it would still be there in another week or so.

She was supposed to be writing postcards while Hillary followed Bobby around on evening stables, but the lure of the dwindling sunshine had drawn her outdoors. Tomorrow was a scheduled wet day, the norm rather than the exception, but she doubted it would sway Hillary from their planned excursion into London. As a tour guide she was inexhaustible. Jack was looking forward to it, although she suspected that not even the Turner exhibit at the Tate Museum would outclass the other sightseeing they'd accomplished in the last week.

What they'd already seen had left her breathless, in awe, and hungry for more. Jack had been entranced by the fabulous medieval Warwick Castle, overwhelmed by the depth of mystery and fact surrounding Uffington White Horse, and charmed by the Red Lion, the picturesque village pub just down the road from the Goodwyns' training stables in the Cotswold hills. On a two-day sprint north and east, she'd found herself captivated by the melancholy ruins of Saint Mary's Abbey in the shadow of York Minster, then dazzled by the cathedral itself. A walking tour through the spectacular colleges that made up Cambridge University had been followed by a leisurely hour's punting on the river Cam, with an undergraduate at the helm who'd wielded the long pole with an ease Hillary pointed out was deceptive. She'd tried punting with Bobby, she said, and the experience had taught her to engage the services of a professional.

Oxford University had its own day. Following an afternoon wandering amid the dreaming spires and secretive quads, Bobby had taken them out for dinner at Exeter College, where, as a favor to his father who didn't approve of his affinity for all things equine, he had studied politics, philosophy, and economics.

Hillary had filled Jack's first week with enough sight-seeing to leave even the most hardened tourist winded. In this, the first quiet moment since her arrival, Jack took deep breaths of the crisp country air and wished life's choices had presented an English option, because she surely would have taken it.

"I thought I'd imagined you."

Jack swung around, startled yet not afraid, although the man confronting her was a giant—by her or anyone else's standards. He towered over her, the last rays of the sun defining the strong lines of his face. His light-colored eyes were narrowed against the sun, and his dark hair was brushed back from his face and lay thick on his collar. Her gaze fell to his shoulders, broad and straight beneath a sport jacket she didn't have to touch to know was cashmere. His shirt collar was open, with no tie or ascot in sight. The rest of his clothing was equally casual and expensive, a combination she found curious, because his accent was English, and as far as she'd been able to ascertain, the word *casual* meant something entirely different to Englishmen than to Americans.

Curiouser and curiouser.

The rail at her back bit into her shoulder blades, but nothing could make Jack ease off so much as an inch, because that would bring her too close to the stranger. She wasn't afraid, just circumspect. Any nearer and she'd be tempted to reach up and touch his cheek where a scar, white from age, slashed from eye to ear.

She didn't think he'd appreciate the gesture of familiarity, particularly if he was sensitive about it.

He stood quietly under her perusal, his hands loose at his sides, his chest rising and falling with every breath, the rhythm even and solid. She guessed she'd been staring long enough to qualify for a trophy in rudeness when he spoke again.

"You're Hillary's friend," he said.

She nodded, her fingers finding the next rail down and curling around it. "From college. It's been years . . ." The thought trailed off, incomplete because she'd forgotten the beginning. His eyes were gray, she realized as the sun dipped lower, throwing a shadow across his face.

"I'm Alex Hastings. Hillary and Bobby invited me for drinks."

"I know," she said, hiding her smile. Hillary's description of this man had been woefully inadequate, mere adjectives when exaggerations would have been closer to the truth. Still, of all the people invited that evening for drinks, Alex Hastings was the only one who'd been described as tall, dark, and interesting.

The man standing before her was all that and more.

"I didn't mean to frighten you, but there was no one inside. I was going on to the stables when I saw you—"

"I'm not frightened," she interrupted, uncertain why she felt it important that he understand that.

He didn't look as though he believed her. "You're all but glued to that fence."

"If we were any closer, I'd get a crick in my neck looking up at you," she said, a grin lifting the corners of her mouth.

He appeared to notice for the first time that she stood at least a foot shorter than he. An expression she couldn't decipher flickered in his eyes, and he said, "You're short enough to get lost in a crowd easily."

"Well . . . yes." She couldn't think of a better response to that rather obscure statement, and was quite content to look at him without having to say anything at all. He was giving her the same kind of thorough perusal, and Jack didn't think it at all odd when several minutes passed without a word between them.

She wondered what he saw when he looked at her and what it was about Alex Hastings that so fascinated her. It wasn't that he was handsome, because he wasn't, not in any traditional sense. He was too rugged for handsome, his face too harsh, his stature too overwhelming.

She was attracted without knowing why, beguiled by a man who touched her soul without laying a finger on her.

The sound of a door slamming shattered the intimacy of the moment, but in that split second before reality intruded, Jack met his eyes and knew he shared her disappointment.

"There will be other moments," he said, his voice low and husky. Then he turned to greet Hillary who was coming across the grass, wiping her hands on the backside of her soiled slacks and tsking when an inspection of her palms was clearly unsatisfactory.

"Great! You two have already met. No, don't touch me if you don't want to get mucky." Alex's hand dropped back to his side as Hillary halted beside him, her short copper-colored hair glinting in the sun's dying rays that managed to highlight bits of straw among the curls.

Alex lifted a brow. "You're the only person I've ever known who can turn the evening walk-around into a mud bath. What was it this time?"

"Jupiter's lad lost a contact lens—glass, not plastic. If Bobby hadn't been so afraid Jupiter would eat it, we would have left it there and bought him a new one."

Jack edged away from the fence to stand beside Hillary, but didn't feel any less overwhelmed by the man who faced them. "Does Bobby look as bad as you?" she asked. She'd rarely seen Hillary's husband looking anything less than immaculate, no small feat for a trainer who, when necessary, worked alongside his lads as though he were one of them.

Hillary shook her head, her mouth twisting in an expression of disgust and humor. "The master went on with his rounds while I stayed behind to help Jupiter's lad."

"I assume you met with success," Alex said.

"I wouldn't be here otherwise. You know Bobby once he decides on something." She wiped her hands again, checked the results, then sighed. "I'll have to clean up. Jack, why don't you walk down with Alex to see Golden Legs." Turning to Alex, she said, "Golden Legs has been moved to a box in the west quad. Bobby said he'd wait there for you."

She hurried away, leaving Jack with a man who was now staring at her with disbelief. "Jack?" he said, his brows climbing a fraction in what she intuitively realized was as much surprise as he liked to show.

"Short for Jacqueline, but no one's called me that in years." Except her mother, but that was different. A chill went through her, making her aware the sun had dropped completely below the hills.

"Jacqueline," he said, wrapping the syllables in a hint of French that stripped her name of the formality she'd always hated and replaced it with something much more interesting.

Something breathlessly intimate.

"Jacqueline," he said again, then nodded as though he'd decided something. He narrowed that cool, gray gaze on her. "May I call you that?"

"It's all right," she said, shivering now and knowing better than to blame it on the cold evening breeze.

"Jacqueline what?"

"Sommers." Another shiver made her realize that perhaps the way he said her name was secondary to the case of pneumonia she'd get if she stayed outside any longer with only a thin sweater between her and the quickly cooling air. "We'd better go on down to the yard before I freeze."

He shook his head, his eyes not missing the way she'd wrapped her arms around herself. "Go inside, Jacqueline, get warm. Bobby and I will be back soon."

She nodded, but something he'd said before kept her rooted to the spot. She couldn't not ask. Lifting her chin to meet his gaze, she said, "Earlier, when you first came, you said something like you thought you'd imagined me." She paused, then added, "What did you mean?"

To her surprise he lifted a hand and cupped her face for a brief moment, almost as though he needed the sense of touch to know what was real and what wasn't. "I'll tell you if you promise to come out with me tomorrow."

The pang of regret was almost physical. "Hillary's taking me to London. I can't."

"Tomorrow night, then," he said smoothly. "There's a place near Oxford where the food is rather good."

"I'd like that." An understatement, she realized, then concentrated on not showing her disappointment when his hand dropped away.

He was walking toward the gate leading to the yard before she remembered he hadn't told her what he'd meant. "Alex?"

He turned, and shook his head. "Tomorrow, Jacqueline. Consider it a bribe to ensure you don't change your mind."

"I wouldn't," she said softly, and knew he'd heard her because the look he gave her was full of masculine appreciation.

The shiver, when it came, was a purely feminine response.

Alex closed the gate and headed toward the stables without looking back, knowing that if he did, he might skip seeing Golden Legs altogether in favor of spending a few more minutes with a woman he had no business being attracted to.

As he'd feared, Jacqueline was no older than Hillary. Even though she looked closer to twenty than thirty, simple math applied to what he knew about Hillary placed her at around twenty-eight. Too young for him, too naive, too trusting . . . too much of a temptation, yet he embraced it with a burning passion he'd not felt for a century or two.

He wanted her and didn't give a damn about the consequences—not beyond a cold acceptance that she was a visitor, only temporarily in his life, as he was only fleetingly in hers.

By then, he assumed, the physical yearnings she stirred in him would lessen to a degree he could ignore.

When he'd caught sight of her in the garden, her long black hair capturing the sun and turning it into blue fire, he'd known at once she was the woman he'd glimpsed at the races. It was as though an invisible force had dragged him closer, his need to know whether she was also the woman he'd smelled overpowering all rational thought. He'd moved silently to stand behind her, a part of him hoping the illusive scent had been a figment of his imagination, another part feeling compelled by the desire to know there was something more to life than business and the satisfying of physical needs.

Rainbows and lilacs. The scent was no stronger than when it had been a mere whiff of fragrance on the breeze. No stronger, but unmistakably the same. He'd spoken then, startling her into turning around to show him a face so delicate and vibrant, he'd known in that moment he wanted . . . no, he *needed* to be with her. Her response to him—unafraid and, at least in a small way, attracted— had given him license to invite her out.

He turned off the path into the yard and saw Bobby at the far end of a row of horse boxes. The decision regarding Golden Legs' fate would have to be postponed, Alex decided as he walked across the almost pristine yard, which was just one more clue to Bobby's dedication to excellence. The last thing he wanted to do was introduce anxiety into the Goodwyn household when he intended to spend as much time as possible with their guest.

Coming to a stop beside Bobby, he looked into the box now housing Golden Legs and asked after his horse. At the sound of his voice, the stallion stuck his head through the open half of the Dutch door and zeroed in on the carrot Alex held in his palm. The soft, velvety mouth closed delicately over the treat without so much as a hint of the strong teeth that could have taken off a finger or two.

Bobby watched the ritual without comment, then launched into an outline of what additional steps he was taking to discover the reason behind Golden Legs' performance. Alex listened attentively to everything the trainer said, and didn't once bring up the subject of selling the stallion.

Nor, for his own reasons, did Bobby.

Alex Hastings wasn't the only guest for drinks, a circumstance that both disappointed and comforted Jack. The almost surreal encounter in the garden had left her feeling vulnerable, her emotions jostled into a tingling awareness such as nothing she'd ever experienced.

Her defenses, historically reliable to the point of being automatic, had never been so completely subdued. She didn't know what to think about that.

She didn't know anything, except that Alex Hastings had managed in those brief moments to touch her senses with a gentleness and care she found herself responding to.

She wanted to know him better.

Almost a dozen others were present, enough people to keep Hillary busy with introductions, yet too few to allow Jack and Alex the opportunity for private conversation. Everyone there—Jack excepted—was closely involved with racing and spoke the language of horses to the point where Jack felt she might as well be listening to Swahili or Urdu. It would take another week or so, she figured, before she had even an inkling of what was being said around her.

During one of the more incomprehensible moments she glanced across the room to find Alex looking at her, the merest quirk of his eyebrow revealing that he understood and was amused by her predicament. She lifted her shoulders in a shrug that wouldn't be noticed by anyone not paying attention, then looked away before the urge to giggle overcame good manners.

She was sitting with three others near the fireplace. The man she remembered being introduced as Colin Moreton was bemoaning his horse's loss that afternoon, while two women, Deborah and Rita, gave him their full attention.

Moreton said, "He got shut in on the rails, then blew up trying to make it up in the last furlong."

Deborah patted his arm while Rita made sympathetic noises. Jack looked up to find Hillary standing beside her chair and was about to ask for a translation when Rita said, "I heard from Tom Fraser that old Weymouth's 'chaser got cast in his box and broke his leg day before last. The knackers almost didn't come get him, as they'd already put a packet on him with Charlie Lawton."

Jack added a year to her previous calculations regarding this foreign language and got up to follow Hillary when she went into the kitchen. As the door shut behind her, she leaned against it and said, "If that horse really blew up, you'd better not tell me because I think I'll be sick."

Hillary laughed and pulled a tray of salmon croquettes from the refrigerator. Putting it on the counter, she fussed with the sprigs of parsley. "A horse that blows up runs out of energy or wind before the race's end."

"What about getting shut in on the rails?"

"Closed in against the inside rail by other horses." Hillary asked Jack to grab some more cocktail napkins from the drawer, and together they arranged them on a tray. "And before you ask, Weymouth's 'chaser is a stee-plechaser—they jump fences, not hurdles. When a horse gets cast in his box—that's stall, to you—it means it rolled on its back and got stuck with its hooves in the air or against the wall. Easy to break a leg that way." Reaching beneath the counter, she brought out a tin of crackers, which they put on another tray. "And the knackers had a prerace bet with a bookie, Charlie Lawton. They were probably miffed the horse didn't live to run, as bets are nonrefundable. Anything I've missed?"

Jack smoothed her palms over her yellow wool slacks and said, "You know there is. What's a knacker?"

"The guy who hauls dead horses to the dogfood factory." Hillary leaned a hip against the counter and regarded her friend with amusement. "On another subject, what did I interrupt in the garden earlier?"

"Nothing," she said, then blushed when her friend laughed at the quickness of her denial. "Really, Hillary, it was nothing. Alex just asked me out to dinner tomorrow. I said I'd go."

"Oh?"

"Mmm. I didn't think Bobby would mind having you to himself for a change."

"I'm sure that's why you accepted," Hillary said wryly. "Prepare to be wined and dined in grand style. Shelby Denton—she's a woman I know who works at Sotheby's in London—anyway, Alex used to be, er, friendly with her," she said with what Jack interpreted as discretion. "She was really quite bereft when the gold rush was over."

"What do you mean, gold rush?"

"The gifts, Jack. Alex is a generous man and he apparently believes in showering his women with life's simple extravagances." Her sigh was heavy with exaggerated envy. "Anyway, after Alex and Shelby parted ways, she cried on my shoulder for hours. It was the money she missed, I know, more than the man. Despite the fact that he's totally devoid of feeling or emotions, it sounds like he treated her quite well."

Emotionless? No feelings? Jack was surprised, because the man she'd encountered in the garden hadn't struck her that way.

Hillary pushed away from the counter and picked up a tray in each hand. "Now pick up that last tray and let's get back to the crowd. If I get a chance, I'll ask Alex where he's taking you so we'll know what you should wear." Pushing the swinging door open with an elbow, she added over her shoulder, "If his reputation is anything to go by, we'll have to do some shopping in London tomorrow. Can't have you wrapped in wool when the occasion demands silk."

The door swung shut behind her, and Jack didn't immediately follow. Hillary's talk of the "gold rush" had left a sour taste in her mouth, although, to be honest, Jack had to admit she hadn't liked listening to any part of Alex's history with other women. Taking a croquette from the tray, she bit into it and wondered why she should care that a man she hardly knew was generous to his lovers.

It wasn't, after all, any of her business. They were only going out for dinner.

She wasn't going to be in England long enough for anything more.

It wasn't until Hillary and Bobby were waving their guests off that Alex managed to draw Jacqueline aside for a quiet word. In the privacy of Bobby's dimly lit study, he kept his voice low so that only the woman with him could hear.

"Hillary quizzed me about where I was taking you tomorrow," he said.

"She said she would." They stood without touching, close enough that she had to tip her head back to meet his gaze.

"She also warned me against seducing you."

"She did what?"

Alex kept from smiling by sheer force of will. "Perhaps not exactly warned, but the word *seduce* was definitely mentioned."

Bright red color suffused Jacqueline's face, and she looked at him helplessly. "This is *not* how I run my life. I *don't* have intimate conversations with virtual strangers, and, with the exception of my mother or father, no one has *ever* warned a man I dated against seducing me." She clapped her palms to her cheeks and groaned. "I can't believe I had to come all the way to England to die of embarrassment."

He pulled her hands from her face and held them against his chest. "Not to worry, Jacqueline. I told Hillary I had no intention of doing any such thing. She probably won't mention it again."

The noise she made was part gasp, part choke, and he hoped she wouldn't bolt and flee. He had taken the precaution of standing between her and the door, but there was little else he could or would do if she decided the conversation was not to her liking and left.

He was quite pleased when she looked up at him and said, "Tell me, Alex, do all Englishmen provide such assurances before going out with a woman for the first time?" Her eyes glittered with mischief now, and it was all he could do not to lean down and kiss her.

He didn't, though. "I don't know about other men, but I've never said anything quite like that before." He lifted a hand to stroke the hair that fell across her shoulder. "What I didn't tell Hillary was that it would only be a seduction if I corrupted you into doing something you didn't want to do."

"Like robbing banks?"

"I suspect I'd have to seduce long and hard to accomplish that."

Her laughter was bright, filling the room like bells in a crystal tower. When she stopped, he was smiling too. She said, "And here I thought *seduction* implied surrendering one's chastity."

"To some, that probably *is* a form of corruption."

They laughed together this time, and somehow Jack found her fingers clinging to the lapels of his jacket. She looked up into eyes that were warm with humor. "Does all this mean my virtue is safe with you?" Her heart thudded in her chest as he slowly shook his head.

"It means I won't seduce you. Anything we do, we do together." He cupped her chin in his hand and said, "Is that all right with you, Jacqueline?"

"Very much all right."

He let out a deep breath and began to stroke her hair again. "I can't imagine why Hillary would invite me tonight, then warn me off. Can you?"

"I can't believe most of this conversation, much less

Hillary's part in it." The sound of a door shutting made her realize their privacy was about to be interrupted. "I'm twenty-eight years old, Alex, certainly old enough to take responsibility for myself."

He looked thoughtful for a moment, then stepped away from her as Hillary and Bobby came into the room. Declining their offer of another drink, Alex said his good-byes and left.

When he'd gone, Jack found herself thinking that for a man with no feelings, he exerted a powerful influence on her own.

The flowers arrived as Jack and Hillary were heading out to the car for their trip into London. The van from a Cheltenham florist swung into the drive, blocking their exit. They watched curiously as a young man with orange hair slid open the side panel and extracted an enormous bouquet of orchids, camellias, and birds-of-paradise. Hillary rushed back to open the front door as the young man staggered under the load in her wake, leaving Jack to follow in amusement.

"It would be more discreet for your lover to send a potted plant or something," Jack said, laughing outright as Hillary tipped the delivery boy and cleared a space for the flowers on the coffee table. "Bobby isn't exactly going to overlook those."

"They're probably from the owner of the horse that won yesterday. Last time, they sent a case of port. Unfortunately neither Bobby nor I can stand the stuff." Hillary dipped a hand amid the blossoms and came out with a card. A sly smile curved her lips as she turned and held it out to Jack. "They're for you."

With considerably less humor Jack looked at the card. Two names only were on it, hers and Alex's, Jacqueline written with the same bold scrawl as the sender's signature.

She looked up at Hillary and sighed. "I suppose it would hurt his feelings if I told him the flowers are just a bit much."

"I told you last night that Alex doesn't have any feelings," Hillary said. "At least not any that apply to the heart. Some woman supposedly cut that out years ago."

"He didn't seem cold or emotionless to me."

Hillary shrugged and led the way back outside. Instead of getting into the car, she looked at Jack over the top of it and said, "I like Alex, Jack. If I didn't, I wouldn't have introduced you to him."

"So why did you?"

"Because I think you'll be good for him."

Jack lifted a single eyebrow as a new wrinkle to Hillary's invitation surfaced. "You're matchmaking, aren't you?"

Hillary grinned. "Just giving you the holiday of your dreams. And what is more memorable than being catered to by a very interesting and *very* sexy man?"

"If that's how you feel, why did you corner him about seducing me?" Jack had been dying to bring up the subject all morning. "I'd think a seduction was exactly what you had in mind."

"Ouch!" Hillary winced as though Jack's needling had been physical. "So that's what you were talking about in the study."

"What gives, Hillary? Are you afraid Alex is really a big, bad wolf out to ravish the hapless tourist?"

"He *is* huge, isn't he?"

Jack noticed her friend hadn't addressed the wolf part. "That doesn't answer my question."

There was a short silence before Hillary said, "I saw

the way you looked at him, Jack. It suddenly occurred to me you might get hurt."

"I hardly know Alex," Jack said. "I just met him yesterday."

"Exactly," Hillary pounced. "Which is why what I saw in your expression worried me."

"It bothers you that I lust after your neighbor?" she teased.

Hillary laughed and shook her head. "Lust *was* what I was aiming for between you two, but—"

Before Hillary could continue, Jack said, "Then you should be pleased with yourself, not worried. Speaking of which, what happened between last night and this morning? You seem to have conquered any last-minute qualms."

"Bobby overheard what I said to Alex." Hillary had the grace to look chagrinned. "My husband suggested I mind my own business."

"That's never stopped you before," Jack said dryly.

"If that's the way you're going to be, I'm not telling you what else Bobby said."

Jack's curiosity was piqued. "It must be good if your grin is anything to go by."

Hillary ignored Jack's invitation to give, though. They got into the car and were several miles from the farm before Jack noticed Hillary's smile had faded.

"What now?"

"Do me a favor, will you, Jack? Don't forget what I told you about Alex."

"What was that? You've said a lot of things about him."

"The part about having no feelings. I want you to have fun, not get your heart broken."

"Don't worry about it, Hillary. We're only going for dinner," Jack said, and wondered which one of them she was trying to convince. The hours she'd lain awake last night had been wasted on a similar effort. She was attracted to Alex and was trying damn hard to keep her emotions from complicating what was simply a sexual response.

The fact that she'd never had a strictly sexual relationship didn't mean there couldn't be a first time.

"Let's go shopping before we hit the museum," she said. "I'm in the mood to splurge on something slinky."

Hillary shot her an exasperated look and sighed. "Maybe you'd be better off in wool after all."

THREE

The "place near Oxford where the food is rather good" turned out to be Raymond Blanc's Le Manoir aux Quat' Saisons, one of England's most exclusive restaurants. The conversion in the early 1980s of the rambling Cotswold manor house to restaurant and hotel had resulted in an elegant and intimate setting, where one could enjoy fabulous meals accompanied by extraordinary wines.

Hillary had filled Jack in on the restaurant's reputation in the dressing room of one of Regent Street's pricey boutiques, as Jack struggled with her conscience over the purchase of a calf-length ice-blue silk dress that flattered her body and took the wind out of her financial reserves. It was only because the dress made her feel like a million bucks—and incidentally fed Hillary's misgivings—that she swallowed her trepidation and allowed the shop to take an imprint of her credit card in payment.

The thing was, when Alex called for her that evening, Jack could have sworn he hardly noticed what she was wearing. His eyes barely left her face, his gaze steady and warm with pleasure. She lifted a shaking hand to tuck an imaginary strand of hair into the simple knot she'd styled at her nape.

He told her how much he'd looked forward to their evening together, and made her feel special in a way she'd never quite felt before. He had a way about him that made her believe they weren't just words, that he hadn't said them to a dozen other women at some time in his past.

She thanked him for the flowers, realizing then that she'd spent the day hoping he hadn't chosen them because they were expensive but because he'd thought she would like them. She wanted to believe only that and thus pushed the words *gold rush* from her mind as he helped her into the sleek Jaguar and guided the softly purring car down the gravel drive.

On the drive from Cheltenham Alex talked easily about the renowned chef's well-deserved success, putting Jack at ease with stories that ranged from Raymond Blanc's lack of formal training to his passionate and endless search for the freshest foods. She found herself responding to the gentle persuasion of his undemanding conversation, allowing herself to be drawn into telling him about the sights she'd visited over the past week. England was the land of her dreams, she admitted, and then, with a lack of self-consciousness that would have surprised her in any other circumstances, she told him about the magic carpet and Seymour Jenkins's cow.

They arrived at Le Manoir too late to properly view the croquet lawn and rose gardens, which vied with a remarkable herb-and-vegetable garden for space beneath tulip trees and ancient oaks. Almost as though he sensed her disappointment, Alex promised to bring her during the day if she liked. Her heart skipped a beat as he took her hand inside his large one and led her up the path to the door.

The interior was spacious and elegantly comfortable, the atmosphere fairly vibrating with anticipation of the culinary delights to come. At least she imagined it was the food that excited the passions she couldn't help sensing.

It couldn't be anything else—except perhaps a touch of the same magic that made Alex seem larger than life. *More* real, not less.

She knew she could touch him and feel solid flesh beneath her hand. She also knew he could touch her and enchant her senses.

With an effort of will that was as much physical as mental, Jack tried to shake off the almost mystical feeling that had been with her from the moment she'd opened Hillary's door and found Alex waiting on the other side.

"What are you thinking, Jacqueline?"

She looked across the coffee table to where Alex lounged in a flowered brocade armchair, his mulberry-and-smoke-blue tie an elegant complement to the charcoal suit, his hair curling darkly against the collar of the white linen shirt. His mouth was curved in an expression of genuine pleasure and satisfaction, and she wondered if he could sense the anticipation she felt as the evening's adventure unfolded.

She said the first thing that came to her mind: "I've never been to a place like this."

"Not many people have," he said, studying her from behind lowered eyelids. "Do you like it?"

Jack didn't answer, not right away. She scooted back from the edge of the sofa until she was as comfortable as Alex looked and glanced around the sumptuous sitting room, which resembled a country home more than it did a restaurant. The room was empty save for another couple at the far end, and she wondered how a place could stay in business with so few customers. Knowing that the words would expose her naïveté—not to mention her own substantially lower standard of living—she said, "It's a safe bet that tonight's dinner will cost more than my plane ticket from California. I would have been just as happy at the Red Lion, you know."

She needed him to understand the gold rush wasn't necessary.

A flicker of disbelief crossed his face. "The food is much better here."

"That's why you chose it for tonight, and not because you thought I would expect to be entertained in style?"

He hesitated, then said mildly, "I thought you would enjoy it."

With a sense of surprise, Jack realized she'd hurt him in a way Hillary had said wasn't possible. He had feelings, and she'd tripped over them with less grace than a beached jellyfish.

"I'm sorry," she said, and reached out as though to touch him. He was too far away, though, in mind as well as in body. He'd withdrawn from her, taking the magic with him. She could feel the absence and was suddenly panicked that it might never come again.

She dropped her hand to her lap and tried again. "Forgive me for being so stupid. Please. I just wanted you to know I'm not used to all this. I don't expect it."

"But do you like it?" The question was asked so softly, she hardly heard it.

"Yes, I do," she said. "Who wouldn't?"

The truth seemed to mollify him, because the atmosphere lightened immediately. "Then let's just enjoy the evening, shall we?"

If there was a hint of reserve in his expression, Jack knew she had only herself to thank.

The waiter appeared with their drinks—dry sherry for her, Irish whiskey for him—and by the time he'd handed out menus and answered several questions Alex put to him, Jack could almost feel the magic again.

Almost. It wasn't until they'd been ushered into the

dining area and she was distracted by the exciting smells and textures that things began to sparkle once more. At her urging, Alex had ordered for her. She ate everything that was placed before her without, in most cases, being sure exactly what passed her lips to seduce her taste buds. She didn't care.

As Alex had said, the food was rather good. After a hot hors d'oeuvre that brought foie gras, shredded turnips, and wild mushrooms together in a delicious concoction, Jack oohed and aahed halfway through a serving of roast woodcock in a Saint Emilion sauce. Then, with her permission, Alex switched their plates and let her finish his own entrée of roe deer in a poivrade sauce with apples and black currants.

Jack glanced self-consciously at the waiters, who either hadn't noticed the sleight of hand or had superb control over their facial expressions. "If you'd done that at a restaurant in the States, the waiters would probably sneer."

Alex shrugged. "The waiters at Le Manoir are entirely too well trained to do anything of the sort. Besides, a chef should feel complimented that his customers are excited enough about the food to want to try everything."

"I feel as though my taste buds have been cloistered and didn't know it." She took another bite and sighed as the rich flavors spread throughout her mouth. "Whoever it was that said the food in England is boring didn't know what he was talking about."

"This is mostly French," Alex said.

"Yes, but the restaurant is in England. I'd say that counts for something."

He smiled, and she bent her head so he wouldn't notice the flush she felt creeping up her face as his smile warmed her inside and out. A breathless quality of anticipation and excitement filled her, and it was all she could do to pay attention to the wonderful tastes and textures passing her lips.

Incredible as it seemed, the food was of only mild interest to her now that the mystical, magical feeling had returned in force.

Alex looked at Jacqueline's bent head and felt something decidedly pleasant ease past his customary defenses —something that at a less cynical age he would have labeled as emotion but that he now knew was sensual awareness. With Jacqueline, though, that awareness was deeper than he was accustomed to, more thorough, as if she were touching all of him, not just the parts he allowed.

He wasn't worried. There was no danger she'd ever touch any emotions other than passion or simple caring. Emotions were expensive and unnecessary adjuncts to the business of living.

Therefore, he didn't have any.

Even so, the illogic of her conclusion about food in England charmed him, as did almost everything else about Jacqueline. There was a subtle sophistication about her that made her appear at ease in what was a new situation, yet allowed her to respond to the experience with complete honesty. The women with whom he'd been intimately acquainted at one time or another were always so accustomed to the trappings of wealth that whatever enjoyment they gleaned had long ago been disciplined into an attitude of casual acceptance.

Jacqueline was having fun and didn't care who noticed. It was enough to make him forgive her claim that the Red Lion would have done as well. He hadn't believed her of course. It made no sense that she would prefer a noisy pub to an elegant restaurant.

Alex knew better than to imagine her eyes would sparkle as brightly if he'd chosen the pub. She was responding to the environment first and to him—a man—second.

Yes, he knew better, and didn't think less of her for it. It was after all the way of things. He preferred it that way. Money, and all it bought, was tangible in a way that emotions never could be. Possessions could be counted and controlled. Emotions, excluding passion of course, couldn't.

He'd learned that lesson long ago.

A waiter topped off the red wine in their glasses, then melted into the background. Alex took a sip and decided to tease her a bit. "For good English cooking, some of the best can be found at pubs. Perhaps I should take you to the Red Lion for bubble and squeak."

"Bubble and squeak?" Jack laughed delightedly, clearly missing the point. "That sounds like a party game."

"It's cabbage and mashed potatoes fried into a hash." He twirled the stem of his wineglass between thumb and forefinger. "Shall we try it tomorrow, or would you prefer to go somewhere in London where we can get food more along the lines of what they offer here?"

"Tomorrow?" she said, and he couldn't miss the pleasure that flared in her eyes.

"If you're free." At her nod he said, "It will have to be later, about eight. I'll book a table for nine; that will give us an hour to get into town."

"The Red Lion is just around the corner," she said. "You wouldn't have to drive so far."

He controlled his surprise, then realized she was only thinking in terms of convenience. "I don't mind the drive."

She hesitated. Alex was telling himself he shouldn't be disappointed that the elegant restaurant had won out, when she said, "I'd really prefer the Red Lion. I've only had lunch there, and Hillary says they can't take me for dinner because Bobby always orders the duck and it's not on his diet."

"Bobby's on a diet?" He'd always thought Bobby a touch on the thin side, if anything.

"Mmm." Alex watched as Jacqueline checked her plate for any scraps she might have missed. Sighing her disappointment, she put her fork down. "Hillary's been on a low-cholesterol kick ever since Bobby's grandfather died following a heart attack last year."

"He was ninety-two years old. If it hadn't been heart disease, something else would have gotten him."

"Try telling Hillary." Jack shrugged off her exasperation. "In any case Bobby's off duck for the time being. Unless you're serious about making me eat bubble and squeak, duck is exactly what I'd like to have. I swear, Bobby waxes poetic about the crackling when he thinks Hillary isn't listening."

Alex surrendered without understanding if he'd won or lost. The subject, which hadn't been very far from food all night, continued in the same vein once dessert was served. He watched with amused indulgence as Jacqueline expressed her delight over the sinfully rich sweets, then had to press her to take the first bite.

"It's too pretty to eat," she said, catching her lip between her teeth in a way that stimulated responses deep inside him which had nothing to do with food.

"If you can't, I will," he said, and was relieved when she finally picked up her spoon and dipped into the espresso ice cream, which was served in a wafer-thin chocolate cup and saucer. Alex started in on his own choice—sunflowers of pineapple with a kirsch parfait and spiced with cherries and a vanilla sauce—and knew that the night's rich repast would result in a substantially expanded exercise program the next morning. Two desserts would have kept him at it all morning.

Jack felt Alex's gaze on her as she picked up the last remaining bit of the chocolate saucer and popped it into her mouth. She looked up at him and smiled. "You've spoiled me forever, you know. I'll never be able to look at food again without remembering its true potential."

"We'll come again, for lunch so that we can see the gardens properly." He put the starched yellow napkin on the table and stood, holding out his hand for hers as a waiter appeared from nowhere to pull out her chair. "Let's go back to the lounge for coffee, shall we?"

Jack put her hand in his. It was hard to say anything as the magic pulsed through her, but she persevered. "I'm not sure I left room for coffee."

Alex led her to the sofa where they'd begun the odyssey, this time easing down next to her, his thigh almost but not quite touching hers, her hand still firmly in his grip. "Take a few deep breaths and think positively. The petit fours are to die for."

Considering his earlier understatement regarding the food, she was impressed. "Given that recommendation, I think I might be able to manage one or two." She turned her head to meet his gaze and saw a deeper warmth in his eyes than had been there before. The responses within her that had managed to avoid being overly stimulated thus far sat up and took note.

"When you look at me like that, all I can think about is making love to you," he said softly, stroking the back of her hand along the taut muscles of his thigh with a gentleness that softened her reply from outrage to wonder.

"Do you always say what you're thinking?"

"Not usually," he said, "but in my own defense, I'm not used to a woman who is so open with her responses. I find it incredibly seductive."

"And I'm not used to a man who makes me feel like

you do." Her hand trembled inside his clasp as she fought for a mental balance.

He stopped the stroking motion without letting go. "How do I make you feel, Jacqueline?"

She almost didn't answer, but there was something in the magic that made her throw caution to the wind. "Whole," she said softly.

His eyebrows raised as though he were waiting for more, and there was a smoldering edge to his expression that hadn't been there before. "The hotel rooms upstairs have the names of flowers on the doors instead of numbers."

"They do?"

"Hmm. Hollyhock and Mimosa are the only two I remember. I wonder, though, if they have one named Lilac."

He wanted her and he wasn't hiding that want. Jack hesitated, then forced a breath and in the same instant decided to ignore the underlying invitation. "Why Lilac?"

"Because rainbow isn't a flower," he said enigmatically.

The non sequitur threw her, and before she could frame a response, the waiter arrived with coffee and the promised petit fours. When he'd gone, Alex reached for a toothpick upon which was impaled a small ball of chocolate. He brought it to her mouth, waited until her lips parted, then slid it inside. "The best first, I think. Just keep it on your tongue for a bit."

Holding his gaze, Jack did as he said, puzzled until a moment later, when the rich chocolate melted away from the frozen ball of a tangy sorbet or sherbet. The contrast in texture and flavor made her laugh in delight. "It's like a Fabergé egg," she said when her mouth was done reveling in the unique taste. "Quite nice before it's opened, exquisite inside."

"You should write copy for the restaurant," Alex said, then let go of her hand to reach for the coffee. In between sips of the rich, dark brew, they sampled the rest of the treats. As he'd said, the best had been the first, and Jack couldn't bring herself to say no when he offered her the second and last of the chocolate-sorbet balls. The element of surprise was lacking this time, but anticipation made up for it, and she enjoyed it every bit as much as she had the first one.

"This is a night for extremes," she said in a voice filled with wonder. "Between you, the food, and this country, everything is so much more than I've ever known before. I worry that California will seem insipid in comparison."

"What about me?" He took her hand again and lifted it to rub against his cheek. "By extremes, do you mean my size? Does it bother you?"

She laughed at what she felt was an absurd question, and with her free hand smoothed a tendril of hair at her ear that had escaped the knot. "If size were a factor, England wouldn't have a chance against the States," she said, answering him without allowing herself to be drawn back into the kind of intimate dialogue that had preceded the coffee.

Yet. She wanted to know something first. "You promised you'd explain what you meant yesterday afternoon in the garden." He looked at her questioningly, and she prodded his memory with what she remembered of his words. "You said something like you thought you'd imagined me."

The look in his eyes didn't change, and she realized he'd known all along what she was asking. He'd been waiting for the question. Still, when the words came, she sensed he hadn't known until that moment whether or not he would tell her.

"Rainbows and lilacs." He leaned close to her and took a deep breath, then lifted his head and captured her puzzled gaze. "I caught your scent twice at the racetrack, but both times you got away. I was afraid I'd imagined you . . . and the scent."

"Rainbows and lilacs." She caught her lower lip in her teeth—a habit Alex was becoming quite fond of—and looked up at him through long, dark lashes that fluttered over eyes clouded in confusion and, surprisingly, disappointment. She shook her head, and a pin came loose from the knot of hair at her nape. "I don't use perfume. It must have been someone else, another woman."

He caught the pin and pocketed it when she would have pushed it back into the knot. "No, Jacqueline. It's you." He took another deep breath and let it out slowly. "If not perfume, perhaps it's your shampoo."

She shook her head again, and her expression was guarded. "Unscented. That's why I use it." Then a smile lit up her face. "I use lilac sachet in my lingerie drawer. I've done it for so long that I'd forgotten all about it."

"That explains it, then," he murmured, and lifted her hand to his mouth so he could kiss the back of it. Her gaze was fixed on her hand, his mouth, and he felt her shiver as his lips made contact with her flesh.

"Rainbows," she whispered, and shivered again as he nuzzled the soft skin between her knuckles. "You had to have imagined that part."

He shook his head, his lips brushing her hand once more before he lowered it to his thigh. "Rainbows are real. Everyone has seen them."

"They don't have a scent."

"This one does." He looked up and saw the waiter heading toward them. "We should probably go. It's a long drive home, Jacqueline. If you'd like to freshen up, the ladies' room is upstairs." He stood and pulled her up beside him, then gently pushed her toward the door. She walked away, the silk of her dress shifting over her delicate curves, the flared skirt brushing her calves.

She looked over her shoulder at him, just once, her expression unfathomable behind lowered lashes. He sensed her hesitation, then she looked away and disappeared around the corner toward the stairs.

The temptation to have a quiet word with the staff and follow her upstairs was tempered by the knowledge that Jacqueline would respond to his loving without guilt or reserve if he gave her time to get used to the idea. Not much time, though, because three weeks was all they had.

Instead Alex signed the check and tried to imagine the look on her face as she walked down the hallway toward the rest room and saw the names of flowers on the doors.

He'd glimpsed the wariness in her eyes when he'd mentioned the rooms upstairs. It wasn't that she hadn't wanted to say yes or no that had made her avoid answering his invitation. It was, he realized, because she'd jumped to the conclusion that the only way he could know about the flower-named doors was to have stayed in one of the rooms.

As it happened, he hadn't. He'd sent her upstairs to discover that she, too, could possess such knowledge without ever spending a night in the hotel. Unless she asked him, she'd never know whether he'd made love to a woman in this place before.

He couldn't imagine that Jacqueline would ever ask.

FOUR

"Have you ever stayed at Le Manoir?" she asked.

"No." Alex pulled the Jaguar to a stop at the bottom of the long drive leading to the Goodwyns' home and set the brake. Turning to Jacqueline, he smiled as his gaze took in her sleepy eyes, the hair that was coming loose from its knot, the lips that were full and slightly red, even though the last traces of lipstick had long since disappeared.

"You're not surprised I asked," she said.

His smile widened. "Yes, I am. I'm just not bothered."

He switched off the motor, got out of the car, and went around to help her out of the low-slung vehicle. When she was standing, he pushed away the fingers that were attempting to button her coat and did the job himself.

"Why did you park all the way down here?" she asked, her voice a near whisper in the stillness of the night.

"Because I didn't want to wake Bobby by driving to the front door. I know he gets up early to organize the gallops." Leaning back against the car, he slid an arm around her waist and brought her to stand between his parted legs. With his free hand he tilted her face upward, and in the moonlight he saw that the sleepy expression had gone. "Besides, Jacqueline, I wanted to kiss you without denting a lung on the gearshift. Any closer to the house and there would be a certain lack of privacy."

She'd been wondering if he was going to kiss her. She'd been waiting, it seemed, all night. "Will you tell me something else?" she asked.

"What?" His head dipped toward her, and the warm, firm brush of his lips across her forehead almost drove that last rational thought from her mind.

"If I'd said yes tonight, would we have stayed at the hotel or would you have taken me to your home?" She felt him stiffen in surprise and she held her breath until his gentle laugh told her how he'd taken her question.

"Does it matter?" he asked, tilting her face to the moonlight.

She lifted her hands to his chest and curled her fingers around the lapels of his unfastened overcoat. "Only because I would have felt self-conscious leaving the hotel in the morning, dressed like this."

"That's all?"

"Yes."

"I'm too much of an Englishman to allow you that sort of embarrassment," he said, his long fingers digging into the knot of hair at her nape and pulling out the pins that held it together. He put them into the breast pocket of his suit coat that contained the one he'd taken earlier, then smoothed the long, heavy waves over her shoulders. "I shouldn't have told you I wanted to make love to you. That wasn't very kind of me."

"Why?"

He bent his head and rested his forehead against hers. "Because when it comes to love affairs, I suspect I live by different rules than you. It wasn't fair of me to announce my intentions before I'd made sure you understood them."

Jack had known this was coming, but hearing him say the words aloud took something bright and precious from the night. She dipped her head because she couldn't look at him and let him realize his words were a disappointment. "You mean your no-strings, no happily-ever-after, no-expectations-leads-to-no-disappointment rule?"

"Hillary's assessment, I gather." His fingers caressed the back of her neck, and he kissed her on the cheek. "I'm surprised you still came out with me."

"Admittedly I've never discussed having sex with a man I'd only just met—"

"Don't make it sound so cheap," he growled, his fingers testing the soft hollow at her nape. "It won't be like that between us."

She didn't doubt him, and credited what was left of the magic for making that possible. With a tremulous smile she said, "What I meant to say was that I'm not accustomed to talking about it or doing it—"

"Making love, you mean?" When she nodded hesitantly, he chuckled and gathered handfuls of her hair into his fists. With a slight pressure he tilted her face until she was once again looking up at him. "I didn't think you were. But as long as we're on the subject, how long has it been since you've had a lover?"

"Why?" Her reply was more a squeak than a word, the accompanying shiver a direct consequence of the seductive quality of his voice.

"Just curious. Your response to me is so intense, so uninhibited." He touched his lips to the soft hollow beneath her ear. "When I touch you, I can feel the electricity pass between us. I'm almost afraid to kiss you for fear lightning will strike us down where we stand."

"And here I thought you were just heeding Hillary's warning."

His laugh was rich and full. "I never promised not to kiss you, Jacqueline." Then his hand slid down to the small of her back, and he urged her closer. Jack leaned into him, his heat penetrating the layers of clothing with a subtle persuasion that eased her deep into the realm of sensual awareness he'd created especially, it seemed, for her.

His kiss, when it finally came, took her deeper still. Alex settled his mouth against hers, shifted the tilt of her head with a firm touch, and parted her lips to slip his tongue inside. Jack yielded to his lead and, in the dance that followed, delighted in the expertise that brought her such incredible pleasure.

His taste was warm and pleasing, his lips firm and persuasive. Her eyelids fluttered closed as his tongue stroked along hers, and the moan she gave came from the far reaches of her soul. His kiss was hot and slow and demanding, and she wanted it never to end. The heat gathered inside her, pooling between her thighs, filling her breasts. Her heart thudded almost painfully in her chest, the pounding filling her ears, and her last rational thought was how perfect her life would be if she could spend the rest of it kissing Alex.

With a shocked gasp she wrenched her mouth from his.

"What's wrong, Jacqueline?" There was a roughness to his voice that hadn't been there before. "Did I hurt you?"

"No!" She pushed against his chest and tried to back away. He let her, but only far enough to put a few inches between them. His hands curled around her arms, stilling her flight with the same firm touch that he'd used on her just moments ago when they'd been kissing.

Just kissing, she reminded herself, that was all. Two adults, fully dressed, kissing in the moonlight after a pleasant dinner together. Normal for some, she guessed, but a new experience for her. All the pieces had been in place before, but she'd never wanted a man's kisses the way she wanted Alex's.

The strength of that wanting scared her more than she liked to admit.

"Jacqueline, what is it?"

She felt like a fool, and to explain what she was feeling would only make it worse. Alex liked his women sophisticated, Hillary had said, and Jack knew that was just another word for experienced. She wasn't, not very anyway, and didn't want to bring a precipitate end to things by admitting it.

That is, if he didn't already know.

Alex shook her gently, then cupped her chin and tilted up her face when she still didn't answer. The worry in her eyes would have caused him concern if he hadn't been fairly sure what caused it. "Are you going to tell me about it, Jacqueline?"

Her hesitation was brief. "I thought I heard something . . . a car . . ." Her words trailed off at the slow shake of his head.

"No, you didn't." He rubbed her swollen bottom lip with his thumb, the fingers of his other hand sinking into her hair. "The beat of your heart was too loud in your ears for you to hear anything else. I know because that's exactly what happened to me."

"Really?" Her voice had a breathless quality that made him want to kiss her again. He didn't, though, because they'd both had enough temptation for one night.

As long as they were going to sleep apart, he needed to keep better control over the powerful responses she raised in him.

He couldn't resist smoothing her brow with a fleeting touch of his lips. "Really, Jacqueline. Kissing you was more excitement than I've had in a very long time. Does it surprise you that I can admit that?"

She nodded, and he laughed against her hair. "It surprises me too. I knew I was attracted to you, but this goes way beyond anything I've felt with a woman in years."

"It scared me when I realized how deeply, how easily I respond to you," she said in a shaky voice.

"You have no need to be frightened of me, Jacqueline. I won't hurt you, not ever."

It wasn't him she was afraid of, Jack thought. It was herself, and the way she was beginning to feel. "Does that mean you want to see me again?"

He looked at her strangely. "I want to make love with you, Jacqueline. Until then I want to spend every moment possible with you."

The intensity of his reply took her breath away. After a long moment in which common sense warred with the passionate needs he had stirred within her, she filled her lungs with clean night air and said, "I've only three weeks left in England."

"I know." He bent his head and kissed her before she realized what he was about. When it was over, he said, "The anticipation is probably going to drive me mad."

"Then why wait?" The words came out before she could stop them, and she waited breathlessly for his reply.

He closed his eyes and groaned. When he looked at her again, not even the darkness could hide the passion in his expression. "We wait because it will be better that way."

And that, it seemed, was that. Jack cleared her throat and took a step backward. He let her go this time, and she pushed her shaking hands into her coat pockets as she looked at him.

"I'd better go in now," she said.

He nodded and slipped his hand beneath her elbow as she turned to walk up the drive. "I'll pick you up at eight, if that's all right. We'll eat at a pub I like near Burford."

"What's wrong with the Red Lion?" She asked the question in the same hushed voice Alex used now that they were near the house.

They reached the door before he answered. "Too many people will know me there. I'd rather not share your company, and I'd end up doing just that if we went to the Red Lion." He took the key Bobby had given her and unlocked the door. "Not to worry, Jacqueline. You'll get your duck."

He pushed the door open, handed her the key, and walked to the bottom of the steps before looking back. The moon caught the silver glint of his eyes, but she could read nothing in his expression that might be a reflection of the sensual upheaval she was feeling.

"Go inside, sweet," he said, then turned and headed back down the drive.

Without kissing her again. She hated the empty feeling that gave her.

Alex walked through the ground floor of the sprawling country house he'd purchased ten years earlier from a man who'd used it as a weekend retreat until his third wife had decided a large manor house in Kent was more to her liking. The brick-and-stone-faced house had been built nearly two centuries earlier, and rebuilt on the inside several times, the most recent being under Alex's direction when he'd rewired, replumbed, and generally reconditioned everything while leaving as many original walls with their wood carvings and plaster moldings as humanly possible. The result was a spacious, comfortable home—

big enough for a large family but not overwhelming for a single man who enjoyed his privacy.

The prospect of bringing a wife to that home was what guided Alex's steps into the walnut-paneled study. He poured himself a snifter of brandy and went to sit in one of the two leather-covered wing chairs facing the fireplace. The logs were set, the flue open, and all it would have taken was to touch a match to the kindling for the whole thing to burst into instant warmth and color. He didn't bother, though, because he didn't intend to sit there any longer than it took to drink the brandy and make a decision about Jacqueline.

His pulse quickened, and the sexual tension that had been with him all evening spread throughout his body until there wasn't a part of him untouched by her heat. Jacqueline's heat, and the passion that simmered in her eyes, her touch.

The only thing that had kept him from reacting too blatantly to the sensual invitation was the realization that she hadn't known it was there. That much had been obvious from her quick blushes, the fluttering of her eyelashes, the tiny gasps of surprise when he'd allowed hints of his own excitement to show.

She'd thought she was responding to him, when in reality he was responding to her. The extraordinary symmetry of their sexual attraction was something he'd never encountered.

It hadn't been until he'd put the chocolate-covered sorbet into her mouth that the notion of marriage had occurred to him. Her response to the delicacy had been as unexpected as it was delightful. She'd made the analogy to the Fabergé egg, then laughed with such enjoyment that he'd felt as though he'd actually given her the fabulously expensive egg.

He'd realized then that he could do worse than marry

a woman who gave him pleasure simply by embracing him in her own. That, added to the undoubtable sexual attraction, was more than enough to get him thinking along the lines of something permanent.

He wasn't even bothered that until that night he'd considered marriage only as a necessary prelude to children. Now, having met Jacqueline, he imagined it might even be enjoyable. All that was left to be done was think it through and make sure there were no obvious deterrents of a practical nature.

No matter how good the sex was, the concept of marriage was nonsense if the people involved weren't compatible outside of the bedroom as well as in.

Alex loosened the knot of his tie, then slipped the button beneath it free as he settled himself comfortably in the deeply cushioned chair. The brandy was an undemanding companion, warming him without making a fuss about it. He took another sip, then set his mind to the task of sorting through the impressions and facts he'd been accumulating all night. Unfortunately the facts were few, as most of their conversations had revolved around sightseeing and food. He concentrated first on his impressions of the petite, black-haired woman who had managed, with no apparent effort, to keep his interest at peak level all evening.

As far as he could discern, Jacqueline was intelligent, naturally vivacious, and self-confident. Those traits were as important to him as they were obvious. She spoke carefully and easily about things she was familiar with and wasn't afraid to ask questions about those she wasn't. Her enthusiasm for sightseeing was clearly an extension of a lively personality, and there was a quiet confidence in her manner that revealed she was content with who she was.

She was also totally without guile—something he'd not accepted without resistance. It wasn't precisely his fault, he allowed. He'd never known a woman quite so honest or sincere, or, for that matter, one who didn't prefer riches to rags. The fuss over the restaurant had seemed false because he wasn't accustomed to dating women who would have been satisfied with the Red Lion when Le Manoir was on offer.

It had taken him most of the evening to realize Jacqueline had told the truth in that as in everything else.

He swirled the brandy in the cut-crystal snifter, thinking she would be less resistant to the little luxuries once she became accustomed to them. He presumed she'd soon come to enjoy them, as she had Le Manoir, and wondered if she would continue to project an air of excitement once those luxuries were the norm rather than the exception.

He shifted in the chair, conscious that he was relying heavily on instinct when it came to interpreting what he knew about Jacqueline. They hadn't been together long enough for more, although he would wager a fortune his assumptions about her were sufficiently close to the truth so as to make no difference in the end.

Impressions and instinct aside, the facts were scarce. All he had managed to learn was that she was a teacher, lived near her family, and valued her independence. Each time he'd tried to probe into her life in California, she'd said little, then brought the conversation back to England. His question about her home life had been channeled into a near-hysterical account of the lunch she and Hillary had shared with a muster of peacocks at Warwick Castle. When he'd asked about her career, they'd somehow ended up debating the merits of punting on the river Cam versus the Isis, which flowed through Oxford.

There was also the story about the pheasant and why Hillary wouldn't let her drive. He'd found himself wondering if he should be the one to teach her to drive on what was, for her, the wrong side of the road or if England would be better off without Jacqueline attempting to perfect that particular skill.

That was, of course, before the idea of marriage had occurred to him. Now he realized there would be no choice. Jacqueline would have to master driving in England, and the pheasant population would just have to make the best of it.

If she chose to stay. There was nothing obvious in her background that would prevent her from living her life in England rather than California. Alex gave only fleeting notice to the chance she'd say no to his proposal. As in business, success was dependent upon the effort that went into the proposition. More than in any act of business, though, this time failure was unacceptable.

The heat of his arousal pulsed through his body, a powerful reminder of how Jacqueline, even in her absence, affected him.

Alex got up and poured himself another measure of brandy, then shut out the lights and stood at the wide bay window overlooking the rose gardens behind the house. He'd never given much thought to marrying, except those times when he'd been forced to sidestep the machinations of one female or another. In fact he'd become quite adept at the marriage-avoidance game following an episode in his early twenties, when young Sylvia Canterleigh had taken his proposal seriously until she'd learned his college roommate had better prospects. The fact that Alex loved her had meant nothing.

The roommate had eventually thrown Sylvia over for a duke's daughter, by which time Alex had learned that emotions were crippling nonessentials that one could live much better without. So long as Jacqueline understood that, they would do quite well together. Alex didn't imagine that would be a problem and supposed he could thank Hillary for that.

He couldn't believe Hillary would go to the trouble of warning Jacqueline of his no-strings rule without telling her what an emotionless bastard he was. He was aware of Hillary's friendship with Shelby Denton and assumed Shelby wouldn't have hesitated to share her views on Alex's lack of emotional depth, as she'd called it. She'd certainly complained enough about it when they'd been together.

If Jacqueline had minded, she wouldn't have come out with him. Even on short acquaintance, he guessed, she was intelligent enough to realize a man of his age couldn't change something so intrinsic to his character. Alex took a final sip of brandy, put the glass down on the desk at his back, and nodded in satisfaction at his assessment.

The pieces were all there. Jacqueline would do nicely as his wife. She suited him. All he had to do now was convince her he wasn't a mad Englishman given to impulsive behavior.

He would have to court her. Not in the traditional sense where hearts confused the facts, but at a pragmatic level. He would give her a taste of the kind of life they would lead together, treat her to new experiences, new levels of pleasure. Over the next couple of weeks he would learn all about her and in the process teach her about himself. By the time he proposed, she'd know that he would protect her and provide for her to the best of his ability.

For the next week or so it would be necessary, he decided, to keep the sexual element in the background as much as possible. The attraction between them was too powerful, too intense. He could easily imagine they would be absorbed by it to the exclusion of all else. With only a short time to achieve the trust and knowledge both would need prior to agreeing to marriage, sex and all that it entailed would only be in the way.

He groaned aloud, acknowledging the physical pain that waiting would bring.

Alex stared out into the garden, where moonbeams cast ghostly images beside the thick, grotesquely shaped trunks of rosebushes that were more ancient that the plumbing he'd replaced ten years past. Bringing Jacqueline into his life was more than a matter of logic and thought, he admitted. It was a necessity.

From the moment he'd first caught her scent, he'd wanted her with a passion that awakened all his hunter instincts and ripped at his control. Sex would be extraordinary with Jacqueline. He was too experienced, too aware of his own responses to imagine otherwise.

She would make love with him without promises, he knew.

But she couldn't promise to stay, and he knew that a week or a month would never be enough.

He wanted her for a lifetime.

FIVE

Hillary poured coffee into two mugs, then added a healthy dollop of milk to her own before carrying them both over to the coffee table as Jack plucked a wilted leaf from the flowers Alex had sent two days earlier. She put Jack's mug on a coaster, then eased down onto the sofa.

"Bobby told me at breakfast that he was considering never speaking to you again," Hillary said.

Jack curled her fingers over the leaf and sat down opposite her friend. "Bobby threatens that every time he catches me laughing at Ian." Ian, Bobby's head lad, was a short, wiry Irishman who was incapable of speaking without a liberal dose of obscenities seasoning the already incomprehensible—to her—horse talk. Far from being offended, Jack thought it was hysterical that the only words she understood were the four-letter ones.

"It's got nothing to do with Ian this time," Hillary said. "Bobby's mad about the duck."

Jack blinked and felt her jaw drop. "What did he do, smell it on me when I came in last night?"

"Alex was up at the gallops this morning. He told."

Her heart beat a little faster, as it always did when she

heard his name. She met Hillary's laughing gaze with what she hoped was mild curiosity in her own. "Oh?"

"Mmm. Alex keeps close tabs on Golden Legs when he's in town. He either comes to see the horses work in the morning or shows up at evening stables. That's why Bobby usually sends Golden Legs out with the first string, so Alex can watch."

"Do all owners do that?" The subject of horses was safe so long as they kept the words short.

"Not as regularly," Hillary admitted. "Bobby says Alex treats Golden Legs more like a pet than a racehorse, but he wouldn't dare tell him so."

No, Jack thought, one wouldn't. She nudged the conversation back to the duck. "What else did Alex have to say about dinner?"

"You'll have to ask Bobby. He was so miffed about the duck, he couldn't talk about anything else."

Asking Bobby what Alex had said about their duck dinner didn't appeal to Jack, mostly because she'd spent the last six years of her life watching teenage hearts soar or break after hearing events retold from the other person's perspective.

She might feel giddy as a teenager, but she was doing her best not to act like one.

Hillary gave her a peeved look over the rim of her coffee cup. "I can't tell you how much I appreciate your getting Bobby started in on duck again."

"You're overreacting, Hillary. The occasional treat won't hurt him." Jack reached for her coffee and held the mug under her nose, where she could better inhale the aroma of hazelnut. "I was going to sneak him a drumstick, but was afraid you'd find it in the fridge and stick it under my pillow. Besides, Alex wouldn't donate his drumstick to the cause, and I'd already eaten mine when I thought of it."

"Speaking of Alex . . ." Hillary looked at her expectantly.

"What about him?" If Hillary wasn't going to tell her what Bobby had said, Jack wasn't going to tell her anything either. Two could play that game, Jack decided.

"Just that you haven't said yet whether you'll be home for dinner, that's all."

Hillary played the game well.

Jack surrendered gracefully. "I told him I'd check if it would be all right to leave you two alone again tonight. He's going to call later."

"You don't have to ask our permission, Jack."

"I'm a guest in your house," Jack said with a hint of apology. "This will be the third night in a row I'm deserting you."

"Bobby and I have had six years of getting used to entertaining each other. Another night shouldn't be a strain."

"You're being deliberately obtuse." Jack finished her coffee and put the cup on the table. "I, on the other hand, am trying to be polite."

Hillary sniffed and waggled her fingers negligently in the air. "Be polite to someone else. In the meantime, I want details about your date and I want them now."

Jack had no more opened her mouth to speak when Hillary interrupted. "And it had better be good this time. I want to know more than what you ate."

Jack felt a grin poking at the corners of her mouth. "I remember telling you I had a great time."

"You also told me about the rooms upstairs with porcelain flowers on the doors. I let you get away with that once, but not today." She leaned forward with elbows on knees and an earnest look on her face. "You've been moody all morning, Jack. What happened last night?"

If she knew that, she'd have a better idea herself how

to deal with it. Jack sighed and was about to launch into an edited summary of the evening, when the phone rang and Hillary ran off to answer it. When she came back, it was to say she had to run over to the vet's to pick up something for Bobby and would return soon.

"Be ready to leave for Oxford when I get back," she said over her shoulder. They were doing the Ashmolean Museum that afternoon, followed by a buzz through Cheltenham's antique stores.

Jack looked down at her fuzzy robe and slippers and thought a day off wouldn't go amiss, particularly after yesterday, when they'd spent hours exploring the ancient spas in nearby Bath. The door closed behind Hillary with a bang, and Jack immediately forgot her friend's admonition to get ready. Instead she settled more comfortably into the deep chair and wondered if telling Hillary about the previous evening would help Jack herself understand exactly what had happened.

Then again, how would talking about it help make sense of anything? There was only the niggling feeling that something was going on that she didn't understand, a feeling that Alex knew something she didn't.

It wasn't that she hadn't had a wonderful time, because she had—beginning, she knew, with the look of pleasure in his eyes when she'd thanked him for the painting that had been delivered just moments before he arrived. It was a vibrant watercolor of Oxford at dawn, the sun's first rays splitting in dazzling array across the knobby spires and rooftops. The night before, she'd mentioned the artist in passing, not saying much more than that she'd seen some of his work in Oxford and thought it good.

The painting was superb—not horribly extravagant, but more than he should have given someone she hardly knew. More than she could accept. Alarmed by her decision, Hillary had been quick to point out the painting had probably cost no more than the flowers, and she hadn't fussed about those, had she?

No, she hadn't, Jack agreed, then remembered how easily Alex's feelings had been bruised the night before over the choice of restaurants. So she'd thanked him nicely, and his smile of pleasure had been worth more than any flowers or painting.

When he told her he'd been advised the watercolor would double in value within a year, her pleasure had dimmed for a moment before she convinced herself he hadn't bought it as an investment.

He'd given it to her because she liked the artist.

At dinner Alex had been attentive, courteous, and interested in everything she said. Halfway through the meal of roast duck with cranberry sauce, Jack remembered thinking she'd never talked so much about herself, but when she tried to stop, he became insistent. And when she finally managed to reverse things, he'd willingly answered her questions, telling her about his life and work with such ease, she'd only had to prompt him here and there.

He'd told her about how he'd invested most of the trust left him by his grandfather in gold, and how those earnings had become a solid basis for the companies he'd either bought or started in the ensuing years. His business interests were diverse and substantial, with the larger concerns being real estate and commercial construction. When he wasn't occupied with those, there was a small pottery works he'd bought in Wales that was doing quite well this year, a men's custom-tailoring establishment on Saville Row, and a theater on the fringes of the West End that he was thinking of selling a half interest in, because he didn't seem to have the time to give it the attention it required.

Jack was astonished at how much detail he shared with

her. She'd guessed he was well off financially, but she came away from dinner knowing his wealth went way beyond any level she'd imagined.

When she'd dared ask about his family, he'd told her about his parents, who had died several years earlier in unrelated accidents, and about his sister, who lived in Argentina with a man she'd met at college. There were no other relatives with whom he kept in touch, he said, then asked her about her own family.

There wasn't anything, it seemed, that he wouldn't tell her. It surprised her, because she'd pictured Alex as an intensely private man who shared the details of his life if and only when necessary.

The magic of the previous night was still in full force, but the conversation seemed to deflect its intensity. Jack realized she was comfortable with Alex in a way she hadn't been at Le Manoir, and wondered if that had been his intent all along. By the time they arrived back at Bobby and Hillary's, she felt as though she'd spent the evening with a very close friend. The magic was still there, but she was somehow at ease with it.

Jack heard the sound of a car coming up the drive, and went to the window to see Hillary alighting from her blue Audi. No, she decided, there was nothing to be confused about. The night had been perfect, up to and including the kiss they'd shared at the bottom of the drive.

The intensity had returned at the first touch of his mouth on hers, and she'd been both frustrated and amused when it had ended much the same as the night before, with Alex walking her to the door and neither of them breathing evenly.

As he'd said that first night, the anticipation was probably going to drive them both mad.

Jack thought the sheer perfection of her time with Alex would get her first.

Hillary came through the door and gave Jack a disgusted look. "You're not ready."

"Why don't we take a day off? We could do housework or help Bobby with something." Jack yawned and snuggled deeper into her robe. "Maybe I'll take a nap first."

"Not used to late nights anymore?"

"We were in by eleven, as you very well know. I saw you peeking out your window as we came up the drive." She yawned again and reached for the empty mug with the intention of getting more coffee. "It's not late nights that's getting me. It's all this dashing around the countryside. Haven't you had enough yet?"

Hillary's mouth curved into a self-satisfied smirk. "This from the woman who swore a month wasn't enough to see everything? I'm disappointed."

"A month isn't enough time," Jack said, "but without a day off I won't last the week."

Hillary shook her head. "We'll talk about days off on our way into Oxford. The Ashmoleon won't be open tomorrow, and anyway I've promised Ian I'd pick up a scarf for his mother's birthday from the Liberty shop in Oxford. We *have* to go."

They went. Jack slept both ways and even managed to dissuade Hillary from stopping in Cheltenham. Antiques, she said, could wait. They'd had enough practice.

Upon their return they learned from Bobby that Alex had called and, yes, he'd relayed Jack's message that she'd be ready at seven. A bushel of tulips—Bobby's words— had also been delivered in their absence. Even Hillary was rendered speechless when they saw the delicate pink blooms sprouting from an exquisite crystal vase. Out of season and too numerous to count, the tulips were extravagant and beautiful and, Jack decided with a sigh, precisely the kind of gift he must have sent other women.

She mentally tied a string around her finger to remind herself to thank Alex for the flowers, then promptly put them out of her mind.

The two naps she'd enjoyed had completely revived her, so while Hillary dealt with some bookkeeping she'd let slide, Jack trailed along behind Bobby at evening stables.

Ian taught her how to give Golden Legs one of the carrots she'd brought without getting her fingers bit off, and another lad—a girl of about eighteen who was classified a lad by occupation, not by gender—let her practice her newfound skill on the three horses in her charge. When the lad who took care of Matchless—a nine-year-old gelding that was due to race the next day—told Bobby the horse was "jumping out of his skin," the only thing that kept Jack from voicing her concern was Bobby's total lack of it.

The language barrier remained as formidable as always.

She was determined to overcome it, and frustrated by the knowledge that in another two weeks it would no longer matter.

SIX

That night Alex took her to a country hotel north of Oxford that had originally been a manor, then a priory, then a barracks during World War II before being converted into its present form. The setting was on a grander scale than Le Manoir, more English than French in flavor, and on the drafty side. Following Alex's suggestion, she'd dressed warmly, in a slim-fitting white knit dress with a paisley scarf in shades of lavender wrapped around her shoulders. As they lingered over predinner drinks in the lounge, Jack pulled the scarf tighter and wondered why centuries of Englishmen had built homes that were impossible to heat. Alex sat beside her on the long sofa, his arm resting across the back and the heat from his body reaching her even though they weren't touching.

All in all, Jack mused, things were going along predictably—almost irritatingly so. The evening figured to be the third in a string of perfect dates, and she couldn't figure out why that made her uneasy. It was almost as though they were both performing according to a script from which the direction allowed no deviation. Alex was courteous, attentive, and totally charming. She was a nervous wreck and wondered if her acting was good enough that he didn't notice.

She loved being with him—what woman in her right mind wouldn't!—but she couldn't help remembering the last time a man had put the rush on her . . . and how it had ended. He'd been frustrated and she'd been annoyed that just because he bought her a few dinners, he'd assumed he'd paid his way into her bed.

The way Alex was treating her was nothing like that, yet the parallel was there. He was attracted, but seemed to be waiting for something. Did he have a magic formula that produced perfect results? she wondered. Did three nights of wonderful dinners plus flowers plus whatever else took his fancy to send her add up to a roll in the sack?

Or was he waiting for her to make the invitation? No, that wasn't it. Somehow Alex didn't seem like the kind of man who would completely yield the sexual initiative to a woman. He wouldn't push, but neither would he let his masculine instincts remain subdued as he waited for the woman to decide the time was appropriate.

His sensual nature was too much a part of him to allow for such docility. She inhaled sharply, stunned at how much she knew about him without knowing how it could be possible. Feeling Alex's eyes on her, Jack shivered beneath her shawl even though she was anything but cold.

"You're awfully quiet, Jacqueline. What are you thinking?"

She had to scramble for it, but came up with something neutral. "When Bobby took us to dinner at College, I about froze to death."

"You're cold?" he asked, and put his arm around her shoulders before she could summon an answer.

"Thanks." His nearness didn't do anything toward helping her relax.

"I understand from Bobby that you lost the snuff competition that night."

Jack laughed softly, remembering the night with a vividness she hoped would never pale. "When they first passed around the little silver box and I saw a gentleman at the end of the table put some on his hand and inhale it, I have to admit I was a bit worried."

"I can imagine," he said dryly.

"By the time it came around to me, I was too curious not to look inside." She rested her head against his arm and looked up at him. "It was almost black—not white, as I'd feared. By the time I put two and two together and figured out what it was, this retired brigadier next to me was offering to teach me the ritual. He put the snuff on his own hand, and showed me how to inhale it without making a mess."

Alex grinned, and raised a hand to brush from her eyes an errant curl that had escaped her chignon. "Bobby said you sneezed in two seconds flat."

"I didn't know until afterward that people around the table made bets on the whole thing. Apparently those who do snuff are timed, the winner being the one with the longest interval between inhaling and sneezing." She sniffled reflexively. "Poor Hillary was sitting there pretending she was mortified, although I think that was for show, because she said later she's always wanted to try it but Bobby won't let her."

"Women generally don't," Alex agreed, "but then, very few men do snuff these days either."

"If I'd known it was powdered tobacco, I probably wouldn't have tried it either . . . although I have to admit my sinuses felt like they'd been vacuumed. It was terrific."

The waiter appeared, and they got up to follow him into the dining room. Alex walked beside her with a hand at her waist, and Jack wondered if he could feel the tremor his touch provoked.

Dinner was excellent, but Jack found herself eating without paying much attention to the food. Alex, as ever a commanding figure in a dark blue suit, light gray shirt, and striped tie, absorbed her thoughts to the exclusion of nearly everything else. She was used to his size, his rugged good looks, the effortless way he dominated the room— used to it all, but immune to none of it.

It was a night much like the one before, filled with magic but lacking the intimately sensual dialogue they'd exchanged at Le Manoir. He delved deeper into her life and led her casually through his. By the time they finished dinner, he'd heard all about the leg she'd broken in her one and only slalom ski race, the car she'd almost lost to the fierce Pacific Ocean tide, and the man who had nearly convinced her to marry him. The last bit had come out of nowhere—the script perhaps—and it wasn't until later that Jack realized his questions had been guided, more or less, to that piece of information.

When he asked her what had gone wrong to prevent the marriage, she said simply that it just hadn't been right . . . and silently wished the director of the play they were starring in would let her read ahead far enough to erect a few defenses. Old romances shouldn't be material for casual dinner conversation, she thought. Alex shouldn't even be interested.

The fact that he was put her more on edge than before.

For each piece of her life that she shared, he gave her one of his own. By the time they went back into the sitting room for coffee, she discovered Alex had rowed with the Oxford Blues against Cambridge, preferred Austrian ski holidays over French or Swiss, and had recently bought a twin-engine Sky King that he couldn't seem to find time to learn to fly.

"So why did you buy it?" Jack asked, thinking an airplane was an expensive toy, even by Alex's standards. She smoothed her skirt and settled comfortably in the deep chair beside the fire, thinking it had been warmer before dinner, with Alex beside her on the sofa.

He poured their coffee from the silver pot and handed her a cup before settling into the chair opposite. "I spend a lot of time flying around England, checking up on various business interests. It made sense to invest in a plane."

"Won't it rot or something if you don't use it?"

He smiled. "It's leased to the charter company I usually use. The pilots are quite good about showing me what they're doing as we go along, but I've got to get some ground school out of the way before they'll let me take the controls."

"Nice to hear you're being sensible," she murmured, and didn't repeat herself when he asked. Instead she changed the subject to Golden Legs. "Bobby mentioned the other day that you were talking about selling him. Is that true?"

He shrugged. "Probably. Bobby wants to race him in three weeks at Cheltenham, but I'm not sure it's a good idea."

Three weeks. She wouldn't be there to watch. Jack kept the regret to herself and said, "Why not?"

"Every time he loses, his value goes down."

"He might win," she said.

"He might not."

Jack put the delicate cup and saucer on the table between them and looked at him curiously. "Who's going to feed Golden Legs his carrots if you're not there to do it?"

He hesitated, and the silver gaze was almost completely shuttered behind lowered eyelids. "His new owner, I expect."

"And if he doesn't?"

"Carrots aren't essential," he said evenly. "Whoever buys Golden Legs will feed him well. It would be senseless to do otherwise."

She didn't argue with him, but neither did she believe he was so uncaring that Golden Legs' future was of no consequence to him. A man who fed his investment carrots was looking beyond dollar signs, whether he knew it or not.

A smile tickled her lips, and she rephrased the thought, using pounds this time, not dollars. It wouldn't take long, she imagined, to change the habits of a lifetime.

It wasn't much later, when they were driving away from the hotel, that Alex asked if she would come out for dinner the next night.

Jack didn't know if she had it in her to endure yet another perfect date. On the other hand, there was nowhere else she'd rather be than with Alex. That realization unnerved her almost as much as their scripted dialogue.

"I really shouldn't," she hedged. "Hillary will begin to forget who I am if I miss another dinner."

"I have to go to the States—New York—the following morning. Hillary will have you all to herself for three days." He reached over and took her hand, bringing it to rest on his hard thigh without taking his eyes from the narrow, winding road. "I've gotten used to being with you in the evenings. The idea of spending the time alone when you're just down the road at Hillary's doesn't appeal to me."

A tiny grin found its way to her lips. "I'm not sure whether you're saying you're going to miss me or that you hate being alone."

"I've never minded being alone," he said simply.

The thought of not seeing him bothered Jack more than she liked to admit. "Why do you have to go?"

"Business." His hand moved to the gearshift, and she felt a slight ripple in his powerful leg muscles as he turned the Jaguar onto the motorway and accelerated. "I'd take you with me, Jacqueline, but it wouldn't be much fun for you. You're better off here with Hillary."

The unexpectedness of his words took her breath away. It wasn't so much that he'd considered taking her that astonished Jack. Rather it was the way he said it, as though he knew she'd go if he asked.

Even knowing he was right wasn't enough to over-come the pique she felt at having the decision handed to her ready-made. The perfect script was wearing thin.

"I suppose someone has to stay here and make sure Golden Legs gets his carrots," she said, well aware that the annoyed tone of her voice wouldn't go over big with the director. Out of the corner of her eye she caught the movement of Alex's head as he glanced at her.

"That wasn't a casual invitation, Jacqueline," he said quietly. "If I were a touch more selfish, I'd do what I want —which is to take you with me."

"I'm not sure that I wouldn't prefer a selfish man to a control freak," she muttered.

"Excuse me?"

She continued as though he hadn't spoken. "At least then I'd get to say my own lines."

There was a short pause, then he said, "You're not making any sense."

"That's because you never learned to ad lib."

Jack could sense his irritation and was extraordinarily pleased by it. Unfortunately, her annoyance was revived by his next words.

"I can't disregard the fact that by taking you to New York, I'd be stealing part of your vacation."

Stealing seemed too harsh a term, and she made a mental note to consult the scriptwriter. Maybe she could arrange a little easing of Alex's control complex at the same time.

"I've never seen New York," she said aloud.

"You wouldn't see it with me either. I doubt I'd have any time with you outside of the hotel."

He sounded sincerely regretful, but she was more inclined to believe he was peeved at having to make the trip alone when he would customarily have feminine company. Something inside her bristled at the implication that if she were any other woman—one who lived in England, to be precise—he wouldn't think twice about taking her along. She lifted her hand from his thigh and hid it in the folds of her coat that lay on her lap.

If that was his problem, she knew how to fix it.

"That's the trouble with tourists," she said. "So much to see, so little time to do it in. I'm sure if you put your mind to it, you'll find someone to take along who doesn't have such a tight schedule."

"What are you suggesting?"

She shrugged. "Look, Alex, I'm not naive enough to think a few dinners give me the right to be annoyed if you choose to take someone else to the States. I won't go with you, so you should feel perfectly free to find someone who will." What she didn't say was that she'd be devastated, not annoyed, and that when he came back, he could take his traveling companion for dinner, not Jack.

She might not have any rights over him, but she had her pride.

The car swerved slightly, and Jack could feel it begin to slow down as Alex eased out of the fast lane. He took the next exit, steering the Jaguar through a small roundabout and onto a two-lane road as Jack wondered where they were going because the exit wasn't the one they'd used earlier. He slowed down and pulled into a roadside parking area, and she shifted uneasily in her seat as he threw the gearshift into neutral, jerked on the hand brake, and shut off the headlights.

Then he just sat there for a few minutes, staring through the windshield, not looking at her, his chest rising and falling with deep, even breaths. She couldn't help but look at him, the meager light from the dashboard disguising his expression in shadowy angles and shafts of unnatural color.

Jack wasn't certain, but she had the impression he was just the slightest bit angry. That notion wasn't dispelled when he finally turned to her and said, "I had hoped that after all the time we've spent together, you would know me better than that."

"Three days isn't—"

"Four," he interrupted harshly. "At least get it right."

He *was* angry, but it didn't occur to Jack to be frightened. "Four days, then," she said evenly. "But only three dinners, Alex. That's not much time in anyone's book." Four days, and she was already more vulnerable to him than any man she'd ever known. A tremor ripped through her. She knew he sensed it, because his gaze narrowed on her face and there was a tightening of the muscles around his mouth.

He spoke as though it took an effort to say the words without shouting them. "It should have been enough time for you to know I wouldn't sleep with another woman while I was seeing you."

A hot flush rose on her cheeks, but she refused to be daunted. "You just said it yourself, Alex. You're *seeing* me, not sleeping with me. There's a difference, one that gives you some leeway."

"Make up your mind, Jacqueline," he said roughly. "Are you angry because you're afraid I'll sleep with another woman, or because I haven't made love to you yet?"

"Neither!" she said, and knew it was both.

His hands fisted on his thighs, and he shut his eyes for a long moment. When his eyelids finally opened and he fixed his gaze on her, she could almost feel the cold slice of steel through her nerves. "I'm not in the habit of taking women along on business trips, Jacqueline. You would have been an exception."

Her breath wedged in her throat. Alex had avoided addressing the matter of whether or not he ever intended to make love to her while setting her mind at ease about the other. It was, she realized, the most she could expect from a situation that was already out of her control.

She swallowed with difficulty, then took a couple of breaths and said, "I apologize, Alex. I guess I'm trying so hard to be casual about this that I got carried away."

"Casual about what?"

"Us," she said simply. "I know that I haven't got your experience, but I'm smart enough to know I shouldn't get so involved that I smother you with demands and expectations."

He hesitated, then said, "That disappoints me, Jacqueline."

"Why?"

"Because, you see, I *do* have expectations when it comes to us. It's why I haven't made love to you yet, even though every nerve in my body is screaming at the delay."

So much for thinking he wasn't going to comment on that detail. Jack waited with every sense on full alert as he slowly reached one hand toward her. When he cupped her heated face with his cool palm, it was both reassuring and tantalizing.

"I suppose it's a good thing we're in the car and not

somewhere else," he murmured as his hand slid down to her shoulder.

"Why?" she asked, a shaky whisper being all she could manage.

"Because if we were someplace that was both comfortable and private, I would be buried deep inside of you right now, and then all the anticipation and waiting would be over. I don't think either of us is ready for that yet, do you?"

Her gasp filled the air, and Alex shifted in his seat so that his back was to the road. "Or do you disagree with me, Jacqueline? Do you wish we were somewhere comfortable and private?" His fingers glided over the delicate line of her collarbone. "Do you want to make love to me as much as I want to make love to you?"

He didn't give her a chance to answer, but instead bent forward to brush his lips across hers in a gentle, restrained kiss. "I have to admit it's been a trial to keep my hands off you," he said softly. "But I knew by our sexual reactions to each other that once we made love, it would be all-consuming."

"I guess I can't see what could possibly be wrong with that." Her voice was wobbly as he eased backward without stopping the sweet caress of his fingers on the bare skin above her dress.

His eyes flashed in the darkness, and she experienced a brief surge of power as his hand fisted against her shoulder. He was less in control than she'd imagined, and the knowledge excited her.

He chuckled then, and gradually eased his clenched fist. "Touché, Jacqueline. That one went deep."

"I meant what I said," she murmured as his hand warmed her shoulder. "I don't see why we're waiting."

"Call me old-fashioned, but I want to know you better

first," he said, skimming a finger up the side of her neck
to her ear. "You're a bit old-fashioned, too, Jacqueline."

"I'm not."

"Any woman who fills her lingerie drawers with lilac
sachets has a touch of the Old World about her."

He leaned forward again, his mouth covering hers
with more heat this time, more fire. This wasn't a man
needing to coax a response from a nervous girl, and Alex
knew it. His tongue delved inside her mouth, stroking,
teasing, learning again the taste of her as she learned his.
He groaned deep in his throat as Jacqueline threaded her
fingers into his hair, and he clenched his hand with as
much restraint as he could manage around her shoulders.

It wasn't enough, though, and he tried to pull her
closer so that her breasts could rub against his chest, her
nipples teasing him in their pointed readiness. He wanted
to unbutton his shirt and her dress, let them be naked in a
way that was exciting and so incredibly necessary. He
wanted to take those nipples into his mouth, to suck and
lick and listen as Jacqueline began her descent to the
erotic whirlpool of—

A faint rumbling sound penetrated his consciousness.
Breathing hard, he glanced up and saw the taillights of a
small lorry disappearing around the bend.

It wasn't the proverbial splash of cold water, but it
served as well. With a reluctance that he didn't bother
hiding, he gave Jacqueline a final, lingering kiss, then
pulled her hands away and held them in her lap. She
looked as dazed as he felt, and the frustration that raged
inside him was in her gaze as well.

"Wrong time, wrong place," he said with forced light-
ness, "but it did serve to prove a point."

"What point?"

"That if we'd made love that first night, I wouldn't
know much more about you beyond how you respond to

me sexually. I'd be too busy making love to you to realize there was anything more."

"Why does that even matter?"

"It just does." He stroked her cheek. "Have patience, Jacqueline. It will be better this way."

"Mad dogs and Englishmen," Jack muttered, then took a deep breath in an attempt to clear the erotic fog from her brain. "It must be the air over here in England."

"What do you mean?"

She looked at him and sighed. "I mean that you only have to look at me and I want to do things with you that I'm pretty sure I've never even imagined doing with anyone else."

"Is that a problem?"

"Only in the wee hours of the morning when I think about it and wonder what the hell happened to my morals."

"Nothing is wrong with your morals, Jacqueline." There was a harshness in his voice that hadn't been there before. "Are you afraid I've seduced you into wanting me after all?"

"No!" She shook her head abruptly. "It's not you, Alex. It's me. I'm terrified I'll go back to California and spend the rest of my life wondering if it was the excitement of being in England that fanned the flames or if what I feel for you was something else."

"Something else," he said. "I've lived in England most of my life, so I can safely say the strength of the attraction is unique."

"You're sure?"

He cocked his head, and she breathed a sigh of relief when a smile tugged at the corner of his mouth. "That's why I invited you to New York. I want *you* with me, not some other woman. As I told you earlier, I have expectations about us, even if you don't."

There was that word again: expectations.

Jack knew she'd misunderstood, *had* to have misunderstood, because otherwise it sounded very much like he'd said—twice now—that he had expectations. About them. *Us*.

It was impractical. Imprudent. Imbecilic.

All of those. Jack took a moment to regroup, replaying the *"ims"* until she was sure she had a firm grasp of the concept.

Impractical.

Their lives were already firmly established, with thousands of miles creating an unconquerable barrier between them.

Imprudent.

In two weeks she would return to a life that was secure and rewarding, far away from the kind of excitement she felt in his presence.

Imbecilic.

So long as she remembered that, her heart would be safe. The last thing she needed was to lose her heart to an Englishman who wouldn't know what to do with it.

Impudent.

Jack wished he would define what he meant by expectations.

"Jacqueline?"

She looked up, and found Alex watching her with a touch of worry furrowing his brow. "What's wrong now?" he said.

Impetuous!

"You *didn't* invite me to New York," she said, smiling for no good reason except that something warm and tender made her feel like doing it. "If I remember correctly, you said I'd be better off with Hillary and that I wouldn't have much fun anyway."

His eyes narrowed to unreadable slits, and she waited

for what seemed forever before he said, "Are you saying you want to go with me to New York?"

Impossible.

Making her own decisions wasn't all it was cracked up to be. The temptation to say yes was nearly overwhelming, but common sense raised its fearsome head and dragged her down in its wake. To say yes would mean admitting she'd rather be with Alex than anywhere. To say no would prove she was still in control—of her life *and* her heart.

Immaterial.

She forced a smile from a disgusting well of sadness and said, "No, Alex, I don't want to go to New York. But thanks for asking."

"I should have done so in the first place."

"You like being in control too much to do that," she said with a forgiving smile. *That's why the director chose you,* she added silently. Her thoughts were in such turmoil, she decided not to force a discussion of "the perfect script."

"You called me a control freak," he said. "I'm not sure I like that."

Impaired—but not beyond salvaging.

"I don't blame you. But don't worry, you have other redeeming qualities."

He reached across the console and took her hand in his. Keeping his eyes on her face, he threaded his fingers between hers.

"You're sure you won't come with me?" His voice was low and had a smile in it that almost made her change her mind.

Imperfect.

She couldn't afford to risk it. "You go, Alex. Alone, if you don't mind me saying so."

"I don't mind."

Impasse.

SEVEN

At Alex's invitation Jack climbed out of bed on the wrong side of first light and, without doing much more than pulling on warm clothing and dragging a brush through her hair, she trudged down to the stables. The first string was already winding its way through the gate and across the road toward the downland track. She jumped into the Land Rover beside Bobby seconds before he pulled out to follow the procession.

"What's got you up so early . . . as if I didn't know?" he asked, his eyes twinkling beneath a lock of straight hair that had escaped the knit cap he wore against the cold.

"Alex said you were going to let Golden Legs run for the first time since his race. He thought I might like to watch."

A curious look crossed his face, but Bobby just nodded as though she'd said something profound. "Just half-speed gallops, though. I've given Golden Legs a few days' rest—walking, trotting, and a short canter yesterday. It's time to let him run a bit now and get the cobwebs out."

"Do you always do it that way after a race?"

He shrugged. "Depends on the horse. Since Golden Legs' second loss, I've tried working different combinations. Maybe this one will bring him back to us."

She caught the worried note in his voice. "Is it normal for a horse to have a losing streak like this?"

"Again, it depends on the horse." He slowed down as the last of the string ambled over the hill ahead, then urged the Land Rover over the crest. "I shouldn't have thought something like this would happen to Golden Legs, though. His breeding is top rate, and his form has been consistently good for the four years he's been doing hurdles. The races he's run lately haven't been out of his class, yet except for the other day when he came in fourth, he's been either at the rear or close to it." He sighed heavily and eased the truck to a stop. "Something's going on with that horse. I know I can figure it out sooner or later."

"And in the meantime all you have to do is convince Alex not to sell."

Bobby grinned. "Just don't use the *sell* word in front of Alex. I've got a feeling he's willing to be distracted from decision making for a few weeks. That may be all the time I need."

Her grin was one of knowing complicity, and they were both laughing when another truck pulled up alongside. Alex got out and came around the hood as she slid from the Land Rover. Field glasses hung from a leather string around his neck, and he looked ruggedly handsome in the navy-blue pea coat with a wool scarf around his neck and boots up to his knees.

Jack took the hand he offered and replied to his soft-spoken "Good morning" with a murmur that carried with it all the shyness she felt as she looked into his eyes and knew he was remembering every word and kiss from the night before. He squeezed her hand, and Jack worked on steadying her pulse as he greeted Bobby in a louder voice.

Together they followed Bobby to the edge of the all-weather gallop and waited quietly as he watched the tail end of the string disappear over a rise.

As this was the first time she'd come to watch the horses exercise, Bobby explained what was happening. "I've already given the lads their instructions in the yard. They'll come past us in groups of two or three at whatever speed we've decided. They're all at different stages of preparation: A couple will race this weekend, others soon after. I'll make the final decisions after I see them work."

She scanned the all-weather track that was surfaced with wood chips, looking to no avail for fences or hurdles. "Where are the jumps?"

"Over that next hill," Bobby said, "but we won't be doing any schooling today. The ground is too frozen."

"In which group is Golden Legs?" Alex asked.

There was a brief silence before Bobby answered. "I left him for the second string. Thought he might work better when it gets warmer."

Jack saw the sharp, puzzled stare Alex shot Bobby, but the sound of thundering hooves distracted her. Over the ridge came the first three, sweeping down as if on wings, past where they stood and onward until they simultaneously pulled up. Even at half speed the noise and excitement of the spectacle was more intense than she'd experienced at the track, and she couldn't help noticing the excitement that bubbled inside of her.

Without thinking she looked up at Alex and said, "How could you even dream of selling Golden Legs? Isn't it just the most glorious thing in the world to see him run and know he's running for you?"

"If he were truly running for me, he'd win." Alex studied her face and decided it was important she understand the principle of the thing. "I bought Golden Legs as an investment. I have neither the time nor the inclination to turn this investment into a hobby."

"I don't believe you," she said, and it was all Alex could do not to kiss her chin that jutted out in stubborn disbelief.

"Bobby does," he said, and switched his gaze to the man at her other side. "Right, Bobby?"

Bobby glared at Jack. "I told you not to use the *sell* word."

Alex stifled a smile, then told Bobby he might as well go to work, as Golden Legs wasn't there. Something that resembled satisfaction flickered across Bobby's expression, but Alex filed the impression for later when Jacqueline wasn't there to distract him.

He gave her hand a little tug and was pleased when she turned to walk with him to his truck, because it signaled her acceptance of his decision regarding Golden Legs.

If all disagreements ended so easily, their life together would be very pleasant indeed.

It was already dark when Alex arrived home from work. When he'd called Jacqueline on the car phone to apologize in advance for being late, she'd yawned and said she'd only just awakened from a nap. Hillary had finally taken her to Stonehenge, she said, as well as Salisbury Cathedral and an obscure stone monument that dated back one millennium or two, depending on which book you read.

The nap had been essential.

She suggested he take his time because she'd be late getting ready, as the only way she knew to wake up was to stick her head under a cold shower. The delay, she said, would be caused by the length of time necessary to dry her hair.

He'd told her not to rush, then tried not to drive into a ditch as he pictured the cold water running down her body, her nipples puckered and hard, her hair sleek and shimmering between her shoulder blades . . . the nest of curls between her legs smoothing under the water's pressure.

Out of necessity his own shower had also been on the cold side.

Alex straightened his green-and-gray striped tie and brushed a piece of lint from the lapel of his dark gray pinstriped suit, then turned away from the beveled hallway mirror and looked critically at the things that really mattered. The hallway itself was wide, well lit, and warmed by Oriental carpets that overlapped one another all the way from the front entrance to the kitchen door. The house was neatly divided by the hallway, with the kitchen, breakfast room, and an American-style family room taking up the smaller side. A wide staircase on that side of the hall led to an assortment of bedrooms, his included, as well as a room specially fitted with exercise equipment. Another room that faced east might easily be used for sewing or painting or whatever someone wanted.

His study was at the back of the house opposite the kitchen. Next on that side came a formal dining room, with glassed-in French doors opening directly into the lounge—or living room, as Jacqueline would call it. Alex walked through the wide doorway and tried to look at his possessions through a woman's eyes.

Jacqueline's eyes.

Like his study the lounge was designed for comfort and pleasure. Several groupings of upholstered chairs and sofas lent a sense of intimacy to the room, while the Sarouk rug and polished wood floor that bordered it exuded luxury. An ebony grand piano commanded attention at one end of the room, while a multipaned bay window drew one's eye to the other. Exquisite jade carvings graced conveniently placed side tables, and there was a massive Remington bronze of a wild stallion atop a gleaming mahogany buffet against one wall. The intricately carved fireplace was as old as the house, although the tile hearth wasn't more than a century old.

Alex looked at it all and was satisfied with what he saw. Someday soon, he decided, he would bring Jacqueline. If she liked what she saw, all the better.

If she didn't, he would heave it all out and buy new things. With a wry smile he revised the word *heave* to *sell* —or store until selling made sense.

They were, after all, only possessions.

The front doorbell rang, and even though Jack knew Hillary was on hand to answer it, she hurriedly picked up her gloves and coat and left the bedside light shining as she closed the door behind her. She went down the stairs wearing the blue silk dress she'd bought in London and slid her hand into Alex's as though it was the most natural thing in the world. Bobby and Hillary, both with raised eyebrows and questions in their eyes, asked only where they were going.

"Knightsbridge," Alex said, and told them briefly about the small Italian restaurant he frequented on nights he had to stay overnight in London.

Muttering something about rich sauces and creamy desserts, Bobby took a chocolate from the open box on the table beside him and popped it into his mouth. Hillary scolded him for ruining his dinner. Jack thanked Alex in one breath for sending the fifteen-pound box of Godiva chocolates, then chastised him in the next for sending so many.

He smiled indulgently at her. "But you *like* chocolates, and you said you'd never had this kind before."

"Yes, but even with Bobby and Hillary's help I won't get through fifteen pounds before I leave for California." Not if she wanted to wear anything she owned, she thought.

"Share them with the horses," he suggested.

Bobby promptly spit out the one in his mouth. "God, Alex! Don't you know chocolates generally contain theobromine, not to mention caffeine. Feed it to a horse and the Stewards will warn me off for doping."

Hillary shot an exasperated look at Alex. "He didn't mean it, Bobby. Tell him, Alex. Tell him you didn't mean it."

"I didn't mean it," Alex said blandly, then told Jack he'd meant to say "horses' lads," not "horses."

Jack nodded without believing a word, and realized for the first time that Alex had a very wicked sense of humor.

He helped her into her coat and steered her around the bits of chocolate scattered across the parquet flooring. "I'll see you at morning exercise, Bobby."

Bobby glared, obviously suspicious, but said he'd make sure Golden Legs went out with the first string. As the door swung closed behind them, Jack could hear Hillary telling Bobby to get his fingers out of the chocolate box. Bobby's reply was unprintable. She glanced up at Alex then and saw the satisfied amusement in his expression.

"You did that on purpose," she said.

"Did what?"

"Baited him about the chocolates. Come on, Alex, what gives?"

"Bobby didn't bring Golden Legs up with the first

string this morning, so I didn't get to see him work. It took me all morning to figure out he was getting back at me for the duck."

"You're joking!"

He shook his head. "I have to admit I shared a few more details about the duck than strictly necessary. By the time I finished describing the crackling in raspberry sauce, he was positively drooling."

"You can't seriously believe Bobby would keep you from watching Golden Legs over something like that? Bobby isn't that devious." When he didn't reply, she said, "Is he?"

He was saved from answering by the ringing of the car phone. He urged Jack into the car, reached across her to pluck the phone from the center console, then stood beside her door as he talked. Alex's side of the conversation was an uninformative string of monosyllables, and when he disconnected, there was a hint of annoyance in his manner. He waited until he'd slid behind the wheel and started the car before telling her the problem.

"That was my office. They're working late tonight putting together the package I need to take with me on my trip, and I've got some numbers they need in my briefcase." He reached for her hand and squeezed it gently. "We'll have to detour by the house and get them."

"Will you have to go to your office afterward?"

"No, just call." He checked his watch and shrugged. "We're already late for dinner, but the restaurant will hold our table for a while longer."

Moments later he pulled into the drive Hillary had said was his. Although she'd been past it many times, Jack had never so much as glimpsed the house, hidden from the road as it was behind a thick stand of trees. Alex made quick work of the drive, rounding the blind corner past the trees with the kind of confidence that came from knowing he owned the road.

She was excited by the prospect of finally seeing where he lived, and disappointed because the night was black and would hide much from view. Almost as though he read her thoughts, Alex reached into the glove compartment and pulled out something that resembled a garage door opener. When he pointed it ahead, lights flared from a dozen points, illuminating the grounds and house.

Although Hillary had warned her to expect something on the large size, Jack was nevertheless astonished by the structure that loomed proud and elegant at the far side of the circular drive. It wasn't so much that it was bigger than she'd expected—which it was—or elegant—which it couldn't help being. What really amazed Jack was how it could be big and elegant and *cozy*, of all things.

It was a home in the best definition of the word.

She turned to Alex as he pulled to a stop and expressed her approval. "Wow."

"The lights?" he asked as he helped her from the car. "I had them tuned to a remote so that I didn't smash into the side of the house on a dark night."

"The lights are good," she said. "The house is better. I like it a lot."

He pushed a key into the front door and paused to look down at her. "How can you tell from the outside?"

"You don't have to cut into a melon to know if it's ripe."

While Alex had misgivings about the melon parallel, he couldn't help but believe Jacqueline knew what she was talking about. She didn't just like the house, she told him after a tour of the first floor. She loved it, and why did he have a piano if he couldn't play?

"It came with the house."

"That's absurd," she said. "Worse, in fact, than having an airplane you can't fly."

"Why?"

"A piano needs love." She ran her fingers across the highly polished wood. "Dusting and tuning isn't enough."

"How do you know I bother to have it tuned, Jacqueline?"

"The same reason you give carrots to Golden Legs. Habit, and because it gives you pleasure."

She was wrong, but all Alex said was, "I get the piano tuned for the same reason I lease out the Cessna: to keep it from rotting." He excused himself and went upstairs to find the required papers. By the time he called the office and got assurances that he would be met at the airport with the finished proposal, he realized they were already over an hour late for dinner. He took a moment to call the restaurant. The woman who answered told him it was a quiet night and they would be seated whenever they finally arrived.

Now all he had to do was get Jacqueline out of his home before he gave into temptation and asked her to stay the night. Under ordinary circumstances he wouldn't hesitate doing that very thing. But these weren't ordinary circumstances. His flight to New York left just after seven, which meant he had to be at Heathrow no later than half past five.

When he made love with Jacqueline for the first time, he didn't want to do it with one eye on the clock. She deserved better.

He was also aware that once he finally lay naked with her, it would be days, not hours, before he would want to do anything else.

Alex left his bedroom suite, thinking that another

three days of abstinence would be possible only because Jacqueline wouldn't be there.

He wished she would change her mind and come.

The first notes of her music caught him much as her scent had, subtly, easing into his awareness, filling a void he hadn't known was there until it was gone. The melody was familiar: Mozart, Alex thought, although it could have been Bach or Bartok and it wouldn't have made any difference. It was the way Jacqueline played and not the sequence of notes that enticed his senses.

He paused midway down the staircase and listened to the gentle care she took with the melody. Her touch was light and sure, her precision more than a passing nod to the composer's intent. Yet there was a bond between Jacqueline and the music, one that filled the notes with an intimate warmth. Jacqueline didn't play music, Alex realized as he quietly descended the stairs. She felt it. Her talent . . . her *gift* . . . was that she made him feel it too.

With her scent she aroused him. And now, with her music, she caressed him, stroking him in places no one had ever reached, creating within him a heat that was at flash point.

Alex forgot all about dinner, his hunger for Jacqueline far outweighing lesser needs. He forgot about his early flight to New York, and about wanting their first time together to be long and uninterrupted.

He forgot everything except that he'd wanted Jacqueline for what seemed a very long lifetime.

Alex walked into the lounge, his steps silenced by the thick rug. Her back was to him, and though he hadn't made a sound since entering the room, he knew when she stumbled over a passage that she was aware of him. His gaze rested on the bare nape of her neck, and he thought he heard the hiss of a sudden breath. He stood quietly, breathing in her unique scent, willing her to go on, to recover the melody . . . wondering if she would continue to play when he finally touched her.

Wanting it all.

EIGHT

One moment Jack was alone, then she wasn't. Her fingers stumbled over the keys, and she drew in a sharp breath to ease the sudden rush of fiery awareness that Alex always provoked.

She couldn't see him, hadn't heard him come in, yet she knew he was there. Close enough to touch, she realized, and didn't question how she knew that. His presence was unique.

She took a deep breath, then forced herself to continue playing. If the rhythm wasn't as precise as it should be, it was because her attention was on the man, not the music.

When at last she felt the hardness of his thighs against her back and the light touch of his hands on her shoulders, she closed her eyes and let her head fall back, her hands slipping from the keys.

"Don't stop, Jacqueline," he said as his fingers traced the line of her collarbone. "You play beautifully."

"I can't—"

"You can," he murmured, then slid his hands down her arms and lifted her hands to the keys. His mouth was close to her ear, and the heat of his breath made her skin tingle. "Pretend you're alone—"

"I'm not—" she began, but he didn't seem to notice the interruption.

"Alone, Jacqueline. In a field of lilacs." He stood tall again, straightening behind her so that his voice seemed to come from far away. His thighs were warm against her back, his hands unmoving on her shoulders.

"Lilacs grow on trees, not in fields," she said, her fingers motionless on the keys because his touch had driven the music from her mind.

"Bushes, I think, and rainbows don't have a scent, but that doesn't stop me from smelling them."

Jack smiled, captivated by the whimsy of his suggestion. Emotions tangled with common sense, leaving her wondering what was common or sensible about any of this . . . or if it even mattered. She'd known from the beginning that the sexual chemistry between herself and Alex was strong and compelling. She had made a conscious decision to accept it for what it was rather than try to make it different and lose it all.

If Alex was satisfied with a relationship that excluded emotions, then she could be too. Just this once.

He drew a line with a single finger down the side of her neck and felt immense pleasure when she shivered in reaction. "Would you finish the melody if I went and sat down?" He began to ease away from her, but a lightning-quick hand reached up and encircled his wrist before he'd moved so much as an inch.

"Stay." The word carried a husky invitation that Alex knew had nothing to do with music. He stayed.

She started the melody from the beginning, her fingers hesitant at first on the keys, then stronger as she went along. The melody ranged from one end of the keyboard to the other, and as she moved with the music, her back grazed his thighs. The caress was innocently provocative, and he luxuriated in the sensation of his growing arousal. Her scent and her music filled the air, and it was with only the greatest restraint that he refrained from slipping his hands from her shoulders to her breasts.

By the time Jacqueline played the last chord, Alex felt as though he'd been through a prolonged session of foreplay with an experienced seductress. He took a deep breath in an attempt to tame his arousal, then another when the first didn't work.

It didn't matter, though, because Jacqueline had ideas of her own. Without turning, she reached up and curled her hands around his wrists . . . then pulled his hands downward until his palms were covering her breasts.

He knew it wouldn't be long before he was deep inside her.

"I had planned to make love to you in my bed the first time," he said as he found her nipples beneath the silk dress and rolled them between his fingers. "But while you were playing, I realized how exciting it would be to make love to you here at the piano."

Her gasp was soft and, he thought, tinged more with intrigue than shock. Her fingers tightened around his wrists and she said in a breathy kind of voice, "How, exactly, does one make love on a piano?"

"Do you want me to show you or tell you?" When she didn't immediately answer, he said, "I should probably do both. That way you can choose."

"You're outrageous, Alex Hastings."

"And you're delightful, Jacqueline Sommers. How can I resist making love to you in a place where you made such beautiful music?" Gently he broke her grip on his wrists and pushed her hands down.

"Put your hands behind you, sweet," he said as his own returned to her breasts. "Put them around my legs."

"Why?"

"Because I want my hands free to touch you," he said, and was pleased when she did as he asked. "The other reason is because when you sit like that, your breasts thrust forward so prettily."

Her head fell back against him as he began to tease the nipples that were erect and proud beneath the silk dress. In the glossy wood above the keys there was a mirrorlike reflection of her face and his hands as they caressed her breasts. He watched her eyelids close as her pleasure increased, felt the slight arching of her back as he slipped his hand inside the silk neckline.

"About the piano," he began in a voice that was husky with his own arousal. "One way would be to back you against the keys, enter you standing up. It wouldn't be too comfortable, but if you're interested—"

Her fingernails bit into his calves as he unclasped her bra with one hand and began to unzip her dress with the other.

"Another option would be a variation on making love," he said, brushing aside the delicate silk and watching in the limited reflection as it fell to her waist. He had to take a deep breath before continuing, and knew his fingers trembled as he slid the straps of her bra down her arms. "Making sure the lid is down, of course, I'd lift you to sit on the end—you know, the way a chanteuse sits during a favorite song. The difference, though, would become clear when I spread your legs and made love to you with my mouth."

Her shudder of response was so strong that Alex knew he'd have to try that particular option—later, though, after he'd satisfied his own raging arousal.

"And there's always the bench, Jacqueline. You would sit facing me, your legs on mine, and I would lift you up—"

"Enough!" Jack said, and abruptly stood and turned to face him. The piano bench was her only buffer from Alex as her dress pooled at her feet, leaving her clothed in only stockings, panties, and heels. Her almost naked state was the last thing on her mind, though, because he was driving her insane and she meant to put a stop to it.

"Is there a problem, sweet?" he asked, but the heat in his eyes belied his easy words.

"The problem is I want to make love, and you seem to be stalling."

He looked at her without touching her, his gaze blazing an almost tactile path from her breasts downward . . . down, past her stomach to the tops of her thigh-high stockings . . . then back up to the place between her legs that was shielded by lace and satin. When his eyes returned to her face, the pupils had expanded until only a faint circle of silver surrounded them. The effect was one of mystery and excitement, and desire such as she'd never seen.

"Right, then," he said, and drew her around the bench with a gentle touch on her arm. "No more stalling."

His arms went around her, drawing her close, enveloping her in a world that was suddenly spinning out of control. Jacqueline gasped as his large hand flattened on her buttocks and half lifted, half pulled her against his hips, into his heat. The tips of her breasts brushed the fine wool of his suit coat, then his mouth was covering hers, and all thought evaporated.

In its place was feeling, sensations that were bold and exciting reflections of this man who stole her fantasies and made them real. His mouth was a devouring rogue that commanded a response from her and rewarded her with more demands, and more rewards.

His hands slipped the remaining clothing from her body without altering the focus of his mouth, then he stripped off his own in the same manner. She felt the urgency of his arousal against her belly, knew there would be nothing gentle about his invasion of her body . . . and reveled in that knowledge. When his fingers delved between her legs, she was exhilarated when they came away slickened by her readiness.

Velvet, soft and deep, was at her back. The lights he'd left on were dancing beyond eyelids half closed from the pleasure he gave her. He touched her everywhere with his hands and mouth, then again . . . and again. Words of praise were punctuated by groans of approval, and she sensed that life as she'd always known it would be forever colored by this night's loving.

Her fingers stroked the part of him that was all male and fully aroused. She heard a distant cry of frustration that was too high to be his, then cried out again as he slowly began to do what he'd promised her. He pushed her legs wide, then was thrusting inside her, deeply, thoroughly, filling her with his maleness as she surrounded him with her uniquely female sheath.

And that was only the beginning.

She awakened as he carried her up the stairs, but Alex knew she was fast asleep again before he'd laid her down on his bed. He let her rest for an hour, then wakened her with the light touch of his hands on her body, touching her breasts without soothing them, teasing the sensitive nub beneath the soft black curls with his tongue as she floated toward awareness.

He took his time with her, making their love last until neither could bear the pain. When it was over, he offered food, but sleep was her choice.

He held her in his arms and promised her unconscious form a life of luxury and, he hoped, happiness, then he stroked her to an arousal that accepted him without any real awareness on her part.

He loved her with his body, and took what she offered in the same vein.

Jacqueline would be a good wife, he decided, and was satisfied with the way things were turning out.

Alex made it to the airport by a whisker, then kept the flight waiting another minute as he scribbled a short note on the back of his business card. He gave it to his assistant with instructions to tuck it inside the jeweler's case that would be delivered to Jacqueline the afternoon he returned.

As he ran down the jetway, his one regret was that he hadn't had the bracelet on hand last night. Unfortunately the one he'd chosen had had to be sized down so that it wouldn't fall off Jacqueline's slender wrist. His plan to give it to her after they'd made love the first time had been circumvented by impulse.

Alex allowed the flight attendant to hustle him into his first-class seat, and let out several long breaths as the jet was pushed away from the terminal. It had been more than an impulse, he admitted, that had caused him to throw away his careful plans and make love to Jacqueline ahead of schedule.

It had been, almost, a compulsion.

As the airplane lumbered toward the runway, Alex closed his eyes and remembered the look of sleepy satisfaction on her face when he'd awakened her to make love one more time. It was the same look that had been on her face when he'd dropped her on Bobby's doorstep en route to the airport. He'd teased her about it, then kissed her one last time and told her how much pleasure she'd given him that night.

He, too, was sleepy and satisfied, and aware that the next three days—and nights—would be among the longest in his life. The corner of his mouth kicked up in a grin as he imagined the look on her face when she saw the bracelet.

He was rather looking forward to it.

NINE

Nothing was so good it lasted forever. Jack just hadn't expected it to fall apart so quickly.

She stared down at the diamond tennis bracelet that lay nestled in its black velvet case and wondered what she could have done to make things happen differently. Perhaps if she'd put her foot down in the beginning when the gifts had first started, she wouldn't be holding a fabulously expensive bracelet and feeling like she'd been bought and paid for.

No better than a whore.

How dare he!

Even the card was an insult: "*Next time wear this . . . only this.*" She couldn't tell by the look on the courier's face if he'd read the note, but God knew how many others were privy to what was no longer private.

How could he!

A sense of unreality clouded Jack's thought processes, enabling her to sign her name on the delivery form with one hand as she crushed Alex's card in her other. She nodded in uncaring acknowledgment as the courier explained about insurance and security. When not on her wrist, the bracelet had to be kept in a safe, or the policy was void. Hillary mumbled something about the safe upstairs and assured the courier everything would be taken care of. She showed the man out, then came back to look over Jack's shoulder at the sparkling tennis bracelet.

"Each of those diamonds must weigh at least half a carat," Hillary said with a breathlessness that proclaimed her awe. "More, probably. Lord, Jack! This is a bit extravagant, even for Alex."

"I hope he thinks he got his money's worth," Jack muttered.

"What?"

"I said maybe he got it on sale." A shiver of distaste made her thrust the case into Hillary's hands. "Here, you do something with it."

"Aren't you even going to try it on?" Hillary asked, a concerned look furrowing her brow.

"By the looks of it, it's too short for a noose. Useless."

Hillary glanced from Jack to the bracelet, then back to Jack again. "You're upset."

"Something like that."

A kind of rage like nothing she'd ever known pulsed through her, and Jack knew she had to do something about it or burst. In quick strides she went over to the front door, swung it open, and threw out Alex's card. Next she strode over to the coffee table and picked up what was left of the flower arrangement he had sent her that first day. She chucked that out the door too—ceramic vase and all—and watched with enormous satisfaction as the vase cracked into a dozen pieces, strewing flowers all down the stairs. Turning her back on the mess, she headed across the room to the buffet and picked up the vase of pink tulips. Hillary caught up with her just as she got set to heave it out to join the first mess.

"*Not that, Jack!*" Hillary had tucked the velvet case

under one arm and now had both hands on the crystal vase.

"Why not? He'll just send more." She put more muscle into her effort, but Hillary was equally as determined.

"The vase is a Steuben."

"Steuben!" Jack shouted in disbelief, then nearly qualified for self-inflicted whiplash when she swung her head around to take a closer look at the shards of pottery scattered across the front steps. "Do *not* tell me that bowl was valuable too!"

"I wouldn't know," Hillary said mildly. "Pottery isn't my specialty."

"Why didn't you tell me the vase was Steuben when the tulips came?" Water sloshed all over the hall as Jack abruptly surrendered the object in question to Hillary's reverent care. It was one thing to break a piece of glass, but art was sacred.

She hoped Alex liked it, because he was getting it back. Biting off a cry of frustration, she scared Hillary again by reaching for the vase, only to grab the flowers out of it and pitch them outside.

"Well, now," Hillary said. "That certainly solves everything."

Jack reached aside to slam the door. "So why didn't you tell me about the vase, Hillary?"

"I didn't tell you because I didn't want you to get mad at Alex." After drying the base of the heavily leaded crystal vase with her sweater, Hillary put it on the gateleg table at the bottom of the stairs and heaved a sigh of relief. "Just like I didn't tell you that fifteen pounds of Godiva chocolates cost at least as much as that dress you bought. I decided you were better off not knowing."

Jack felt a sinking sensation in the vicinity of her stomach that was getting worse by the second. "You mean a box of candy cost as much as that horribly expensive dress that maxed out my credit card?"

Hillary shrugged, and the bracelet case slipped from her armpit to the floor. Neither woman bent to pick it up. "That dress wasn't *horribly* expensive, Jack. Just a little on the pricey side for someone who wouldn't pay a hundred dollars for a pair of shoes."

"And you would?"

"Every time I think I can get away with it," she said, a grin lighting up her face. "Now, then, Jack, don't you think it's time to settle down and look at this from Alex's perspective?"

"I will *not* be treated like all his other women."

"I've never heard of him giving away diamonds before," Hillary said, then bent to pick up the case. "It doesn't sound to me like he's treating you like all the others."

"That's not my point," Jack fumed, crossing her arms defensively. "I don't want the presents."

"You told me you think he has feelings, Jack. What if it gives him pleasure to give you things?"

"He's too extravagant—"

Hillary interrupted neatly, "He's rich."

"What does that make me?"

"Lucky?" Hillary said, then backed off a few steps when Jack scowled. "He's going to be here soon, Jack. Don't you think you should clean up the mess on the front steps before then?"

"No."

Hillary paused, then tried to give Jack the case. "At least try on the bracelet before you give it back."

"Why?"

"Memories?"

"I'd rather put it through the garbage disposal," Jack said belligerently.

Hillary snapped the case back to her chest. "Then it's a good thing we don't have one."

"Ask Alex for one," Jack retorted. "Tell him it's for me."

"I'm going to the stables until you simmer down," Hillary said.

Jack reached past her, grabbed Hillary's coat from the hooks by the door, and gave it to her. "It might take a while."

"Don't break anything important." She looked down at the case, then smiled at Jack. "I'll just keep this with me for now."

"Don't trust me?"

"It's nothing to do with trust. I want to show it to Bobby. With runners in both the Grand National and the Cheltenham Gold Cup, chances are the owner of Goodwyn Stables might see fit to reward the lady in residence with a token of his appreciation for her forbearance. It won't hurt to prime the pump."

Jack stared after her with more questions than answers going through her mind. "What *are* you talking about, Hillary?"

"The bracelet, Jack. No reason I can't set my sights high." She flipped open the case and sighed. "It's absolutely gorgeous. Alex has impeccable taste."

"I doubt he's even seen it." The jeweler was British, not American, and there hadn't been time for Alex to shop before leaving for the States.

Hillary headed toward the back door, the bracelet case clutched firmly in her hand. "Bobby is never going to forgive Alex for this."

Neither, Jack thought, would she.

It was midafternoon when Alex parked the Jaguar in front of Bobby's and got out. He'd tried calling from the car to tell Jacqueline he'd be a little early, but no one at the Goodwyn residence had answered. He hurried up the flagstone walk and was thinking she wouldn't need to pack much when he noticed he was treading on flowers. Lots of flowers, most of which were pink tulips . . . very much like those he'd sent Jacqueline. He tried walking between the stems and felt something hard crunch under his foot.

Gingerly Alex lifted his foot and stared down at the bits of partially crushed pottery. There was a larger shard on the flagstone just a few inches away, and it occurred to him the design was familiar.

Never a slouch when it came to adding two and two together, Alex contemplated the mess at his feet and guessed Jacqueline had thrown a tantrum. Oddly enough, the thought that she was capable of doing so bothered him not at all.

It was the fear that he wouldn't be able to talk her around whatever had set her off that made his blood run cold, but Alex dismissed the panic as easily as it had surfaced.

He hadn't gotten where he was today by letting events control his life. There was nothing that he couldn't fix once he set his mind to it.

A quick glance around the immediate area yielded no sightings of shattered crystal, which indicated that even in anger she wasn't so careless as to destroy a valuable piece of art. A pity she hadn't realized the value of the pottery vase, he mused, and made a decision not to tell her. The insurance would cover it.

A further perusal of the scattered remains revealed no trace of chocolate—but he assumed Bobby might have gone through them before the tantrum occurred. The painting had probably survived for the same reason she hadn't destroyed the Steuben vase.

Alex didn't bother looking for the diamond bracelet amid the rubble. If it was there, it could wait.

A cool breeze teased the wilting flowers, and out of the corner of his eye he saw a crumpled wad of paper roll toward the grass. He knew what it was before he picked it up and flattened it on his palm.

"Next time, wear this . . . only this."

From the looks of things Jacqueline was less than enthralled with the prospect of a next time. He slipped the card into the breast pocket of his coat and turned to go up the front steps, his mind sorting through the information available and coming up blank.

Whatever had set her off was a mystery to him.

He was almost relieved when Hillary answered the door instead of Jacqueline.

She looked past his shoulder to the debris, then shook her head ruefully. "I was hoping you wouldn't see that," she said as he came inside and followed her into the lounge.

"It would have been difficult to miss."

"Actually I meant that I'd hoped Jack would clean it up before you came," she said with a wry grin. "I guess she hasn't gotten over being miffed yet."

If this was an example of miffed, he wondered what she'd do in a towering rage. It would, he imagined, be something to see.

"Would it be breaking a confidence for you to tell me what caused all this?" he asked, declining her offer of a drink. There wasn't time, not if they were to be at the airport on schedule.

Hillary looked down at the coffee table, and he saw the velvet case lying there.

"She didn't like it?" he asked.

"No, Alex, I don't like it."

He turned to see Jacqueline standing in the doorway. She was wearing peach-colored stretch pants, a matching knit top that covered her thighs, and a scowl on her face he assumed was directed at him.

"Is that what all this is about?" he asked mildly. "A difference in taste?" Personally he thought a tantrum a bit extreme for something that could be resolved with a trip to the jeweler. Behind him he heard Hillary escape into the kitchen and pull the door shut. "If that's all it is, we can exchange it for another. It's of no difference to me, Jacqueline."

She walked toward him, her hands fisted at her sides and an air of fury surrounding her like a cloak. "I don't like it because it makes me feel like a whore."

He was confused. "I beg your pardon?"

She stopped when she was just inches away, then had to tilt her head to meet his gaze. "A whore. A woman you pay for performing sexual acts."

"Oh." He was still confused. "It's not that I don't understand the word, Jacqueline. I just can't figure out why you should imagine it applies to you." Alex judged she was moving from "miffed" to "towering rage" as her eyes took on a look as hard and bright as the diamonds that had caused it all.

"If I had spent the weekend with you instead of just a few hours, would I have earned a necklace too?"

It seemed prudent not to answer that. Instead he said, "I've been buying things for women all my adult life, and not one of them has ever reacted like this." He knew that was a mistake the minute he said it, but with her scent wafting into his nostrils, he was having trouble concentrating.

"Then you can safely assume I don't wish to be treated like one of your other women," she said, enunciating each word precisely. "I don't want expensive presents, not for making love to a man I've grown rather fond of."

A man I've grown rather fond of. There was, he thought, a bright side to everything. Even anger.

"I never dreamed you'd see it that way," he said. "It appears my timing was unfortunate, to say the least."

"You know that Hillary told me how generous you are with women," she said, sniffing. "She called it the gold rush."

He almost smiled. "That's the first time I've heard that expression used in conjunction with my personal life."

"I don't want to be bought," she said, and he sensed her anger was beginning to fade. "I don't even want to be rented."

"I can't imagine that you would," he said softly. The brightness in her eyes was blurred by unshed tears, and Alex had to use every iota of his willpower not to take her into his arms and comfort her. "I sent you the bracelet because it gives me pleasure to give you things, not as payment for services rendered. I also thought it would, in a small way, convey how much joy you give me—all the time, not just on occasion."

"But it *isn't* small! It's awfully expensive." She pointed angrily at the Steuben vase. "Just like that thing. If Hillary hadn't stopped me, that would be in a million pieces right now, and it would be all your fault."

"Why my fault?" he asked, making a note to thank Hillary for intervening. Too bad she hadn't been quick enough to save the pottery one.

"Because it never occurred to me you'd do something stupid like send a Steuben vase under all those flowers. As I told you that night at Le Manoir, I'm not *used* to all this extravagance. I don't *expect* it!"

"And all I care about is whether you like what I give

you," he said, putting a touch of firmness into his words. "The price of things is my concern, not yours."

Her bottom lip trembled. "Maybe if I thought you'd at least taken the trouble to pick the bracelet out yourself, it wouldn't feel so . . . impersonal."

"But I *did* pick it out, Jacqueline. The day before I left for the States." He lifted his hand and brushed a tear from her cheek. "I thought if I had it delivered before I returned, you'd forgive me for leaving you for so long."

"Three days isn't that long," Jack whispered, thinking it had been an eternity.

"It was forever."

His hand cupped her face, and she felt herself leaning toward him as the anger drained out of her. "You really picked it out?"

He nodded. "It's why I was late calling for you that night. I took off an hour in the afternoon to go to the jeweler's, then had to work late to clear my desk before the trip."

Her objections disintegrated in the face of Alex's reasonable explanations. In short, the cost was none of her business, the timing unfortunate, and the choice of baubles his and his alone.

There was still the matter of the note, however. Swift and sure, the anger that had nearly deserted her rose again, making her back away and shrug off his touch. "It seems you have an answer for everything, Alex. How are you going to explain how you dared write what you did on that card?"

There was a puzzled look on his face as he pulled something from his pocket. By the time she realized it was the business card in question, his expression had deepened to one of real concern. "Next time, wear this . . . only this," he read aloud, then looked up at her. "I don't know whether you're angry because I assumed there would be a next time or because this suggests a scenario that makes you uncomfortable."

When she just stared at him in stunned disbelief, he shook his head and sighed. "Forgive me for whichever it is, Jacqueline. Honestly, though, I imagined our lovemaking was pleasurable enough to warrant repeating. I also got the impression you were sexually stimulated by erotic suggestions. The note was—"

"The note was read by *other people*—the courier, the jeweler, and everybody in between!" she shouted, not caring if Hillary or Bobby or even Golden Legs could hear her. "How do you think I felt knowing the courier was probably imagining how I'd look wearing nothing more than that stupid bracelet?"

Alex closed the distance between them with two long strides and grasped her forearms. "Did he say *anything* to make you feel like that?" He wasn't satisfied with the reluctant shake of her head. "Are you sure? I mean, did he even look at you strangely?"

"No, but—"

His grip on her arms softened, and he let out a harsh breath. "You had me worried, Jacqueline, but really, you should know I wouldn't subject you to anything so tawdry."

"I should know?" she asked, hearing the flippant note in her voice and hoping Alex heard it too.

If he did, he ignored it. "Yes, you should. And on the practical side, anyone who would dare invade my privacy like that wouldn't have a job for any longer than it took me to pick up the phone and get him fired."

"The courier doesn't even work for you."

"That's immaterial."

"But what about all the others?" Her frustration rose as she began to realize he truly didn't understand.

"There are no others." His fingers slid down to her

fisted hands and began to massage them. "The only person who saw that note was my personal assistant, who, I assume, placed it into the box before giving it to the courier. It's part of his job to guard my privacy, so I have to believe he is the only one besides yourself who would have the opportunity to read what I wrote. And if he did chance to read it, he wouldn't dream of thinking anything one way or the other. He's paid not to."

"How can you be so sure?"

"I have to be," he said shortly. "I couldn't function if I didn't trust at least a few key people."

His air of total confidence succeeded where mere words might have failed. Her fury dissolved from the inside out, the steady relaxing of her guard beginning with her heart and ending with her fingers relaxing until he was able to thread his between them.

With her hand enclosed in his, Alex tilted her chin up until she was looking into his eyes. "It would be nice if you could trust me too. I would never do anything to make you unhappy, Jacqueline."

"I know that now, Alex. It's just that when I saw the bracelet . . ." She shook her head helplessly. "I didn't like being reminded that I'm merely the latest target of your generous nature. Not the first and certainly not the last. Silly, isn't it?"

His gaze narrowed thoughtfully, and he hesitated before replying. "No, Jacqueline, it's not silly. You're special. I thought the bracelet would make that clear."

As mud. How could he say she was special and not know her well enough to realize it would be the man she remembered when it was over, not his generosity?

There was, she supposed, no way to make him understand. Not in the short time left to them.

She gave in with a tired smile. "The bracelet is beautiful, Alex. Thank you."

"You're sure? As I told you before, it's a simple matter to exchange it."

She wished he hadn't said that. Whatever sentiment she might attach to the bracelet in the future would be tempered by Alex's lack of it. Before she could dwell on the bruise that knowledge left on her heart, he pulled her over to the table and picked up the case.

"Now, put it on, Jacqueline, so we can make sure it fits. We can't take it with us if it doesn't."

"Where are we going?" Le Manoir, she supposed, or somewhere equally elegant where the bracelet wouldn't be out of place. She lifted her arm, and he fastened the glittering chain of diamonds around her wrist.

"Austria." He tried to edge the bracelet off her hand and murmured in satisfaction when it wouldn't go.

The bracelet was rather pretty, she thought, and she had opened her mouth to thank him again when what he'd said sank in. "Austria?"

He nodded. "Only for the night, I'm afraid. We'll ski tomorrow, then come back after. I've got a meeting early the following morning."

"Austria? Are you crazy?"

"I don't think so." He smiled down at her. "Did you have other plans for tomorrow that won't wait?"

Nothing she could think of, but that was likely because her thinking was temporarily handicapped. "It's just that flying off to another country isn't something I do at the drop of a hat."

"Put it into perspective, Jacqueline. It's no different than if you went from California to Las Vegas for a weekend."

"You don't need a visa for Las Vegas."

"Austria, either, although we'll need passports. Don't forget to pack yours."

Her heart began to speed as the excitement of seeing

Austria caught her imagination. "But I don't have any clothes for skiing."

"Hillary does, and whatever doesn't fit we'll take care of when we get there." He lifted his arm to check his watch. "We need to hurry if we're going to get there before dinner. Why don't I tell Hillary while you put a few things into a bag."

"But—"

"And I'll ask her to give one of the lads a few quid for cleaning up your mess," he said as though he hadn't heard her.

"But—"

He noticed. "You thought of something I haven't?"

Before she could think which words needed to come out, he made his own conclusions. "But . . . I haven't even kissed you yet. Is that what's bothering you?"

A slow smile spread across her lips. "Come to think of it . . ."

"To be honest, sweet, we don't have time for that either." He put his hands on her shoulders and turned her toward the stairs, nudging her gently between the shoulder blades. "Now, run along and get started. I'll send Hillary up as soon as I've spoken with her."

For not the first time since meeting Alex, Jack felt as though things were spinning out of control. As she hurried up the stairs, she admitted it wasn't such a bad feeling at all.

It was in fact rather exciting.

TEN

Inside the private jet he'd chartered to whisk them to the Alps, Alex made up for his earlier omission of not kissing her. By the time they arrived at Salzburg, Jack's lips were swollen and she felt just the slightest bit dazed. Alex teased her about the first and must have noticed the second because he was extra careful with her as he ushered her through customs and immigration, then into a Mercedes sedan.

Then he leaned over and kissed her again in a decadent claiming that left her wanting more.

Breathless, she sank back in the luxurious passenger seat and watched Alex maneuver the car through the well-lit byways of the city's outskirts. Even though it was still early evening on the clock, winter's night was already well established, and she couldn't see anything beyond a few houses that lined the road. Her disappointment was short-lived, though, because Alex promised her they'd be returning early enough the next day to see a bit of the city.

It occurred to Jack she hadn't considered or protested the expense of the trip, but the loose thought was quickly reconciled by the realization that it wasn't a "thing" he'd given her.

It was time together, and that was more precious than any trinket or expensive gift. A day with Alex was something she would value forever. She wished she could tell him, but in a relationship that could never be anything but temporary, there wasn't any use.

Her stomach rumbled, and Alex slid a sideways glance at her. "I told you to eat something on the plane, Jacqueline."

"I wasn't hungry then." Not for food, anyway. "Besides, I seem to remember my mouth being otherwise occupied."

He inhaled harshly and reached for her hand. "Don't say things like that when I'm driving, sweet. It's not safe."

He had a point. "Hillary told me she and Bobby went skiing with you last spring," she said.

"Hmm. We went to Ellmau then too. It's a quiet town without too much nightlife. I prefer it to resorts like Kitzbühel or St. Anton."

"I'm surprised you were able to pry Bobby away from his horses."

"So was Hillary. I think the only reason we got away with it was because we had him on the plane and halfway across the Channel before he realized we weren't going to Scotland to look at some horses."

"Speaking of going somewhere else, Hillary and I were supposed to go to Leeds tomorrow."

"You can go to Leeds anytime. This was the only chance I'd have all month to go to Austria."

Jack agreed, but for other reasons. "Hillary is probably relieved to get me out of her hair for a while. We went to Tintagel while you were gone and spent the night. Between that and all the other sightseeing we've done lately, I imagine she's glad to spend some time alone with

Bobby." She slid him a flirting look. "Too bad it's only one night."

"I know," he said, and she realized he was quite serious. "But don't worry about Hillary wanting you out of the way. She's having the time of her life with you here. Bobby told me she's been waiting years for you to come."

"And it will be years before I come back," she said with a sigh of regret. "That's why I'm so frantic to see everything."

Alex could have told her that she'd have her whole life to visit England's sights and she wouldn't have to travel from California to do it. He didn't, though, because the assumption was premature by about twenty-four hours.

Sometime tomorrow he would ask her to be his wife. By the time they landed in England, Jacqueline would either be wearing his ring or at least thinking about it. Either way it would be out in the open. He squeezed her hand and felt the imprint of the tennis bracelet against his wrist.

It was a reminder that he couldn't afford any more mistakes.

He couldn't help but give her expensive things; it was as much a part of him as breathing and thinking. She'd just have to get used to it. He could, however, make sure she knew he'd picked out whatever it was—whether he had or not. It seemed important to her.

As was the timing. He thought about the items in the flat case at the bottom of his shaving kit and wondered how he'd manage to give them to Jacqueline without offending her sensibilities. He couldn't, he decided, make love to her in one breath and hand over her present in the next.

He would have to be more clever than that if he didn't want another argument on his hands. He would have to choose a moment when the gift couldn't possibly be linked to sex—recent or in general.

Perhaps, he thought, when she brushed her teeth. . . .

They drove out of Salzburg toward the WildeKaiser Mountains, leaving Austria for about half an hour as the road took them through a small bit of Germany. The shortcut saved hours, Alex explained, and cost them only the time it took to show passports at either end. Jack was delighted to notch her expanding list of countries visited and insisted the immigration officer stamp her passport for proof.

The ski area was WildeKaiser Brixental, a ski circus of mammoth proportions that sprawled across a series of mountains and valleys. They stayed in Ellmau, one of a half-dozen towns connected in winter by the masses of lifts and runs—pistes, Alex called them. She thought he was teasing until she saw a woman walking through the hotel lobby wearing a sweatshirt from the French resort of Val d'Isère that had OFF PISTE emblazoned in huge letters across the front.

Jack wanted that sweatshirt.

Alex checked them in at the desk, then rushed her back outside and down the street to a ski shop that was five minutes from closing. In less time than it usually took Jack to sort out the best mushrooms at the grocery store, he'd filled in the gaps in her wardrobe, rented them both equipment, and arranged to have everything delivered that night.

They hurried back to the hotel, took a total of five minutes to find their room and freshen up, then lingered over dinner because, according to Alex, no one cared how long they took to eat so long as they were seated by eight.

"Why do I get the feeling we'd have starved if our plane had arrived half an hour later?" Jack asked, taking her first unhurried breath since arriving in Ellmau.

"There aren't many places to eat outside of the hotel, and those are mostly pizza or sandwich shops. The food here is much better." He poured more wine into their glasses and regarded her from across the table. "Sorry about the rush, though. I had planned to get here earlier."

She thought about that for a moment, and the light dawned. "In other words we'd be eating pizza now if I'd argued about the bracelet five minutes longer."

Alex shrugged a single brow—yes, *shrugged* was the word for it, she realized. What most people needed a whole shoulder for, Alex accomplished with an eyebrow. "Actually I was thinking about the kiss we didn't take time for. That, I imagine, would have thrown the entire schedule into disarray."

She felt her cheeks warm, and knew it was as much because of the way he was looking at her as it was the memory of how close they'd come to not stopping at just kissing aboard the jet. Alex had wanted to make love then and there and had only refrained, she knew, because she hadn't been able to relax—not with the cabin crew on the other side of the door.

He'd understood without commenting, and it warmed her heart to realize he'd learned something important from that afternoon's argument.

Dinner was served with a minimum of fuss, slowly, like Alex had promised, and in a combination of French, German, and English. Jack's French—she wouldn't have tried it except she heard the waiter speaking in that language to the people at the next table—was only marginally less successful than Alex's stab at German, and neither was as good as the waiter's heavily accented English. By the time dinner was over and they'd moved to the lounge for coffee in front of the fire, Jack was wishing she'd paid more attention in the German course she'd taken in high school.

A waiter brought the brandy-laced drinks, and Alex dug into his pocket and pulled out some folded banknotes before the waiter said he would charge their drinks to the room. With a hand on his arm, Jack stopped Alex from returning the cash to his pocket.

"I've never seen anything like that," she said. "May I look at it?"

Alex looked at her strangely. "The money?"

"The clip," she said, laughing. "It's gorgeous. Where did you find it?"

He unclipped it from the cash and handed it to her. "My father gave it to me when I left university."

"What a wonderful gift." She turned it over and peered closely at the engraving. "What is the crest?"

"The university's." When she handed it back, he put it around the cash and back into his pocket.

"You surprise me, Alex," she said. "I wouldn't have thought you were sentimental enough to carry a memento with you. I think it's sweet."

"It's twenty-four-karat gold," he said with a shrug. "If it had been tin, I doubt I'd know where it is, much less carry it every day."

She couldn't believe he was serious. "Pull the other leg, Alex. You carry it because your father gave it to you, not because it's a precious metal."

"I carry it because it suits me, Jacqueline," he said as he leaned back and pulled her against him. "Besides, my father wouldn't have given me tin."

Jack decided to retreat rather than risk losing an argument she wasn't in the mood to fight. She looked around the sparsely populated room and snuggled closer to Alex, who had his feet propped on the hearth and his arm around her shoulders. "For as many people as there were at dinner, not many of them stayed around," she said. "Is there a disco or something close?"

"Mmm, but I doubt they went anywhere but to bed. Most are here for a week or two," he said lazily, then put his cup aside and rubbed his knuckles across her cheek. "After a full day's skiing, day after day, they tend to wear out fairly early."

"When I was in college, we'd ski all day and party all night."

He laughed and brushed a kiss across the bridge of her nose. "I hate to admit this to you, sweet, but in case you haven't noticed, I'm a bit past college age. Let's go to bed."

"You haven't even been skiing yet," she teased, but didn't protest when he took her cup from her fingers and put it down.

His eyes darkened with desire and excitement, and she didn't look away as he pulled her to her feet. "I never said I was sleepy, Jacqueline. Only that we're going to bed. Come along, now, before jet lag catches up with me."

From the way he was looking at her, Jack didn't think he'd allow even that to get in his way.

Much later, as she lay with Alex under the thick duvet with her head pillowed on his chest and his arms holding her close, she listened to his steady heartbeat and knew the day's travel had finally caught up with him. That, along with some very intense lovemaking.

It was the latter that made her own eyelids droop, but she fought sleep with a sense of frustration that was as illogical as it was compelling. To sleep was to waste time that would be irrecoverable next month or next year—moments with Alex precious even though he was sound asleep. Time, that thing that had never seemed so critical, was spending itself with a speed that wrenched at her heart.

When Jack's eyes finally drifted shut, her dreams were filled with images of Alex standing next to a longcase clock that kept perfect time with the beat of his heart. It wasn't until he reached out and slowed the swinging pendulum that she fell into a deep and untroubled sleep.

Morning dawned bright and clear with skies that were bluer than any Jack ever remembered seeing. They had an early breakfast along with most of the other eager beavers who'd gotten a long night's rest, then took the ski bus to the Hartkaiser Bahn. The funicular hauled a hundred or so skiers up the side of the mountain in one go, and Jack followed Alex through the pressing herd outside to where everyone was snapping on skis. The general spirit was to rush, and, as opposed to the preceding day, she was eager to do so. She pushed off the ledge and went where Alex had indicated; he followed her to ensure she was at least skilled enough on skis to manage the gentle slope.

It was easier, she imagined, than if he went first and had to track back up the hill if she made a mess of it.

Fortunately for them both she was as competent as she was confident—as good as Alex in fact—and within minutes Alex passed her to take a fast lead. She followed him a short distance to the bottom of a T-bar lift, where they joined a wedge of people all waiting for a ride up the hill. Jack looked around in disbelief.

"Why don't they organize people into orderly lift lines like they do in the States?" she asked.

"Probably for the same reason the ski maps are illegible," he said. "This is the way it's always been done, and no one here sees any reason to change it."

Jack watched as a matronly-looking woman elbowed

her way deep into the wedge, walking on other people's skis and using her poles when someone refused to move. Jack was appalled. "This is ridiculous!"

"No, this is Austria." He put an arm around her waist and pushed her between two people where she hadn't thought there would be enough room to stand. There was, just barely, and even less a moment later when he came up beside her.

She looked at him in exasperation. "What were you saying about the maps?"

"They only work if you know your way around in the first place. Otherwise it's mostly guesswork." He pulled one out of his coat pocket and showed it to her as a child no more than four feet tall squeezed between them on his way forward. "The lifts and pistes are numbered, which should help but doesn't because the map doesn't show where they intersect. Now, as far as lifts are concerned, the numbers only apply to the map. You never see a number on an actual lift. Sometimes they're named, but never numbered."

"That doesn't make any sense."

"Neither do the maps."

They'd finally made their way to the front of the wedge. Repeating the procedure she'd learned at the Hartkaiser Bahn, Jack slipped the ski pass she wore on an elastic string around her neck into a machine, which spit it back at her. A quick learner, she grabbed it before the elastic snapped the thing in her face and shuffled through the turnstile.

She sniffled and looked around for a box of Kleenex. Alex pulled one from the same pocket where he'd put the map and handed it to her.

"We're in Austria, Jacqueline," he reminded her. "Making tissues available for anyone who comes through the queue is yet another American innovation that hasn't arrived here."

She blew her nose and stuffed the tissue into the top of her bib coverall. "Runny noses are endemic to skiing, Alex. Tissues are even more important than maps."

"And it costs a lot more to ski in America than at Ellmau," he said reasonably. "Perhaps it's because everyone remembers to bring their own."

Good for them, she thought. She'd barely had time to pack a toothbrush!

They finally reached the head of the line, where a nice-looking man was waiting to snap the T-bar against their butts. Unfortunately for Alex, the bar didn't quite reach as high as that because Jacqueline was shorter, enough to make a difference. That and the disparity in their weights made the ride difficult and uncomfortable. By the time they arrived at the top—and they were, she knew, lucky to get there at all—Alex suggested that in deference to his knees they should try to avoid any more T-bars. So they headed over toward the Hohe Salve, the highest mountain in the WildeKaiser ski circus where the lifts were mostly chairs.

The trip took an hour, but it only took Jack ten minutes to realize she was having the time of her life. Skiing had never been better, and it wasn't just because the snow was perfect, the sky was blue, and there was a hut around every bend with refreshment for the weary traveler.

It was because Alex was with her, and because she'd never been with a man who was so unafraid of letting her know how much he, too, was enjoying himself. It showed in every glance, in his laughter and in his smile. The women who had called him unfeeling had been blind, she realized. They had obviously been looking for one thing —the gold rush—and had thus missed the very essence of the man. Alex had feelings that were deep and real, and just as valid as the next person's. They were different, though, and it was that difference that beguiled her.

It was the intensity of those feelings that drew her to him, and the fact that he wasn't even aware of them.

Either that, or she was seeing things that weren't there in order to justify the fact that she'd fallen in love with him.

The simple words stunned her, and in her inattention the tip of her ski embedded itself in a bump. Jack flipped onto her face and began a descent that was considerably less elegant than her form only moments ago, with skis, poles, and miscellaneous gear flying every which way. She heard Alex shout at her as she passed him, but his words were garbled in the avalanche of sound resulting from the spread-eagle swath she was cutting through the moguls. After what seemed an eternity, she finally quit sliding and came to an abrupt stop at the base of a stronger-than-it-looked sapling at the side of the run. *Piste*, she corrected herself.

So much for how she felt.

She was wiping the snow from her face when Alex slid to a stop just above her. She looked up at him and asked, "Am I going the right way?"

"Your sense of direction is splendid, Jacqueline," he said with a chuckle. "It's your style that needs work."

"For someone who has a long climb ahead of him, you're pretty cocky."

"Climb?" he asked innocently, glancing over his shoulder at the array of gear she'd discarded on the trip down.

"Climb *up*, Alex. As in 'fetch.' I'm much too shattered to collect all those bits and pieces myself." She sighed dramatically and leaned back against the small tree, crossing her feet at the ankles and her hands behind her head in her best exaggeration of a relaxed posture. The heavy boots lent the pose emphasis, if not necessarily grace.

"You'll have to buy me a beer for this."

"I'll buy you two," she said. Then her grin widened, and she added, "But you'll have to pay. I don't have any marks."

"They use shillings here."

"I don't have any of those either."

In the end a trio of Russian tourists picked up the rubble on their way down the slope and returned it with many smiles in Jack's direction and wary glances in Alex's. Their ski guide, an English girl in a bright yellow parka, handed over Jack's sunglasses and translated thank-yous before herding her charges down and away.

Jack reassembled herself for a short trip around the next bend to a welcoming Juesen hut, where they sat at wooden table in the corner of the deck and drank a Jagatee, not beer. The mixture of tea and alcohol was so strong that when Alex unzipped a pocket and pulled a string of diamonds from it, her brain was sluggish enough that for a moment she imagined it was her tennis bracelet.

It was about the time Jack remembered she'd put the bracelet into her own pocket that she realized the one he was showing her was different. It was longer than hers, at least twice as long, and she thought the diamonds were just a touch larger.

Alex arranged it into a circle on the table between them, and she looked up to find him watching her. Her throat was dry, her heart pounding almost painfully in her chest, and the only thing that kept her from screaming was the unmistakable look of pleasure in his eyes.

He spoke before she could figure out what to say. "I thought I'd better give you this before you broke your neck."

"It's a bit on the expensive side for a good-luck piece,"

she said, and remembered Hillary's comment about the bracelet: *"This is a bit extravagant, even for Alex."* Wait until she saw the necklace.

"I told you to let me worry about what things cost," he said lightly. "And as for any of the other objections you might have, I personally chose it and delivered it. I believe I've already explained about the timing."

She looked blankly at him.

He explained. "It's not big enough to fit around a neck brace."

"Ha ha," she said in a shaky voice, and thought it would, however, fit around the arm cast she'd be wearing after she cracked her forearm across his head.

Jack would have done it, too, if she'd thought it would knock some sense into him. She blinked rapidly and focused on the necklace, wishing she knew what it would take to make Alex understand he was blowing her mind with his lavish gifts.

The glittering circle of diamonds was mesmerizing in its brilliance, a seduction of fire and ice that flared with passion even as it chilled her heart. A shiver curled through her, and it had nothing to do with the snow just a few feet away.

"It would give me a great deal of pleasure to see you wearing this, Jacqueline," he said, and reached across the table to cover her trembling hands with his. "Please?"

She tried to be logical with him. "I'd be too frightened to wear it in public," she said weakly. "Between that and the bracelet, you could pay off the debt for the entire California school system and have change left over."

"It's not that dear."

"But what if I lost it?"

He shrugged offhandedly. "It's insured, sweet. So is the bracelet."

His total lack of concern would have worried her had she not known he did care, but was so used to denying it that it was a habit. She *had* to believe Alex cared, needed to. He cared about Golden Legs—she knew he did. He cared about his home; it wouldn't have that warm, cozy feeling if he'd been indifferent to it. He cared about Bobby and Hillary and about the money clip in his pocket.

He cared about her, too, she realized, and suddenly what he'd said a few days earlier began to make sense. *"I have expectations about us."*

Was it possible? Against all odds, was Alex contemplating a future that included her? She looked into his eyes and knew that she wanted to be right more than she'd wanted anything in her life.

Loving Alex made her want it all.

Later Jack decided the Jagatee must have been messing with her mind, because one moment she was looking for more excuses not to take the necklace and the next Alex was fastening it around her neck. It was a snug fit, and he covered it securely with her turtleneck just in case she took another tumble and it came off.

They skied some more, had lunch, and in the early afternoon headed back across the mountains toward Ellmau. Alex gave her the earrings as they were riding up the chairlift, then he nearly dropped them when he grabbed her to keep her from pitching forward off the chair.

She didn't know whether to be more upset because she'd nearly died or because he'd almost dropped the huge emerald-cut diamonds into the snow. Either way the combination of shocks served to mitigate her initial and oft-repeated protest against his extravagance. By the time they walked back into the hotel, Jack was consoling herself with the argument that if she was wrong about Alex and he didn't care a whit about her, she could always return the jewelry to him. That would at least salvage her pride.

Her heart, however, wouldn't be so easily mended.

ELEVEN

Alex lifted himself up on one elbow and began to stroke Jacqueline's naked back, bottom, and thighs. Her hair was a thick shawl across her shoulders, and the diamond bracelet sparkled around her wrist. She'd insisted on wearing it even with the slight crimp in the white gold setting that she'd discovered upon removing the bracelet from the pocket of her ski suit. She had been frantic at the damage that must have resulted from her spectacular fall on the mountain, and Alex had had to soothe her with promises that he'd arrange to have it fixed without sending it away.

It amused him that she couldn't bear to be parted from the bracelet. The same couldn't be said for the other jewelry, though. The earrings, he thought, were in the adjoining sitting room, and the necklace was somewhere in the tumble of sheets. A lazy, satisfied smile touched his mouth, and he knew he'd never be able to look at any of the jewels without remembering that afternoon.

He felt himself growing hard again, but this time the delicate scrape of her necklace around his erection was a product of his imagination and not the wickedly erotic torment Jacqueline had subjected him to earlier.

She moaned something into the pillow, then made what appeared to be an enormous effort to lift her head and look at him.

"Don't you think we've had enough exercise for one day?" she asked, then dropped her face back into the pillow.

"You don't have to do anything but lie there. I'll do all the work." He continued to pet her, savoring the contrast of her silky skin against his callused hand.

She groaned and turned her head so that she could breathe. "You're insatiable, Alex."

He'd thought it was the other way around. "Is that a problem?"

"Only if you don't want to have to carry me through the airport."

The airport. He sighed and spanked her lightly on her bottom. Too bad one of them was being sensible, he thought. "You're going to make us late for our plane if you don't get into the shower. As it is, it will be too dark to see much of Salzburg."

"You can be first," she offered with a yawn.

"You take longer getting dressed, Jacqueline." He rolled her onto her back and pushed her legs toward the edge of the bed. "Get moving, sweet. You can sleep on the plane."

She grumbled some more, but eased off the bed and stretched with complete disregard for the effect her naked body had on him. Alex had a hell of a time letting her walk unmolested into the bathroom, but eventually she was out of sight, and the temptation to make love to her just one more time was somewhat lessened.

He waited until he heard her step into the shower before reaching into the bedside table for the box he'd hidden there earlier. Snapping open the flip-top box, he looked at the emerald-cut diamond ring that was larger than her earrings, but otherwise a perfect match. He'd planned to give it to her that afternoon, but their love-making had taken his mind off the schedule, and now there wasn't time.

It would have to be on the jet, he decided, and got up to tuck the ring into his coat pocket. He just hoped she'd manage to stay awake long enough for him to put it on her finger.

While Alex waited for the clerk to prepare their bill, Jack picked through the postcards at the end of the reception desk. She chose the one that had *Ellmau* written in gold letters along the bottom.

As if she'd ever forget.

She turned to give it to Alex because she still didn't have any money that worked in Austria, and was just in time to see a tall, stunning brunette lay her hand on his arm in a gesture of such familiarity, Jack wanted to bite her. The only thing that saved her—the woman—was the way Alex brushed off the offending hand before speaking.

Somewhat relieved, Jack stayed where she was and watched to see what would happen next.

"Anita," Alex said in a mild voice, "what on earth are you doing here? I thought Switzerland or France were more your style."

Jack thought he sounded annoyed, but couldn't be sure because her own feelings were a little on the aggressive side.

"We've only stopped for a drink on our way to Kitzbühel. Eric insisted on taking the scenic route."

"Eric?" Alex said.

"Eric Hanson. But never mind him, Alex, I should ask what you're doing here. Ellmau isn't exactly your scene either. When we went skiing together, it was usually at Gstaad or Val d'Isère."

"My tastes have changed."

Jack realized she was looking at one of Alex's past lovers. It shouldn't surprise her, she mused. From what Hillary had said, there were enough of them scattered about that it was inevitable she'd run across one sooner or later.

She would have preferred later.

Alex, it appeared, shared her feelings. He shot a rueful glance toward Jack and held out his hand in invitation for her to join him. Jack went to him with a sense of unease dragging at her heels.

She put her hand into his in time to hear Anita say, "But, Alex, darling, Ellmau is so . . . quiet. And small. Anyway, I heard you were in New York."

Alex pulled Jack against his side and put an arm around her shoulders. "That was business. This is pleasure. I don't believe you've met Jacqueline Sommers. Jacqueline, this is Anita Carroll. She has a nightclub in London."

Until that moment Anita had acted as though Alex were the only other person in the room. She looked briefly at Jack, then dismissed her without so much as a hello. "I see Ellmau isn't the only thing you like quiet and small," she said, then turned on her heel and walked quickly out of the lobby and into the adjacent lounge.

Jack looked up at Alex and said, "Are all your past lovers as onery as that one?"

"Is it the fact we were lovers or because she's got a nasty streak that has those gorgeous blue eyes firing daggers?" he asked instead of answering her question.

"Neither. I think it was the way she touched you that got my back up." She grinned at him. "I could tell you didn't like it either."

"Thank God for a perceptive woman." He hugged her closer and leaned back against the counter. "Anita was someone I knew a very long time ago," he said in a more serious tone. "She's nothing to do with you and me."

"How long ago?" she asked, teasing now because she knew she could.

He thought about it and said, "It's been about fifteen years, I suppose. Look, Jacqueline, I'm sorry we had to run into her, but I can't promise you it won't happen again—with Anita or another woman."

"I wouldn't expect you to promise any such thing," she said, equally as seriously. "With any luck, though, all the others will have the courtesy to keep their hands to themselves."

He grinned. "I admit you looked as though you wanted to scratch her eyes out."

"Wrong, Alex," she said. "I wanted to bite her."

He dropped a kiss on the bridge of her nose and said he was glad she hadn't done either. Anita wasn't worth the risk of infection.

Jack giggled and handed him the postcard as the clerk came out of the back office with their bill.

A few minutes later Jack was sunning herself on a bench in front of the hotel while Alex went to get the car from behind the hotel, when something moved between her and the sun. Jack opened her eyes and saw Anita looming over her.

"What's wrong, Anita?" she asked easily. "Worried that your parting shot missed?"

The other woman shook her head and sat down without waiting for an invitation. "I came out because I wanted to apologize. I'm sorry for how I behaved in there. It was inexcusable."

Jack wasn't so gullible as to believe Anita had come all the way outside to say something nice. On the other hand it went against her nature to reject a peace pipe when offered.

"It's okay, Anita. Alex is a special man. He would be . . . difficult to forget." *Impossible*, she added to herself, and looked away before the other woman could see the depth of her feelings.

Apparently, though, apologizing wasn't enough. Anita said, "You see, Jacqueline, I don't understand what went wrong between Alex and me, and it makes me a little wild to see him with another woman. The wounds Alex left are still quite raw. That's why I came to Austria in the first place." She sighed and added, "I had hoped Eric could help me forget. Just my luck to run into Alex here of all places."

Jack looked at her in surprise. "Alex told me it all happened a long time ago, Anita. Don't you think that after all these years it's time to put it behind you?"

Anita looked at her strangely. "He told you that?" Jack nodded, and the other woman closed her eyes briefly, then got up to leave.

Almost against her will Jack put out a hand to stop her. "What is it, Anita?"

The brunette looked down at her and shook her head. "I've already said too much." She tried to walk away, but Jack bounded to her feet and blocked her path.

"You don't drop a bomb like that and walk away." Jack shoved her hair behind her shoulders and stared intently at the other woman. "Tell me, Anita. Now, before Alex gets back with the car."

"What difference does it make to you? You've got him for now. Be happy with that."

A feeling of dread was building inside of her, but she couldn't just walk away and pretend the encounter had never happened. Whether or not she believed Anita was something, she'd decide later. For now she wanted to hear what she had to say.

Anita lifted a hand to toy with a magnificent pearl-drop-shaped diamond that hung from a delicate chain around her neck. "Alex gave me this for Christmas, then celebrated New Year's Eve with someone else."

"Fifteen years ago?" Jack asked softly.

Anita shook her head. "No, Jacqueline, not fifteen years ago. Not even one. It hasn't been two months since Alex walked out of my life."

Jack didn't believe her, couldn't believe her.

Wouldn't have believed her . . . until she said one more thing.

"I suppose it would have been easier on me if I'd seen it coming. But, you know what, Jacqueline, I'd fallen in love with him by then and couldn't imagine he'd be that loving or generous with a woman he planned to discard." The laugh she gave was weary and humorless. "I even deluded myself that he felt the same way about me, that he loved me. It only goes to show how wrong a woman can be about a man."

Before Jack could say anything, Anita stepped around her and went back into the hotel. That was just as well, Jack thought as she grabbed her handbag from the bench and hurried down the street.

There wasn't anything left to be said.

Alex pulled up in front of the hotel minutes later, swearing under his breath at the parking attendant who had misplaced the keys to a car blocking the Mercedes. It had taken forever, it seemed, to find someone to move the other car so he could leave.

The luggage was beside the bench where he'd left it, and Alex loaded it into the car boot before going inside to collect Jacqueline. When a quick search of the lobby didn't yield results, he decided she'd gone into the rest room. Five minutes later he sent the desk clerk inside to see if she was ill.

But Jacqueline wasn't even there.

Alex was standing at the desk trying to figure where she'd gone off to when he looked outside and saw Anita slide into a gold-toned sports car at the curb. There was a sinking feeling in the pit of his stomach as he rushed outside and tapped on the car's window. The feeling only got worse when Anita lowered the window and looked at him with an expression that could only be described as one of malicious satisfaction.

"You're too late, darling," she said, her voice a vicious purr as she showed him the necklace. "This little diamond you gave me at Christmas made your little girlfriend so unhappy that she ran off."

The man in the driver's seat said, "Anita, what are you talking about? You said you bought that last summer in South Africa."

Alex cut him off with a dark look. "You know very well I didn't give you that diamond—last Christmas or any other."

"I know it and you know it. Unfortunately little Jacqueline doesn't." Anita smiled spitefully. "In the future keep your nose out of my business, Alex. I didn't appreciate having my weekend at the Greshams' ruined."

Alex channeled his fury into a simple edict. "If anything happens to Jacqueline because of your bitchy interference, Anita, the consequences will exceed your worst nightmares." He didn't bother looking to see if she believed him because whether or not she did was unimportant. He never made idle threats. Nor was Anita's response a priority.

At that moment the only person on his mind was Jacqueline.

He had to find her.

She wasn't anywhere to be found. Alex searched Ellmau top to bottom, then did it again as the light began to wane. When he failed even to find someone who had seen her, he went back to the hotel and left money for her in case she returned. She had no Austrian shillings, he knew, but he wasn't sure whether she had other cash or credit cards.

It terrified him to think she might be wandering around with no money and no way of getting back to England.

It was pitch-dark when he forced himself to admit there was nothing more he could do in Ellmau. The police weren't interested, because it had only been a few hours, and lovers' tiffs weren't their problem. The people at the hotel promised they'd watch for her, but with all the tourists that passed through there, Alex wasn't confident they'd notice her.

He called the pilot in case Jacqueline showed up at the airport. She hadn't yet, but the pilot promised to canvas the airlines while he waited for Alex to arrive. By the time Alex pulled the car into the car park at the airport, it was four hours since she'd disappeared. He grabbed their things from the boot—she hadn't even taken hers, he realized—and ran to the end of the terminal where private aircraft were handled. The pilot met him outside Immigration with the news that no one had seen her. She hadn't booked a flight, and no one he'd questioned remembered seeing a black-haired woman of Jacqueline's description in the terminal.

Alex gave him their bags, then walked the length of the terminal himself. The effort yielded nothing. Jacqueline either wasn't coming to Salzburg or she'd slipped through and they'd somehow missed her.

On the off chance he was wrong, Alex prowled the airport for another hour, leaving messages for Jacqueline at all airline desks and airport shops. Finally the pilot found him and said they had to leave for England or be forced to wait until the next morning.

Alex knew staying in Salzburg would accomplish nothing. If Jacqueline was still in Austria, he had no way of finding her. And if she was on her way back to England, he wanted to be there when she arrived. He followed the pilot to the jet and ducked his head to climb aboard.

He would give her until morning, he decided. If she hadn't found her way home by then, he'd come back with an army of men who knew how to track people.

Alex knew he wouldn't sleep until she was found.

Jack didn't know what she would have done without Audrey. She doubted she'd even be alive without her.

Anita's revelations had sent her mind into such a tailspin, she'd been incapable of paying even rudimentary attention to where she was going as she ran from the hotel. All she remembered was a shout, then a hand pulling her out of the way of an oncoming bus. With the shattering realization of what she'd nearly done had come recognition of the English ski guide.

Gathering her wits, Jack had asked the girl where she could find transportation out of Ellmau. After a few questions—none of which were about Alex, Jack was relieved to note—Audrey had introduced herself and offered her a ride to Innsbruck. She'd been going there anyway to visit a cousin. Jack accepted gratefully, but her relief at seeing Ellmau disappear in the distance was short-lived. She had no money with her other than the English equivalent of about twenty dollars, and her credit card was still wincing from the beating she'd given it at the London boutique.

She couldn't even call Hillary because she and Bobby were spending the night in Scotland, where Bobby had horses running in races today and tomorrow. She was considering testing the expansiveness of her credit card company when the crimped setting of her tennis bracelet snagged on her sweater. With a sigh of frustration she bent her head down as she disentangled it . . . and a better idea occurred to her. She could hock the damn thing and give Alex the pawn ticket when she returned the necklace and earrings.

She couldn't imagine he would bother claiming it.

Audrey had been appalled by the suggestion, but after a minor argument she'd given in so far as to drive Jack to a pawnshop and go inside with her to act as translator. When she'd dropped her at the airport, Audrey had refused payment, but demanded Jacqueline call her at her cousin's to let her know she'd arrived safely.

Two hours later Jack was sitting in the first-class section of a commercial aircraft and wondering how she could be so incredibly stupid. She leaned her forehead against the Perspex window and shut her eyes to the twinkling lights below that reminded her of the bracelet she no longer wore.

"You're an idiot," she said, then nearly jumped out of her seat when the woman next to her said in an English accent, "Excuse me?"

"Not you," Jack said in apology. "I was talking to myself. I'll try to keep the conversation more quiet."

The woman, older than Jack by more than a few years, looked amused. "Do you always call yourself such unkind names?"

"Only when I deserve them." Jack heaved a sigh and winced. "I'm afraid *stupid* is mild compared to what I should be calling myself."

"Do you mind if I ask what you've done to warrant all this self-castigation?"

"I would likely bore you," Jack assured her.

"On the contrary," she said, reaching over to pat Jack's hand. "I've just spent two weeks minding my daughter's four children—none of whom is over ten—and the only civilized conversation I've had is with the milkman, who learned to speak English in the Bronx." She accompanied the word *English* with a shudder. "I'd listen to you lecture about sea anemones if it would get you talking."

The flight attendant interrupted to hand them the drinks they'd ordered earlier, and Jack decided before she'd taken a sip of her red wine that it wouldn't hurt to chat with this woman. If anything, maybe she could give Jack a clue how she was going to fix the mess she'd gotten herself into.

So Jack told her everything—well, everything that was essential to the story—and by the time she got to the point where she hocked the bracelet so that she could pay her way home, the woman was shaking her head in dismay.

"Precisely when did the word *stupid* occur to you?" she asked.

Jack said, "Sometime between takeoff and when I felt the wheels locking into place. Until then I'd been too worried about details."

"Too late to go back, then," the woman said, and waited as the attendant replaced their drinks.

"I doubt he'd still be in Ellmau anyway," Jack said. "I'm sure Anita wouldn't leave without letting him know what she'd done. At that point he won't have any reason to stick around."

"Why not?"

"Would you wait for someone who chose to believe an

ex-lover's lies when you'd already told her the truth?" Jack gulped back a cry of frustration, then drank deeply of her wine. "How could I let myself be tricked so easily?"

"She sounds as though she was very convincing."

Jack shook her head. "That's beside the point. I shouldn't have listened."

"I have to admit I can understand why you were calling yourself names."

Jack would have laughed if she hadn't known it would come out sounding pathetic and defeated. "You know, the worst thing about all this is that now I don't know what to believe."

The woman looked at her sharply. "I thought you'd decided you believe your young man."

"Oh, I know *who* to believe. It's the *what* that's got me scared." Jack looked at her traveling companion and said, "I don't know now if I really love Alex. I thought I knew this afternoon, but how can I say that . . . and bail out on him the first time things aren't perfect?"

TWELVE

The taxi driver wanted what Jack calculated to be over a hundred and fifty dollars to take her from Heathrow to Hillary's, so she did the next worst thing and rented a car. Even though she had enough cash on hand to buy passage on the *QEII*, the rental agency insisted on putting her credit card through their machine. When no alarms went off and the agent began to enter the information into his computer, Jack restrained herself from wondering aloud how that had happened and decided to settle the bill in cash. She grabbed the keys before the machine changed its mind.

Twenty minutes later she was tooling along the motorway toward Oxford with her mind on the traffic and her foot heavy on the accelerator. The blue Ford Escort responded to her urgency with the manners of a polite stranger—helping her along without presuming to interfere. In other words it went fast when she told it to and didn't burden her with a lot of unsolicited advice. As a result she missed the exit she wanted and had to go on to the next and track back. By the time she got through the confusing roundabouts that dotted the northern curve of

Oxford's ring road, she was getting weary of doing all the driving and directing too.

She gave a sigh of relief when Oxford faded into the distance and the only choices she had to make were more familiar ones. That was a good thing, too, because the night was pitch-black, and she had to concentrate on staying on the left side of the road without driving too close to the edge. She'd already made that mistake once—on the way out of the parking lot when she'd overcompensated and hit the outside curb. She knew that if she did the same on a country road, the soft shoulder would suck her in faster than a pheasant could cross the road.

Speaking of pheasants . . . Jack eased off the accelerator and prayed they'd see her coming and do the right thing. Ten minutes later she made the turn into Hillary's driveway and was thinking all the pheasants in Gloucestershire must be asleep, when she noticed another car parked in front of the house.

Alex's car. Jack braked abruptly and watched spellbound as the tall, wide-shouldered man she'd last seen in Ellmau walked into her headlights.

She'd been so busy with the mechanics of driving through a foreign country on the wrong side of the road that she'd blocked everything else out. It came back at her with the punch of a gale-force wind, her insecurities vying with pride and wishful thinking as Alex came around to the driver's door and pulled it open.

She wished she'd had the guts to believe in him . . . in them. Now it was too late, and there wasn't anything she could do about it. Her fingers were curled around the wheel, and she stared straight ahead through the windshield because she couldn't bear to see the expression on his face.

She already knew what she'd see there, and it was more than she could handle at that moment to see the contempt he must be feeling confirmed in his eyes. She felt rather than saw him hunker down in the gravel beside her door. When long moments went by and he didn't speak, she forced herself to turn her head and look at him.

What she saw confused her. There was relief where she'd predicted disdain, caring where she'd expected indifference . . . and hope when she'd anticipated nothing of the kind. In the light of the open door she studied him carefully, noting the strain that had deepened the lines of his face. His tie was loose around his collar, and his shirt sported a few wrinkles. The effect was one of general dishevelment, a state she'd never imagined Alex could achieve.

He looked like she felt. She said, "I thought you'd be angry."

"No, Jacqueline, I was worried." He thrust his fingers through his hair, furthering the deterioration of his normally immaculate appearance. "If I'd known you were driving from the airport, I would have been in a bloody panic."

"I didn't hit anything."

He muttered something under his breath that was likely unfit for her ears, then cleared his throat. "I've been sitting here waiting for you, and I didn't even know if you were in this country. Or if you were hurt or wandering around lost or incapable of coming back because you didn't have any means to do it. I don't want to go through another night like this one ever again. Do you understand me, Jacqueline?"

No, not really. She stayed mute in her confusion.

"Don't *ever* worry me like this again. If we fight and you feel you have to run away, at least have the courtesy to tell me first. Otherwise how can you possibly expect me to stay sane?" The last words were said in a crescendo that was nearly a roar when it ended.

She took several deep breaths to calm her rising expectations. "I didn't do it to worry you. If I tell you how very sorry I am, will you—"

He silenced her with two fingers over her lips, and this time when he spoke, his tone was gentle. "I told you before that I can't change my past, Jacqueline. The only guarantee I can give you is my honesty about it."

Tears welled in the corners of her eyes, and her hand was trembling as she reached out to touch his face. "I knew before the plane took off that I'd been a fool for listening to her."

"Don't blame yourself, sweet. Anita has many talents, and duplicity is at the top of the list." He rubbed his thumb across her bottom lip. "I didn't give her the necklace, last Christmas or any other. It's been fifteen years since I did more than speak to her when necessary."

"How can you be so understanding about all this?" A tear fell down her cheek, and he brushed his thumb across the wet track it left. "I should have trusted you."

His voice was low and husky. "Trust is something that will come in time, Jacqueline, along with everything else we're going to need to make this work."

"What do you mean, everything else?" And silently she asked, *Make* what *work?*

The look he gave her was intent and candid. "Compassion, honor, and fidelity would do nicely as starters. I would expect my wife to adhere to the same standards I set for myself, although I have to admit fidelity is something I never thought I would desire in a marriage."

"Fidelity?" She blinked in tempo with her pounding heart. "Marriage?"

He nodded solemnly. "I suppose I was always on the outside looking in and wondering how two people could possibly be satisfied with only each other. Now I find myself wondering how it could be any other way." His gaze narrowed sharply. "You do believe in fidelity, don't you, Jacqueline?"

"Of course. I—"

"I knew you must, but it's reassuring to hear the words." He reached into his pocket and brought out a small velvet box. "I meant to give this to you this afternoon, but your rather innovative lovemaking threw my schedule off, and then Anita—"

Jack took her turn at interrupting. "Say that woman's name one more time tonight, Alex, and I'll never, *ever* forgive you." She avoided looking at the box he was holding between them, not daring to believe it was what she thought it was, that it meant what she thought it meant. . . .

He snapped his fingers. "Forgiveness. That's another quality I need in a wife."

"Wife?" Her voice was a high squeak that would have done justice to a mouse.

"Wife, Jacqueline. *My* wife." He cupped her face with his free hand and held her gaze with his. "Does the idea appeal to you at all?"

She nodded.

"Will you marry me, Jacqueline?" he asked.

She nodded again, and his laugh was a low rumble in the night air. "I would prefer hearing you say it out loud."

She opened her mouth to speak, then closed it to swallow back the lump in her throat before trying again. "I only realized this afternoon that I loved you, Alex. I guess I'm having trouble keeping up with the pace you set."

A shadow flickered across his expression, and he studied her for a long moment before replying. "Love isn't something I expect to find anywhere, Jacqueline, even in a marriage."

It occurred to her a bit late that he hadn't actually said he loved her. She wished she'd noticed the omission earlier. "You want to marry me, but you don't love me. Is that correct?"

"I care for you."

"But you don't *love* me." She wanted to be sure she had that part straight as the emotional roller coaster she was on plunged downward into a terrifying void.

He shook his head and put the ring box on his knee. "You're misunderstanding, sweet. It's not that I don't love you. It's that I don't *believe* in love."

"Then why marry me?"

"Because we suit. I've spent the last week learning about you, delving into your background and letting you see mine. There's every reason to believe we'd have a good marriage, and nothing that I can see to prevent it. Unless, of course, you're unwilling to move to England. I'm afraid I'll have to insist upon that."

"Insist?" She wasn't sure she liked that word.

He looked confused. "But I thought you liked England, sweet. That's one of the first obstacles I eliminated."

"Obstacles?"

"You have to admit there are a few, only some of which I've resolved to my satisfaction." He ticked them off on his fingers. "Besides the fact you'd have to move, there's the problem of if and where you want to work, whether we were sexually compatible, if you liked my house enough to live in it, whether you could—"

"*Stop!*" Jack interrupted him midlist and glared him into silence. Information was coming in faster than she could assimilate it. She put her fingers to her temples and tried to focus on one thing at a time. It didn't work.

She dropped her hands to her lap and glared at him some more. "I can't believe you actually put sex and my career in the same sentence."

"They're both important," he said reasonably. "Critical, in fact. Sex for the obvious reasons, and your career because if you're not happy with your options, it will impact our life together."

"What if I don't like your house?"

He grinned. "But you do like it."

"But what if I hadn't? Would you still be asking me to marry you?"

"You're being deliberately obtuse, Jacqueline," he said a trifle impatiently. "With a few notable exceptions such as sex and general compatibility, the rest of the considerations are just that: considerations. If there had been too many points where we had obvious disagreements or if the obstacles seemed insurmountable, it would have indicated that we didn't suit after all. That isn't how it turned out."

She stared at him blankly. "So what you're saying is you want to marry me because we suit."

"We suit very well, Jacqueline. You know that as well as I do." He picked up the box and snapped it open. "I'm almost on my knees, and I'm asking you very seriously to become my wife. Will you?"

An enormous emerald-cut diamond flashed brightly against the black background, its brilliance slicing to the heart of the matter with an ease that shocked her. Jack knew that if she took the ring, she would be tied to Alex forever. Even if the marriage didn't work, by taking this step she would be committing her heart and soul to a man who didn't believe in love, a man to whom possessions and wives were chosen because they suited.

She didn't believe it. Alex was a caring, gentle man whose definition of love happened to be complicated by a history that had nothing to do with her. In order to protect his emotions from abuse, he pretended—to himself and to the world—that he didn't have any.

She knew better.

The problem, Jack thought as she stared into the diamond's white-blue core, was proving it. And not only as those feelings and emotions applied to her but as they applied to the rest of his life as well. The kernel of an idea rattled around in her head like a pinball gone wild, and when it finally dropped into the slot, it had evolved into a harebrained scheme that she knew couldn't possibly succeed.

She also knew that it must.

"Well, Jacqueline?"

She looked up at his prompting and held out her left hand. "I will, Alex."

"Good." He took the ring from the box and was about to slide it onto her finger when she jerked her hand back. "What's wrong?"

"Nothing. I just want to make sure you know that I love you and don't intend to stop just because you don't believe in it."

She could have sworn it was pleasure that flared in his eyes, but he blinked and it was gone when she looked again. He said, "If it makes you content to believe that, I won't mind."

"Nice of you," she said smartly, and gave him her hand again.

She snapped it back before the ring reached her first knuckle.

"What now?" he demanded, looking a bit peeved. "My knees are going to be permanently bent if I don't get up soon."

"In a moment," she said. "I also want to make sure you know that I wouldn't mind if someday you decided you loved me too."

His hands fisted on his thighs, and he took several deep breaths before replying. When he did, it was with considerably more patience than she expected. "I've told you how I feel about love, Jacqueline. It's not something I'm capable of. I can, however, give you certain assurances that you might discover you come to value as much."

"What assurances?"

"I've already said that I care for you, sweet." He reached for her hands and held them against his chest as his gaze held hers in a similar kind of captivity. "I care enough to want to keep you safe from harm. I want to laugh with you and to know you'll run to me when the world isn't treating you right. I want to have children with you and to know that you'll stand beside me through good days and bad." He leaned across the gap between them and kissed her lightly on the mouth. When he lifted his head, there was a hunger in his expression that sent her heart spinning toward the stars. "I care for you, Jacqueline, and I'll do everything I can to make you happy for the rest of your life. If we give it a chance, I know we could have a rather good life together."

If that wasn't love, Jack mused, what was? She slipped her left hand from his grasp, and this time when she held it in the air between them, there was a fine tremor in her fingers that she couldn't seem to control. Alex pushed the ring onto her finger, then bent his head and kissed each knuckle separately—twice on her ring finger, but who was counting?

Jack was. She was counting the minutes before she could put her plan to work. She knew better than to imagine this was simply a matter of semantics she was dealing with here. True, Alex loved her, and yes, she would eventually point that out to him if he was too stubborn to see it for himself.

First, though, she would have to demonstrate the difference between valuable possessions and those belongings that enriched one's life in more than a financial sense.

Perhaps then he would understand wives were more than "women who suited."

Wives were intended to be loved, and Jack was determined that Alex adhere to that custom . . . even if it meant taking on the giant.

THIRTEEN

"What do you mean, you 'hocked the bracelet'?" Alex asked.

"Hocked, as in pawned, mortgaged, borrowed. Audrey helped me find a pawnshop in Innsbruck that wasn't too far from the airport." Jack tested the omelet she was cooking, trying not to drool as the aroma of cheese, mushrooms, and bell peppers filled the air. It was early morning by anyone's standards, and the light that came into the east-facing windows of Alex's kitchen was meager at best. Jack turned the heat down under the pan, then looked over her shoulder to where he was setting the table. "Is that a problem, Alex?"

He grinned. "Not in the least. In fact I'm impressed that you thought of it. Well done, Jacqueline."

Wrong answer. She would have thrown the spatula at him if she hadn't needed it for the omelet. Containing her frustration, she returned her attention to the stove. "The ticket is somewhere in that wad of shillings in my purse. I'll need a bit of the cash to pay for the rental car, but you can have the rest back."

"Why? The bracelet was yours. Do what you like with

the money." She heard him pull a chair out from the kitchen table. "Leave the car with me, though. No sense in taking any more chances with it."

"Worried about the car?" she asked.

"You know better than that, sweet. The car is of no difference." His voice dropped to a husky caress. "You, however, are extremely important to me."

She looked down at the diamond on her finger and counted to ten, unsure whether she was frustrated over his lack of concern over the bracelet or miffed at his comment on her driving skills. Both, she decided, and poked his side of the omelet until it took on the appearance of scrambled eggs. Satisfied with her efforts, she served the meal onto two plates and took them to the table.

"If I'm going to be living in England, I'll want to drive occasionally." She ignored Alex's raised eyebrows as he glanced pointedly from his plate to hers. When she cut into the omelet, Alex picked up his own fork and began to eat his scrambled portion as though he hadn't noticed the difference.

"We'll take some time for practice over the next few weeks," he said. "I'm sure you'll do quite well once you find your wheels."

"I thought I did pretty well last night," she said.

"We can't depend on luck to keep you safe, Jacqueline. There is a certain amount of skill required when driving on narrow roads and through roundabouts." He looked at her over the rim of his coffee cup. "Besides, you're not licensed to drive over here."

"I have an International Driver's Permit," she said.

"Not anymore. I put it in a safe place."

"You did what?" She was stunned that he would take something from her.

"I took your license. You can't legally drive in England."

"But why?"

"Because I didn't wish to spend today worrying about you. I'll be glad to go driving with you another day, Jacqueline, but I've got a meeting this morning and can't spare the time." He went back to eating his mangled omelet as though the subject were closed.

If she hadn't been planning a little thievery of her own, she would have resented his interference. As it was, Jack decided she liked the sense of balance it gave her.

Alex had stolen something from her. She was planning to steal something much more valuable from him. By the following morning the score would be one to one.

Alex dropped Jack at Hillary's, then went into town already an hour late for his meeting. Jack went inside, changed into a skirt and sweater, then looked through Hillary's desk until she found a rubber band to put around the pile of shillings. Tucking the wad back into her purse, she snapped it closed and wrote out a note for Hillary in case she returned before Jack did. Then she took the keys to Hillary's blue Audi from the kitchen hook and went outside to start the car.

It was skill—not luck, she assured herself—that saw her safely to the train station, where she left the Audi in the car park and purchased a return ticket to London. As the train zipped toward the city center, Jack studied her map and worked out which Underground line she'd need to take to Regent Street, where she remembered seeing several up-market jewelry shops. First, though, she'd have to stop at a bank and exchange the Austrian shillings for pounds.

An hour later Jack left the bank with her handbag clutched firmly under her arm. Somehow the British pounds seemed more real than the Austrian shillings had, and she was self-conscious about carrying so much cash on her. Accordingly she went into the first jeweler she came across and described what she wanted. They were unable to help her, though. It took two more stops before she found what she was looking for. Jack handed over at least half of the pounds she was carrying and tucked the velvet box into the bottom of her handbag.

By the time she arrived back at the car park where she'd left the Audi, she was exhausted from looking over her shoulder. Still, there was a certain spring in her step that arose from her anticipation of the look on Alex's face when he saw what she'd done.

He was furious, and she hadn't done anything yet.

Jack parked the Audi behind Alex's Jaguar and snuck another look toward the front steps where he was waiting for her. If his ferocious scowl was anything to go by, the man Jack had said she would marry was more than mildly irked with her. She considered putting the car into reverse and leaving until he cooled off, but she suspected that a time delay wouldn't solve matters. With a sigh she let herself out of the car and walked over to the steps.

She paused at the bottom one and looked up to find that his scowl had deepened. Added to the fact that he towered over her in normal circumstances and was now at least three feet higher, she wondered that she had the nerve to stand up to the giant at all.

But Jack did have the nerve, a tenuously thin band of bravado that wrapped around her spine and made her look up at him without cowering. "If you're going to roar at me, Alex, get it over with. I've had a long day and I'd like to sit down and put my feet up."

"By the time I get through with you, *sit* won't be one of your favorite words," he shouted, then raised the decibels in case there was someone in all of Gloucestershire that hadn't heard him. "You'll wish you'd stayed where I put you this morning, my sweet Jacqueline. Do you have *any* idea how worried I've been since Ian told me you'd taken the Audi?"

Jack thought that if he always got angry when he got worried, then last night's gentle concern had either been an aberration or he'd already progressed through the ranting and raving stage by the time she got there. In any case it was interesting to see that he did have a temper and that it was capable of being roused.

She couldn't wait until morning. A temper tantrum was exactly what she was hoping for.

She smiled up at Alex encouragingly, hoping to nudge him from furious back to worried. When he exhaled in an explosive sigh, she imagined her ploy had worked.

It had, to a degree. He was still angry, but his voice had lowered to exclude the immediate neighbors from hearing. "I thought I told you not to drive, Jacqueline."

"No, Alex. You said I couldn't legally drive in England. You didn't say anything about doing it the other way."

"The other way!" he roared, then came down the stairs in one long stride to stand over her. "There *is* no other way. If they catch you driving without a license, they lock you in the Tower."

"*Impossible*," she shouted back. "I've *been* there, and it's not big enough to hold all the people Hillary told me they send there for driving 'very, very badly' *and* the people who drive without licenses."

Before he could get in a word edgewise, she added, "Unless, of course, they have more than one bloody Tower in this bloody country."

"Don't swear," he growled.

"*Bloody* isn't swearing," she returned without missing a beat. "It's short for *by my lady*, or didn't you know that?"

He looked poleaxed, and his voice lowered to a shadow of its former thunder. "You actually believe that?"

"Of course. Why, what do you think it means?"

"*Bloody* is a blasphemous reference to Christ's blood, or so I've been told."

"I like my definition better," she retorted, shifting restively because she'd always thought the word a charming relic of Camelot and knights of olde.

He hesitated, then a reluctant smile pushed at his mouth. "So do I, sweet."

"Really?"

"Mmm-hmm." He slipped a hand beneath the hair at her nape and began massaging the crick she hadn't noticed until then. "Just do me a favor and don't use it around anyone but me."

She closed her eyes so that she could fully appreciate the warm strength of his fingers as they moved on her neck. "Are you giving me permission to swear at you, Alex?"

"I suspect you'll do it with or without my permission," he murmured, and she felt the firm brush of his lips across her cheek. "Just as you drive with or without it."

"I didn't drive to annoy you, Alex," she said, then gave a satisfied moan as his fingers worked their magic. "I drove because I had somewhere to go and no one to take me. I'm used to a certain degree of independence. You're going to have to learn to live with that."

"It isn't the independence I mind," he said, kissing the corners of her mouth, then leaving her wanting more as his lips traveled upward. "In fact that's one of your redeeming qualities. As far as I'm concerned, you may drive any car you wish once I'm satisfied you can do so safely.

Until then I'll make arrangements for a driver. I'm sure Ian or one of the lads will be happy to make a few quid."

"Even your Jag?"

He winced, then nodded reluctantly. "Even my Jaguar."

"And may I swear at Ian?" she asked mischievously.

"He won't notice one way or the other."

Alex silenced her request with a kiss, suspecting it was the only way to interrupt her gloating. As happened more often than not when he kissed Jacqueline, he found himself drawn into a voluptuous whirlwind of passion that was like nothing he'd known with any other woman. Their mouths dueled and mated, and the fact that he was bigger and stronger had no impact on the pleasure given or accepted. She was as forceful as he'd ever dared, and as gentle as a summer's night. She teased, taunted and tamed him, then surrendered in the next breath to his desire to do the same.

Jacqueline was the embodiment of passion, and Alex knew he would never get enough of her.

It must have been quite some time later when he looked up to see Bobby's truck pulling into the drive, because Jacqueline's mouth was swollen and red, and his body virtually thrummed with the need to take her to the nearest bed and make love to her. In an effort to disguise the more visible signs of that need, he pulled Jacqueline to stand in front of him and waved over her shoulder to the approaching truck.

Hillary must have spotted Jacqueline's ring before the truck stopped rolling, because before Alex knew it, he and Jacqueline were subjected to a veritable whirlwind of hugs, kisses, and backslapping. The scene was repeated inside to the accompaniment of champagne and toasts, with Hillary offering a toast to herself in congratulations for having brought the pair together. Alex had been the

first to second her initiative, but privately assured himself
that he'd have found Jacqueline with or without Hillary's
help.

The scent of rainbows and lilacs would have led him
to her eventually.

Alex and Bobby soon went down to the yard for evening stables, where Alex gave Golden Legs the carrot he'd
nicked from the kitchen. Between his trip to New York
and Austria, it had been nearly a week since he'd seen the
horse, and he pressed Bobby for details of the exercise and
schooling Golden Legs had been given.

Bobby looked as though he wished Alex hadn't asked.
"He's not doing as well as I'd hoped," Bobby admitted. "I
thought it would be useful to have Sam Beckett school
him instead of the apprentice who's been on him lately,
but it didn't help. Even from where I was standing, I
could tell Sam was doing more of the work than Golden
Legs."

"How much do you think he'll get in the sales?" Alex
asked, the decision a mere formality now.

Bobby shot him a frustrated look, then named an
amount close to what Alex had estimated. "Do I put him
into the sales or not?"

Alex hesitated. He had a drawerful of carrots in the
refrigerator that would rot if there wasn't a horse to give
them to. In addition Jacqueline was sure to pitch a fit
when she discovered he was selling Golden Legs. He decided to put off the deed until she'd left for the States. In
the meantime he'd warn the housekeeper not to buy any
more carrots.

"Let's wait until after Jacqueline leaves, Bobby," he
said. "Until then don't run him."

"Are you hoping she'll forget about Golden Legs between now and when she moves here?"

Alex shrugged. "She'll have too many other things to

do to worry about a horse. But if she's upset, I'll buy her another."

"It won't be the same," Bobby argued. "She's attached to Golden Legs."

"She hardly knows one end of a horse from the other. Trust me, Bobby, she won't mind."

Bobby shook his head, but didn't offer further comment. "You'll still come watch Golden Legs work?" Bobby asked.

"I'll come." He didn't see any reason not to. After all, Golden Legs was still his horse, and there were all those carrots. . . .

They finished Bobby's walk around without any more discussion regarding Golden Legs, although several times Bobby started to say something, only to shake his head and turn away. On the way back up to the house Alex invited Hillary and Bobby for dinner at the Red Lion. Visions of roast duck had the desired effect on Bobby, and he herded everyone into the truck for the short drive before Hillary or Jacqueline could so much as freshen their lipstick.

Dinner conversation revolved almost entirely around their forthcoming marriage. Hillary was appalled that they hadn't decided when or where the wedding was to take place, and took immediate charge of everything. Before Bobby had taken the first bite of crackling, it had been decided that "when" would be July or early August, right after Jacqueline finished out her teaching contract. England was chosen as "where," because, as Hillary so succinctly put it, "Alex can afford to fly over anyone who wants to come." Besides, Hillary pointed out, preparing for the wedding would give her something to do. Jack, she added, would be busy enough with her work and doing all those things necessary to move from one continent to another.

During the course of the evening Alex noticed that Jacqueline's contribution to the decision making was substantially less than Hillary's. He asked her about it when Bobby and Hillary went over to the dessert cart.

"I'm not only marrying you, Alex," she said softly. "I'm moving my entire world to be with you. It's enough to make the nerves tingle a bit, don't you agree?"

He agreed, but on the off chance there was more to it than a case of nerves, he went through the plans with her as they drove back to his home. Her agreement with Hillary's suggestions stood firm, though, and he was reassured. He found he was pleased they would be beginning their life together as they meant to go on: in England, land of his ancestors . . . land of her dreams.

Later that night as Alex lay propped against the pillows of his bed with Jacqueline sprawled half over him and the covers tangled at their feet, he remembered he hadn't asked her where she'd gone that day in the Audi. In the moonlight that streamed through the windows he looked at her face on his chest and wondered if the closed eyes meant she was sleeping or if she was merely conserving energy. His fingers traced the delicate features of her face, drifting over her cheeks and the tip of her nose to her mouth. She didn't move except to part her lips as he drew a line from one corner of her mouth to the other. He slipped his finger inside where the moist warmth vividly recalled to mind the erotic foreplay that night involving the piano and what Jacqueline termed "fair play."

He shifted beneath her, giving his arousal room as he remembered his original intent and the way she'd turned the tables—or piano—on him. Her wanton enjoyment of his response had amplified his own excitement, and the raging urgency to be inside her had driven him to take her standing up not two feet from the piano where it had all begun.

To make it up to her—something she'd insisted wasn't strictly necessary—Alex had brought her to his bed, where he'd made slow, almost torturous love to her. By the time he finally slipped the reins of his own control, the woman in his arms had been begging for an end, a beginning . . . completion.

Her mouth closed over his finger, and she gave a tiny snore in her sleep. With regret Alex decided to abstain from waking her. There wasn't much left of the night, and the following day would be a busy one. Although he knew waking her was very likely impossible, he was careful as he reached for the quilt and pulled it up over her shoulders.

The ache in his groin lessened after an hour, enough to let him sleep but not enough to keep him from waking Jacqueline with the dawn. They made love with a luxurious sense of having all the time in the world, then rushed into the shower because the day had started without them.

Jack slipped out of the huge glass-sided shower when Alex ducked his head under the streaming water to rinse the soap from his hair. She wrapped a towel around her wet body and raced into the adjoining dressing room. Her fingers trembled as she dug into her handbag for the thing she'd bought in London, even more so when she went over to the dresser where Alex had emptied his pockets. She pulled his money clip from the folded bills and replaced it with the one in her hand. Holding one up to the other, she judged they were close enough in shape to suffer minimal scrutiny. Anything more would reveal the substitution.

She hoped he was in a different county when he noticed the difference.

The shower cut off, and she realized she'd better hide the clip that had been a gift from Alex's father somewhere other than her handbag. She'd already learned he had no qualms going through that. In a panic she sprinted through the open door into the hall, then down several yards until she came to a narrow table against one wall. On it was a vase of silk flowers, and it gave her an idea. Her fingers were still shaking as she dropped the clip into the porcelain vase, whose delicate winter roses would never die.

A deep breath restored her nerve, but she almost lost it again when Alex said from behind her, "Exploring your new home?"

A mouse running across her toes would have startled her less. "Where did you come from?" she demanded.

He looked down at the towel at his hips, then at the one she wore, focusing on the knot between her breasts. "I think we came from the same place, Jacqueline. Did I frighten you?"

Just out of my wits, she said silently. "Startled, not frightened," she said, and it was the truth. She couldn't imagine being frightened of Alex. He snagged her hand and pulled her back into the bedroom. Jack went willingly, relieved to get him away from the vase.

He stopped in the center of the room and tugged at the knot in her towel. When the towel fell to their feet, his voice took on that husky note that promised passion and excitement as his eyes went dark and silver at the same time. "If you don't put some clothes on, sweet, I'll miss all of my meetings, not just the first one."

"You don't sound like you've got meetings on your mind, Alex."

"That's your fault." He bent to touch his mouth to her bare shoulder. "How can you expect me to think of business when I find you walking half naked through the halls?"

Jack shivered as his mouth moved slowly toward her neck. The idea of prolonging their morning together appealed to her. She was just about to check beneath his towel and gauge his interest in business versus pleasure, when he set her away from him with a regretful sigh.

"Sorry, sweet, but I really do need to get to work." He slipped the towel from around his waist and threw it toward the bathroom. "We'd better get dressed."

She looked at his naked body and tried not to laugh. "I don't think they make clothes in that shape."

He glared at her reprovingly, then pulled on the slim-fitting nylon shorts he favored.

She was right. They didn't fit. That didn't stop Alex, though, and she began to pull on her own clothes in a bid to finish first. She really didn't want to be there when he noticed the clip, and there was a chance it would happen the first time he picked it up.

He said, "I'm afraid I don't even have time to make coffee. Do you want to fix something for yourself here, or wait until you're back at Hillary's? I remember hearing her say she wanted you there by ten."

"I'll wait," she said, and shook out the sweater she'd worn the night before. "Ugh. I wish I'd thought to bring fresh clothes. It's a waste to shower, then not have anything clean to put on."

"It's only this once," he said, then opened a drawer and rummaged through it until he found what he wanted. He tossed a key down next to her handbag. "You'll need that so you can come and go as you please. I'll help you bring your things over before dinner." He finished buttoning his shirt and reached for his trousers.

She stopped what she was doing to stare at him. "I never thought about moving in."

"I have no intention of sleeping without you." He matched her stare with a determined one of his own. "You can either move here or I'll spend the nights with you at Bobby's. Do you really think that's a good alternative?"

"No." She gulped, realizing anew how the ring on her finger had changed everything. Alex wasn't a man to be denied what he wanted, and if he wanted her beside him at night, he would do whatever was necessary to make that happen.

She didn't mind at all.

Jack pulled her sweater over her head and went to the mirror. It confirmed that her appearance was as wrinkled as she'd feared. From her handbag she got a brush and dragged it through her hair. Out of the corner of her eye she saw Alex reach for the money clip and put it into his pocket along with some small change.

He hadn't noticed. She calmed her racing heart with a deep breath, then said brightly, "Shall we go, then, Alex?"

He turned from straightening his tie and paused to look at her. A wistful smile curved his lips, and he shook his head slowly. "Even wrinkled, you're more temptation than I deserve to be saddled with first thing in the morning."

"After we're married, maybe I'll just stay in bed while you dress," she suggested as she slipped her hand into his.

The sound he made was more of a groan than a laugh. "If you do that, sweet, I might never get out of bed at all."

Everything considered, Jack didn't think that was such a bad idea.

"Is it my imagination, or did I single-handedly plan your wedding last night?" Hillary asked as she slid into a chair opposite Jack's at the kitchen table.

Jack reached for the coffeepot and refilled both their cups. "It wasn't your imagination, but don't worry. If Alex and I are still engaged by the time I return to California, I'll do my share."

"What do you mean, 'still engaged'?"

"Exactly that." She blew across the top of the cup, not so much to cool the hot liquid but to help the flavor of vanilla into the air. "Unless Alex realizes he's marrying me because he loves me and not because I happen to suit him, I have no intention of going through with it."

Hillary sat back in her chair and frowned. "But he *does* love you, Jack. Even a fool couldn't miss how he looks at you."

"I know it, you know it, and Bobby probably knows it, too, although your husband was so thrilled with his duck, I doubt he noticed much else last night." Jack looked down at her ring and clicked her tongue in annoyance. "Alex is the only one who hasn't figured it out."

Then she told Hillary in great detail about Alex's approach to marriage. When she'd finished, Hillary just shook her head and laughed. "It's obvious that Alex's brain is disproportionate to his size."

"Only in this," Jack said, quick to defend her intended. "Otherwise, I think he's smarter than the average giant."

"He's brilliant," Hillary agreed, "but a pea brain when it comes to love."

"Exactly. Unfortunately I've fallen in love with him, pea brain and all."

"That's also easy to see," Hillary said, "and now that you've explained everything, I've got a question."

"Just one?" Jack mused. "What?"

"With so little to work with—I'm referring to applicable brain size here—how do you intend to get your point across *and* accomplish it before you leave?"

"I've already started." A swarm of butterflies took flight in her stomach as she told Hillary about the money clips. Thanks to sidebars that began with how she'd gotten the money and then regressed to Anita's interference, the story took a pot of coffee and two cheese Danishes each. Then she had to show Hillary the necklace and earrings, neither of which she'd worn the night before. By the time Jack told Hillary where she'd hidden Alex's money clip, she was ready for a nap.

Unfortunately Hillary wasn't about to be fobbed off by exhaustion. "I don't get it, Jack. What does stealing Alex's money clip prove?"

"I didn't steal it," she said loftily. "I merely replaced it with one of approximately the same value. You can't imagine how difficult that was to find. Do you have any idea what twenty-four-karat gold costs?"

Hillary leaned across the table and wagged her finger in Jack's face. "Don't change the subject, Jack. You were about to tell me why stealing from Alex is going to make him realize he loves you."

"Because he said he carries the clip because it suits him, not because he attaches any sentiment to it." She gulped as a pair of daring butterflies worked their way into her throat. "If I can get him to admit he cares enough to want to carry the one from his father and not the nearly identical one I substituted, it will be a step in the right direction."

Hillary shook her head in despair. "The trap here is that he might admit to preferring the clip his father gave him but won't see a parallel to his relationship with you."

"His brain isn't that small." Jack pushed away from the table and walked over to the sink, where she poured out the dregs of her coffee. "The worst scenarios I can imagine are that either he won't notice at all or he won't mind. I can handle the first by pointing it out to him, although I'd really prefer not to be there when it happens, just in case he's a little miffed."

"I can understand that," Hillary said. "But what will

you do if he doesn't mind, if he decides one is as good as the other?"

Jack turned from the sink and leaned back against the counter as she regarded her friend. "Then, Hillary, I steal something bigger."

FOURTEEN

Alex arrived too early for evening stables, and told Bobby he wouldn't wait because he was taking Jacqueline to the theater. They would have to go early if they wanted time to eat something before the curtain went up. Jack walked down to the yard with him so that the carrot he'd brought wouldn't go to waste. Golden Legs had his head through the half door of his box and nickered when he saw them coming. Alex broke the treat in half and handed Jack a piece. As Golden Legs closed his mouth over the carrot, Jack lifted her other hand to cover a yawn.

"We don't have to go to the theater if you're too tired, Jacqueline," he said. "When my friend offered me the tickets to *Piaf*, I tried to call you and ask, but you were out."

She moved aside to lean against the wooden door. "We went to Bourton-on-the-Water and Broadway," she said, naming two of the most visited Cotswold villages. "Hillary was looking for something to send her niece, and I wanted postcards to show my students. I'd neglected to buy them last time we were there."

He rubbed Golden Legs between the ears, then did it

some more when the horse jostled his arm. "We could always give the tickets to Hillary and Bobby and stay in tonight," he suggested. "*Piaf* will still be running when you return from the States."

Her heart leaped at the reminder that she would be coming back, then fell again as she added "maybe" to that assumption. It took an effort of will to stifle her worries and smile up at him. "Let's go tonight, Alex. Elaine Paige might leave the production before August, and I do so want to see her."

"That's what I thought when I took the tickets." He gave Golden Legs a final pat and tucked Jack under his arm as he headed back up to the house. "Did you get your things packed?"

"Enough for a few days. I need to do some laundry before I pack the rest."

"You can do that at my house. If you're worried about getting in the housekeeper's way, don't be. The sooner she gets used to having you around, the better."

"I'd rather do it here," she said, twisting her head to look up at him. "It's one thing to be in your home with you, but I'd rather not be there alone."

He pushed open the garden gate and walked with her toward the fence where they'd first spoken. He leaned back against the rails and held her close. "It's your home, Jacqueline. Not just mine, not anymore."

"Not yet." She turned in his arms until she was facing him. "When we're married, then yes, it will be my home too."

He scowled. "You make me think we should marry now and get it over with."

"Just because I won't do my laundry over there?" she asked, half believing he was serious.

"This isn't about laundry, Jacqueline. Maybe I'm tired

of having to collect you from the neighbors' every day."
He bent down and buried his face in her hair.

"And maybe you like things your own way too much."
She lifted her face for his kiss, but he was more interested
in teasing her ear with his tongue. She moaned as he
delved inside.

"If you were waiting for me at home, we could do
more than neck in the garden," he murmured.

"True. And there would be the bonus of being able to
drive myself back and forth."

He stopped what he was doing and looked at her.
"What do you mean, drive?"

She blinked innocently. "You don't seriously expect
me to walk, do you? It's three miles to your place, Alex,
and—"

He hushed her with a deep, hungry kiss that stopped
long before she was ready. He said, "On second thought
you're probably right about staying here for the time being. I'd hate for you to miss *Piaf* because we were too
involved with other things to watch the time."

She agreed, but only just. "I'm not sure I wouldn't
rather give the tickets to Bobby and Hillary."

"We'll go to the play, Jacqueline," he said, then drew
her with him toward the house. "Trust me. It will be
worth the sacrifice."

"This is definitely worth the sacrifice," Jack said as she
took a small sip of champagne. It was the intermission,
and they were packed shoulder to shoulder in the wine
bar with a hundred other theater goers. Luckily Alex had
arranged their drinks before the play began, so it had been
a simple matter of looking for their number along the wall
and claiming the champagne.

An unfamiliar elbow dug into her back, and she edged

closer to Alex, who towered over the jostling crowd. He made a space for her between himself and the wall and braced his hand beside her head. "This madhouse is worth the sacrifice?"

"The play, silly," she said, then glanced aside to where a man was lamenting his choice of red wine in one breath and promising to have the lady's dress cleaned in the next. She looked back up at Alex. "I have to admit this has its moments too."

"So long as you're not claustrophobic," he said. "If you're feeling too squished, we can go back to our seats."

"I'm fine, thanks. Besides, I doubt we could get out of here if we wanted to."

He nodded, his silver gaze cool and somewhat curious. "Something odd happened when I came in here earlier to order our drinks."

"What?" She took a drink, then nearly spit it back out when he replied.

"I went to pay, and discovered it wasn't my money clip that I was carrying, although I have to admit it's very close in size and weight." He cocked his head and regarded her as though what they were discussing was a mere curiosity and nothing more. "Now, Jacqueline, I've sorted out where and when the exchange took place, and, naturally, the who. But even though I've had the entire first act to think about it, I haven't been able to understand why. Perhaps you might explain it to me?"

The mildness of his request distressed and annoyed her, but she didn't let either show. The emotions she wanted disclosed were his, not hers. "Why, Jacqueline?" She lifted one shoulder in a deliberately careless shrug. "Why not? You told me you only carried it because it suited you, and that you wouldn't carry it if it were tin. Well, the one in your pocket is gold and, as you pointed out, very close in size and weight. What's the problem?"

"There is no problem," he said, "but you still haven't explained why."

Bells rang announcing the intermission's end and people began filtering toward the door. "We should be getting back to our seats," she said.

"Not until you explain why." He put his glass aside and leaned closer. "You have less than a minute, sweet, or we'll miss the second half."

She'd rehearsed for this all day and was able to keep the explanation succinct. "I'm trying to make a point, Alex. I would like for you to admit the clip from your father has sentimental value."

"What would that prove?"

That you have feelings, she wanted to say, but knew he would resist any such suggestion. She had to sneak up on the idea from a different direction. "It would prove there are some things in life that you value beyond their monetary worth."

He shook his head impatiently. "The clip is just a thing, Jacqueline. If I didn't like it, I wouldn't carry it."

"If it didn't suit, you mean." She lifted her chin and met his gaze. "Just like if I didn't suit, you wouldn't marry me."

Anger flared in his eyes. "You're talking nonsense. I wouldn't—"

She cut him off by ducking under his arm and following the last of the stragglers toward the door. Over her shoulder she said, "You can think about all this nonsense during the second act, Alex, while I enjoy the play. Coming?"

He came, and in the brief moment between reaching their seats and the lights going down, his expression lost all impatience and annoyance. In their place was a calm assurance that told her nothing had changed.

Jack sat through the second half of the play and knew Alex paid more attention to it than she did.

On the way home Alex refused to talk about the money clip beyond telling Jack she should retrieve the one from the flower arrangement before it was forgotten. It would be a shame, he said, for it to be lost when she could have it melted down and shaped into something she liked.

The one she'd bought would do very nicely for him, he added. After all, it had taken all day for him to notice the substitution, so it obviously suited him as well as the other.

Jack wanted to hit him for being so stubborn, but Alex subdued her anger with kisses and touches that made hitting seem a waste of effort. She was still angry with him when their lovemaking was over, but not enough to want to sleep anywhere but within his embrace. She could tell by the way he held her that he was aware of her feelings, but he merely kissed her one last time before closing his eyes.

Late in the night, long after Alex had fallen asleep beside her, Jack finally quit worrying about where she'd failed and began to make tentative plans for another attempt. As she'd told Hillary, whatever she stole would have to be bigger. It would also have to mean more to Alex, or as she was forced to look at it, *she* had to believe it would mean more to him. Otherwise there was no sense in trying.

There was only one thing that came to mind, and for the first time since the play's intermission, Jack felt a smile touch her lips.

It was still there when she awoke the next morning,

and not only because Alex had set the alarm early and drew her from sleep with caresses that were gently demanding. They made love with care, neither of them sure the night had been long enough to dispel the last of her anger. When they rose to shower together, Jack reassured Alex with smiles and touches, showing him the issue of the money clip was settled.

If Alex thought Jacqueline's eyes sparkled a little too brightly for someone who had been seriously angry the night before, he put it down to his imagination and counted himself a lucky man. Even in her anger she'd been wise enough to know that nothing should come between a couple at night. She had made love without holding anything back, and she'd slept in his arms even though the anger was still in her.

Precisely why she had been angry was still a mystery to Alex, although he suspected it was because he'd erred when he'd told her she suited him. Not that it wasn't true, but he could understand her annoyance at being likened to a money clip. As he dressed, he watched her carefully and wondered if she had any idea how glad he was that she did, indeed, suit him.

Jacqueline, and no one else.

He decided he would have to make that more clear, and scribbled a mental note to visit the jeweler at his first opportunity. Maybe then she'd forget all that nonsense over the money clip and accept him as he was.

Alex parked in front of the Goodwyns' house, then went straight to the stables because Jacqueline wasn't expecting him quite yet. It was dark when he walked into the yard, and he saw Bobby under a light at the far end of the quad with Ian. They were just finishing evening stables, he guessed, so he saluted the pair with the carrot and went along the row of boxes until he came to the one Golden Legs inhabited. As was usual after Bobby's walkaround, the horses were all shut in for the night. Alex unlatched the top half of the door and pulled it open. When the horse didn't immediately come to him, Alex peered inside. The light from the yard dove into the far corners of the box without stumbling across the horse that should have been inside.

He heard footsteps behind him and turned. "I thought you decided changing Golden Legs' box wasn't the problem, Bobby."

"It wasn't."

The trainer looked uneasy, and Alex imagined he was gearing up to argue about Alex's decision to sell Golden Legs. He checked his watch and figured he could spare ten minutes. "So why have you moved him, Bobby?"

"I didn't. I sold him."

The announcement stunned Alex, but years of practice in the boardroom kept his visible reaction to one of mild curiosity. The trainer pulled a piece of paper from his breast pocket and handed it to him. Alex held it up to the light and skimmed through the document, then read it more slowly to make sure he hadn't misunderstood. He hadn't. It was the bill of sale for one racehorse named Golden Legs.

Jacqueline had stolen his horse. No wonder she'd been so vague about what she was doing when he'd called her during lunch. Obviously it hadn't been a whim that had provoked the prank with his money clip.

It was a crusade.

Alex looked at Bobby with no hint of the exasperation he felt. "Explain."

"I thought you knew."

"Knew what?"

Bobby returned his gaze without flinching. "Jack told me you'd decided to sell Golden Legs. I called a man I'd run into at Cheltenham recently who had expressed an interest in adding to his string. He knew Golden Legs' form and was anxious to make an offer."

"That quickly?"

"Jack made it clear you wanted to be done with it." Bobby pulled at his collar as though it were too tight. "Naturally the bill of sale requires your signature, but I assured the buyer you would sign when payment is confirmed."

"You did, did you?" He couldn't believe Bobby would do such a thing without calling him first. It simply wasn't done. Jacqueline must have talked a pretty good story to keep Bobby from contacting him.

Alex couldn't remember the last time he'd been so furious, and never with a woman.

On the other hand he was in awe at how much Jacqueline had managed to accomplish in the space of one day. Somehow she had coerced Bobby into sanctioning the sale, pushed him into acting without delay, and arranged for the horse to be whisked away—all without even consulting her future husband. He couldn't decide whether to strangle her or to let Bobby do it for him. The trainer was clearly distressed at having lost Golden Legs from his stables.

Bobby nodded toward the paper. "If you've got a problem with all this, you have the right to back out."

"Which would leave you looking like a right prat, wouldn't it?" Alex tossed the carrot into the air and caught it, smiling grimly when Bobby didn't answer. "Especially as you've already shipped the horse to his new home."

"Well, yes, but it's still not too late." Bobby shoved his hands into his pockets and looked almost mournful. "I can have him back tomorrow if that's what you decide."

It suddenly occurred to Alex that all might not be as it appeared. For one thing it didn't make sense that Bobby would have shipped the horse before the financial transaction had been completed. For another he sounded anxious to have Golden Legs back, even if it made him look like an inept mug. Alex knew from experience that Bobby was anything but a fool. Which brought him back to the beginning. Bobby shouldn't have sold Golden Legs without Alex's express approval of the terms on offer.

He rolled the evidence over in his mind until it resembled something that made sense. Bobby hadn't sold Golden Legs at all. Following that logic, he guessed the horse had been moved somewhere else in the yard, not shipped. No wonder Bobby was so anxious to have Alex reverse the sale. Until that happened, he had a hot horse in his stables.

All of which meant Bobby was up to his neck in Jacqueline's little plot. He imagined Hillary was in on it too. It had probably been Bobby's wife who'd convinced his otherwise irreproachable trainer to become involved.

He wished Jacqueline had kept her crusade private.

Alex let the silence drag on, content to watch Bobby fidget under his gaze. Part of him was relieved Golden Legs was still his, but he told himself it was because he wouldn't have appreciated Jacqueline's interference in what was, after all, a business decision. The fact that Golden Legs was somewhere near had nothing to do with his relief. After all, he still intended to sell the animal, but in his own time.

For now, though, he had to pretend he believed the sale had actually taken place. He didn't know of a better way to teach her a lesson. Unfortunately Bobby would have to suffer the consequences, too, but that couldn't be helped. Alex thought it would serve him right for going along with such a harebrained scheme in the first place.

He cleared his throat and regarded his friend curiously. "You do realize, Bobby, that my fiancée, for all intents and purposes, has stolen my horse. In the Wild West they would hang her for such an act."

"She didn't steal it," Bobby argued. "She told you you wanted to sell—"

Alex cut him off with a raised hand. "You should have known I would deliver such a request personally. No, Bobby, she stole Golden Legs in an attempt to force me to admit the horse was more to me than a mere investment. Well, she was wrong. Golden Legs would have gone to the sales the minute Jacqueline boarded the plane for California. By selling him now she's saved me training and stable fees."

"You're going through with it? But Alex—"

"Of course I'm going through with it. I don't see why not. It's a good return on my investment. I do apologize, though, for the awkward position Jacqueline put you in. I can only imagine the story she spun to keep you from calling me." He forced a smile to prove his sincerity in the face of Bobby's horrified disbelief. "I'll go up to the house now and express my appreciation to my sweet fiancée. Once she sees her gambit has failed, perhaps she'll stop trying to make me into something I'm not."

Bobby looked as though he wanted to dig a hole and crawl into it.

"I would appreciate it if you wouldn't let on to Jacqueline I saw through her scheme," Alex continued, pretending not to notice Bobby's discomfort. "The sooner she realizes I won't rise to such bait, the more easily she'll accept things as they are."

He was giving her everything he had to give. It had to be enough.

Bobby nodded, apparently incapable of speech.

Alex filled the silence with chatter designed to make Bobby even more uneasy than he already was. "At least now I don't have to worry about selling Golden Legs in her absence. Funny how things work out, isn't it?" He tossed the carrot into a bin, then told Bobby to ask the buyer to messenger over a bank check the next morning. He'd send the signed bill of sale back with the courier.

Bobby mumbled something under his breath and set a quick pace back up to the house. Jacqueline was hovering anxiously at the back door when they came through it. Alex flashed her a wide grin, then pulled her into his arms and kissed her hard. When he released her, she looked thoroughly perplexed.

"Well done, Jacqueline," he said. "I doubt I could have gotten a better price for Golden Legs at the sales."

Dismay flickered across her expression. "You don't mind?"

"Why should I mind? You've saved Bobby the bother of hauling him to the sales, and me a few weeks' expenses. I wish all my business transactions were so tidy. You deserve a reward for this."

"Reward?" Jack searched his expression for something that resembled anger or frustration, but there wasn't any. There wasn't any room, not with all the pride and satisfaction that was there instead.

Oh, dear. This wasn't going at all as she'd planned.

"Of course you'll be rewarded, Jacqueline," he said, then took her hand and led her toward the lounge, to where Bobby had fled moments earlier. "I'll have to admit you surprised me, though. I thought you would mind when I sold Golden Legs."

"Er, Alex—" she began, but he seemed not to hear her as she struggled with the words she knew she must speak.

"Hello, Hillary," Alex said in such high spirits that Jack cringed inside. "Isn't the news marvelous?"

"Marvelous?" Hillary looked as though she'd swallowed a bee.

"Absolutely." He gave Jack a hearty squeeze and smiled down at her. "It's a shame we couldn't figure out what was wrong with Golden Legs, though. I really enjoyed it while he was winning."

Hillary's smile was determinedly bright. "What if Golden Legs wins for the, er, new owner? Won't you regret selling?"

"Not at all. Business decisions can't be judged by what-ifs. I've got my profit, and that's enough." He paused as Bobby thrust drinks at him and Jack, then said, "Jacqueline, why don't you come into town tomorrow after lunch? Bobby is going to arrange for the check to be delivered in the morning, so we should go shopping for something special. By the way, Bobby, what percentage do bloodstock agents get? Jacqueline has earned that, if not more."

Jack drowned her groan with a huge gulp of the whiskey Bobby had decided she needed, then turned bright red in an effort not to choke on the unaccustomed spirits. Alex turned to say something else to Hillary, and Jack took the opportunity to exchange horrified looks with Bobby. She jerked her chin toward the kitchen, intending that Bobby follow her so she could find out exactly what had happened down at the yard. Unfortunately Alex had other plans. He caught her hand before she could get away and finished his drink in one swallow.

"If you and Bobby will excuse us, I promised David and Missy Gresham we'd meet them for dinner. It's time Jacqueline met some more of my friends." His eyes took on an appreciative glow as his gaze took in Jack's upswept hair, the soft blue knit skirt and sweater that lay loosely against her curves, and the diamonds that sparkled at her ears and throat.

It was, she realized, the first time he'd really looked at her since he'd come in the door. She wondered why that seemed wrong, then let the thought go as she responded to his silent appraisal. A now-familiar heat rushed through her, and it was all she could do to remain standing beside him when she would have rather slipped her hands around his neck to pull his mouth into range.

When he gave a low chuckle, Jack knew he'd read her thoughts. She ducked her head and put down her glass on a nearby table. "I left something upstairs," she told him, then walked toward the stairs before he could second-guess her diversion. Hillary, bless her heart, followed, and a moment later they were whispering frantically behind the closed door of Jack's room.

"What are you going to do?" Hillary demanded. "I thought the plan was to get him riled enough to admit he liked owning that particular horse?"

"I don't know what I'm going to do," Jack said furiously. "I don't even know what he said to Bobby. And how am I supposed to go out with him and pretend everything is fine when I know he's expecting a huge check for Golden Legs tomorrow?"

Hillary put her hand at Jack's forehead. "You could pretend you're sick. You're certainly hot enough."

"That's outrage, not a virus," she muttered.

"You think Alex would know the difference?"

"He hasn't missed a trick yet." Jack paced back and forth in front of the door, shooting glances at it now and then because she wouldn't put it past Alex to come through it if he got impatient waiting. "I either have to confess to the whole plan or find a way to come up with a great deal of money by tomorrow."

Hillary put a stop to Jack's pacing by planting herself in her path. "You have to go down there, Jack. He'll wonder what we're talking about."

"Let him wonder." She hugged herself in an effort to arrest the chill that was growing beneath her frustration, and looked at her friend. "I'm worried, Hillary."

"You should be. It's not every day you have to come up with the price of a racehorse."

"Not about that." She shook her head and knew by Hillary's concerned look that her worry was shared. "I've taken the only things from Alex that I was sure he cared about. There's nothing left to steal."

"You're admitting defeat?" Hillary asked softly.

Jack shook her head. "No, I'm admitting that I'm frightened. Alex isn't responding, Hillary." She swallowed hard, then added, "What if I've been wrong all along? What if Alex truly isn't capable of love?"

Neither woman had an answer to that.

As much as Jack enjoyed meeting Alex's friends, she was relieved to get back home. It had been horribly difficult to keep a smile on her face when she had so many other things on her mind. Golden Legs and all that involved was a minor concern when compared with her failure to get Alex to admit he truly cared about anything. As the evening went on around her, she nodded and murmured and wished she knew what she was going to do.

He'd said he cared about her, but she was terrified that caring wasn't deep enough to sustain them if or when life threw challenges at them. Wanting to be with her because they suited was an inadequate basis for a strong marriage. What if she swerved the car to avoid a pheasant and crippled herself in the resulting crash? Would he still want to spend his life with her? Or what if she chose not to have children—although she really couldn't imagine that would ever happen—would he still think she suited him? What would happen when he discovered she was horribly grouchy the first day of her cycle, then weepy and miserable the second?

How many things could happen to change the original circumstances before Alex began to wonder if she was worth it?

It wasn't enough to care, she knew. He had to love her if there was any chance for them. Just as she loved him.

Their lovemaking that night was a welcome distraction to her increasing preoccupation. As if sensing her distress, Alex revealed a side of himself she'd only glimpsed before. He became a wild and uninhibited lover who seemed to pour his soul into their mating and demanded as much or more from her. It began with seductive words and not-so-innocent touches as they drove home from the Greshams'. By the time they pulled into his private drive, she was so aroused that the journey inside seemed too difficult, too far.

When she confessed her need—something she'd discovered gave him much pleasure—he stopped the car beneath the bare branches of a towering oak and got out of the car. Seconds later she was standing with him, and his hands were tearing at the bits of lace beneath her skirt. Jack had barely enough time to grab his shoulders before he backed her against the hood of the car, spread her legs, and thrust deep inside her.

She came almost at once, convulsing around his solid shaft as he pounded into her, screaming because the pleasure was too intense, too wonderfully perfect. He held her in his arms, and it was through a daze that she realized he was still inside her, still hard and waiting. When she moved her hips in invitation, he surprised her by cupping her bottom and lifting her away.

Hushed words and promises of more filled the silent night as he held her to his side and walked up to the house, leaving the car for another time. He waited only until he'd shut the heavy door against the night before coming to her again. He urged her down onto the thick carpet just inside the moonlit hall, pushed her skirt to her waist, and lifted her legs to his shoulders, keeping her gaze captive in his as he filled her once again.

He fulfilled all his promises, then made more. As if driven by the same demons that taunted her heart, he made love to her with more passion and more care than he'd ever shown before. It was as though he was afraid it was the last time, and she knew deep inside that her own fears were flowing between them unsaid.

Much later, upstairs in Alex's bed, he was gentle but insistent, not allowing her to rest until, finally, she confessed to a degree of soreness. She could sense his melancholy as he began to speak of their future, the perceptible doubt that was no longer hers alone.

Jack fell asleep in her lover's arms, renewed by those doubts because so long as they were shared, there was hope.

Alex sighed as he felt Jacqueline ease into a deep, exhausted sleep, her face nestled to his chest and one knee thrown across his thigh. He'd been rough with her, he knew, but no more so than she'd demanded. But he'd been gentle, too, aware of her frustration and judging it too deep to be vented in one night's passion.

He could almost sympathize at how she felt at being thwarted in her futile crusade, but knew no other outcome was possible. There were things she couldn't change, and she would have to accept that.

In her sleep her hand crept up his chest to his heart.

Alex covered her hand with his own and closed his eyes for a few hours' sleep, thinking how glad he was Jacqueline hadn't actually stolen Golden Legs. There were all those carrots to be considered, although he conceded they wouldn't have gone to waste, not with a stableful of horses willing to take them off his hands.

Somehow, though, it wouldn't have been the same.

FIFTEEN

Alex felt Jacqueline stir in his arms, but didn't protest when she slipped from bed. She had admitted to being sore last night, and he doubted things had changed much in the few hours since then. He lay in bed as she showered, his deep yawn a reflection of the accumulation of short nights behind them. They would have to get more rest, he realized, and decided they'd have dinner at home that night and retire early. He was sure that if they put their minds to it, they could curtail the ensuing lovemaking to reasonable limits.

The anticipation of the night to come swelled his sex to an unwelcome hardness, and it was all he could do not to join Jacqueline in the shower for immediate relief. Luckily—for one of them, anyway—he heard the shower shut off and other noises as Jacqueline puttered around the dressing room. Ten minutes later she was fully dressed and pulling the brush through her hair as she walked back into the bedroom.

She threw the brush at him to shift him from the bed, then gasped as he stood and revealed his fully aroused state. "If you'd only said something, Alex, I might have waited for you in the shower."

"You're still sore," he grumbled. "Do try to get over it

by tonight, though, will you? You can't expect me to get much work done in this state."

"You looked like that yesterday, and I didn't hear any complaints about your productivity then," she teased. The laughter slid from her eyes, and in its place was the kind of drowsy, sexy look he was used to seeing in the early stages of her arousal. She came toward him, gliding across the carpet with an effortless grace that he loved watching. When she reached him, her lips were slightly parted, and he could hear the gentle rush of air through her mouth.

Before she could touch him, Alex shook his head reluctantly. "You've already showered, sweet."

"I'll take another." She lifted a hand and traced a single finger across his shoulder.

"I have to go to work."

"You're the boss. You don't *have* to do anything." She leaned forward to lick his male nipple.

He groaned and fisted his hands at his sides in a desperate ploy to keep from touching her. "You're sore."

"You're not." She smiled, and her fingernail drew a sharp, tingling path down the center of his chest, through the arrow of hair that led to his groin . . . and lower.

"We can't," he said as her hand closed around him.

"You can," she whispered, her fingers stroking him in the way he'd taught her, contracting and sliding and teasing until he couldn't stand it any longer. He reached for her.

But Jacqueline wasn't there. She was on her knees, her hair a silken shroud around her shoulders, a look of luminous pleasure on her face as she bent toward him. Though he'd guessed her intent before she'd laid a finger on him, the shock that ripped through him sucked the air from his lungs and left him weak and unsteady on his feet.

He threaded shaking fingers into her hair, then lifted

his gaze to the cheval mirror in the corner . . . and watched his own pleasure.

Jack cooked breakfast while Alex showered, then carried kitchen stools out to the grand piano and served it there. She drank orange juice while he stared at his plate, then shrugged when he asked if this was the kind of thing she preferred at that hour.

She cut off a piece of sautéed carrot and put it into her mouth. "My mother taught me not to waste food. There's a whole drawerful of these in the fridge. If we're not careful, they'll spoil."

He picked up a raw carrot and bit down. "The carrots are for Golden Legs—"

"Who is no longer here," she interrupted smoothly.

Alex frowned, thinking she was leaving it a bit late to admit her scheme had failed. He didn't push her, though. If she wanted to wait until after lunch when she came into town, it would be just as well. He was late getting to the office already. A full-blown discussion about horse stealing would take more time than he could afford.

He grimaced as Jacqueline stirred a stick of raw carrot in the soft yolk of her egg and teased him with her smile.

"Give the carrots to Bobby, sweet. Tomorrow I'll cook."

She batted her eyelids innocently. "You don't like my cooking?"

He changed the subject. "Is there a particular reason you decided to eat at the piano?"

"I wanted to." She took another bite of egg-flavored carrot. "Besides, I have a certain fondness for this piece of furniture."

"You do manage to make extremely pleasing music on it," he said.

"I could make 'extremely pleasing music' on almost any piano." She flashed a mischievous grin. "That isn't what I had in mind when I said I was fond of it."

Alex remembered the night of fantasies fulfilled and groaned deep in his throat. "Are you as attached to the other furniture and bits of carpet where we've made love?"

She shook her head. "The piano was the beginning for us. I doubt I'll ever be able to look at it and not be reminded. Are you telling me you could look at this beautiful instrument and not feel something inside?"

"Now that you remind me—" He reached for her, but she slapped his hands away.

"Without me telling you is what I meant," she said. "Doesn't the piano mean anything more to you now than it did a month ago?"

He finally realized where she was going with this and knew he had to put an end to it. "For all I care, Jacqueline, you could replace it with a snooker table and I wouldn't mind. Besides, we made love on the sofa the first time, and no, I don't have any particular feelings for that piece of furniture either."

"We may have finished on the sofa, but the piano is where it all began."

Her eyes took on a glittering edge, and there was an insistent note in her voice that puzzled him, but the striking of the clock kept him from pursuing it. "I think we'd better be going, sweet. Leave the dishes for the housekeeper."

He stood and lifted her from the stool, then pulled her along with him toward the front door. His briefcase wasn't on the hall table where he normally left it, and it took several moments before he realized it was still in the car . . . which was at the far end of the drive.

They ran to the car, and by the time Alex had dropped

Jacqueline at Hillary's and was on the London road, he'd forgotten all about their curious conversation at the piano.

Jack hadn't. In fact she spent the entire morning on activities directly related to that conversation. Hillary helped, using her forceful personality on the phone to convince people to do what Jack wanted them to do. Then she drove with Jack over to Alex's and kept the housekeeper from calling her employer while Jack dealt with the people Hillary had summoned. By lunchtime everything was more or less as she'd asked, although Bobby grumbled about using a horsebox for storage purposes.

"It's only for a day or two," Jack said as she dug into the primavera salad Hillary had put together for their lunch.

"That's what you said about Golden Legs," he reminded her, "and now I've got a horse I can't even take to the gallops because Alex thinks he's in another county."

Hillary put a comforting hand on her husband's shoulder as she slid into the chair next to him. "Don't take it out on Jack just because Alex didn't react as he was supposed to."

Bobby gave a grunt of agreement. "I could have sworn he liked that horse. Speaking of which, you still haven't told me how you're going to wriggle out of that mess."

Jack pulled a silk bag from her pocket and threw it onto the table. She took another mouthful of pasta and chewed it before saying, "That's the necklace and earrings Alex gave me. I have to meet him in town in a couple of hours, but I should have enough time to hock those first. Any ideas where I should go?"

Hillary and Bobby exchanged glances, then Hillary

reached for the bag and pushed it back toward Jack. "We can't let you buy Golden Legs, Jack. Not with that."

"Why not? Alex doesn't mind what I do with the things he gives me." She swallowed the bitterness that fact evoked before it ruined her lunch. "Besides, I don't have any other means of getting the money. I spent nearly the last of what I got from the tennis bracelet this morning. There's only enough left for those cashmere sweaters I'm taking back for Christmas presents."

Hillary opened her mouth to speak, but Bobby stopped her. When he looked at Jack, his expression was determined. "Hillary and I discussed this last night, Jack. We decided to put the money up ourselves."

She put her fork down and stared at Bobby without blinking. "Why?"

"Because I know I can make that horse win." He covered Hillary's hand with his own and forced a smile. "Golden Legs is too valuable to give up on. I'll have all spring to do whatever I can to turn him back into a winner."

"What if you can't?"

"Then he'll go to the sales. If I only race him once between now and then, I won't lose more than ten or fifteen percent off the price Alex agreed to."

Jack shook her head. "That won't work. I can't have you footing the bill for my personal life, and that's what this all comes down to."

Bobby was equally adamant. "I want to train that horse, Jack, and this looks like the only way I'll be able to do it."

"What do you think I'm going to do, ship him to California?" Jack pushed the diamonds back into the center of the table. "No, Bobby, it's my way or not at all."

Hillary groaned and buried her face in her hands. When she looked up again, there was a touch of regret in her expression. "What Bobby is trying to avoid telling you is that the diamonds won't cover the price you offered for Golden Legs."

"They won't?" As the couple shook their heads in unison, she could feel the blood drain from her face and the beginnings of a sick feeling in her stomach. "I suppose I should have looked at that contract before I signed it yesterday."

"You were too busy making up a false name and disguising your writing," Hillary said. Then she told Jack how much Alex expected to receive for Golden Legs.

The sick feeling got worse. "I didn't know horses were worth that much money." Then it occurred to her that all was not lost. "Never mind, you two. It doesn't make sense for any of us to buy Golden Legs. It's not exactly something we'll be able to keep from Alex, so I might as well tell him everything now. The good news is that when he finishes being mad at me, we won't all be flat broke."

"And he'll go right ahead and sell Golden Legs just to prove the point," Bobby said. "I won't have it. I want to train that horse, and if I have to buy it to do so, then so be it." He pulled a folded piece of paper from his pocket and handed it to Jack. "When you tell Alex about your little scheme, give him this. It might save your neck."

Jack looked down at all the zeros on the check and gulped. When she lifted her eyes, Bobby actually looked pleased with himself.

Hillary, on the other hand, looked the slightest bit green. It was, she agreed, a lot of money for a horse.

Following Alex's directions Jack took a taxi from the train station to his office, where he was waiting for her in an office furnished with deep leather chairs and gleaming wood tables. His corner desk was a massive piece of mahogany inlaid with fine leather at the end by his equally massive chair. Beyond it all, the penthouse view was partially obscured by filmy curtains that deflected the unusually bright sunlight. She hardly appreciated any of it, though, because she had something to tell him and needed to get it over with before the anxiety felled her.

He stalled her by folding her into his arms and kissing her until she was breathless and happier than she'd been all morning. By the time he pulled her over to sit in one of the chairs, though, the glow had faded. She was gearing up to tell him everything when he pulled a familiar-looking box from his breast pocket.

"I know I promised to take you shopping, sweet, but I had an idea you might like this instead."

She looked at the box, and a feeling of dread swept through her as he flipped it open and showed her the contents. It was a chain of delicate gold links, a necklace, she thought, but that wasn't all. At the bottom of the loop was a golden charm in the shape of a horse. It seemed as though it was racing the wind, its tail and mane streaming backward, its legs strong and elegant as the animal stretched to cover the distance.

It was beautiful, and she almost cried as Alex fastened it around her neck and kissed her on the forehead. She hated knowing she'd been the one to deprive him of Golden Legs, even if he hadn't minded. She wanted him to have that horse!

"I thought this was appropriate, in view of your help in selling Golden Legs."

Tears threatened, but she was determined to hold them back.

Suddenly he took a good look at her and was startled at what he saw. "I'm sorry, Jacqueline. If I'd known it would make you this miserable, I would have let you off the hook this morning."

"What hook?" She sniffled a little, but didn't cry.

He perched on the thickly padded arm of her chair and lifted her chin in his fingers. "Golden Legs. I knew yesterday that Bobby hadn't sold him after all."

"But he did," she blurted out, and pulled up the hem of her plaid wool skirt so that she could retrieve the check she'd hidden in the top of her stockings. She thrust it into his hands, then smoothed her skirt when he didn't take his eyes off her legs. "Actually Bobby didn't sell Golden Legs. He bought him, which I suppose is the same thing to you so long as you get your money."

He looked at her blankly. "Bobby did what?"

"He bought your horse." She tried on a smile, thinking it might help if he realized this was a good thing, not a bad thing.

"Why?"

"Because he wants to train him. He *believes* in him." She waggled her fingers at the check he still held. "Bobby didn't have time to get a bank check, but you know his personal check is good."

Alex unfolded the check, read it, then frowned at her. "I do wish you'd keep our personal conflicts between us, Jacqueline. Dragging Bobby into this is unconscionable."

"I didn't drag him in," she muttered. "Hillary did. Anyway there's a good side to all this. Bobby wants to train Golden Legs and now won't have to worry about your selling the horse out from under him."

Alex got up and walked over to his desk, where he sorted through some papers until he found what he wanted. He came back and hunkered down in front of Jack, capturing her gaze with a steely one of his own. "Bobby can't buy Golden Legs, Jacqueline. It isn't good business."

She didn't understand. "Why not? You're both getting what you want out of the transaction."

"If Golden Legs suddenly begins to win, there will be whispers in the horse world about whether Bobby could have produced the same results before forcing me to sell."

"But he didn't force you—"

"And who is going to believe him if Golden Legs suddenly makes Bobby very, very rich?" He shook his head firmly. "I won't let Bobby make that kind of mistake, Jacqueline."

"If it's such a mistake, I can't believe Bobby didn't see it."

"You've probably got Bobby so confused with your shenanigans that he isn't thinking straight." Jack watched in horror as he ripped the check and contract in half, then threw the pieces onto a nearby table. "Fortunately for all of us I'm still thinking with my head."

"That's what this was all about, Alex," she said. "For once I wanted you to react without thinking first."

"If I had, what would it have proved?" He eased off his heels until he was sitting on the floor with his back to a chair and his long legs stretched out in front of him. "You've known all along that Golden Legs is nothing more than an investment. Selling him was my intention all along."

"But you feed him carrots," she said. "If he's just an investment, why do you bother?"

Because I like to, Alex thought, but he stopped himself from saying the words aloud because they were precisely the ones she wanted to hear. *He* knew that the pleasure he received from feeding Golden Legs carrots was unrelated to any deep-seated caring.

"It's a matter of enjoying the moment, Jacqueline," he said reasonably. "When the horse is gone, the moments go with it. I won't miss either."

"I don't believe you."

Her softly spoken denial and air of sadness made him

wish he could have given her the response she wanted. But he couldn't, not without lying. Still, there was a way to smooth over the problem that wouldn't involve lies or hard truths.

He said, "There is some good that's come out of this, sweet."

The hope that flickered in her eyes nudged something inside of Alex, leaving him curiously contented. He paused as though hesitation would force that contentment to explain itself, but it didn't happen. Shaking his head at his irrational behavior, he said, "I hadn't realized how determined Bobby was to end Golden Legs' losing streak. With that in mind it would be unreasonable of me to remove the horse from his stables."

She looked at him in stunned amazement. "Because you think the horse will win?"

"Because Bobby does." He shot back the cuff at his wrist to check the time before meeting her gaze again. "He's my friend, and it's within my power to do this for him."

"Even though you might lose a portion of your precious investment?"

He stood abruptly and went over to the corner of the room where there was a bar and reached for glasses. "I'm not the heartless bastard you think I am, Jacqueline. If he wants to train Golden Legs that badly, I'll have to let him do it."

"In other words you'll do for a friend what you won't do for yourself."

Alex avoided looking at her as he handed her a sherry and went to stand at the windows, leaving the Scotch he'd poured for himself on the bar. "There is a difference between doing the right thing for a friend and letting emotions rule one's life. I may not have any of the more sentimental feelings you seem to regard so highly, but I do understand duty and commitment."

Jack put her drink aside and went to stand beside him. When she laid a hand on his arm, he covered it with his own and gave it a gentle squeeze. She said, "I've never questioned your sense of responsibility, Alex. I believe you would do and be everything you promised when you asked me to be your wife."

"But it isn't enough for you, is it, Jacqueline?" He said it without looking at her.

"No, Alex, it's not enough." She rested her head against his arm and looked through the filmy curtain at a day whose sunshine contrasted starkly with the emotions roiling within her. "The things you considered as you made your decision to marry me aren't stagnant facts. They are realities with a vitality of their own, changing with or without our consent or blessings. The—" She hesitated, looking for the right word, then using another when it didn't come to her. "The satisfaction you have in making a commitment to me might be lessened with life's changes."

"I've made a commitment to you, Jacqueline," he said urgently. "Nothing that happens will alter that."

"I know." She reached up and pressed the side of his face until he was looking at her. "But that won't matter if you're no longer satisfied. If you loved me, the commitment wouldn't be all there was holding us together."

His eyes were almost silver in the reflected light. "Love can't ensure our marriage will work."

"And without it we don't stand a chance." She turned away from the almost violent protest she saw in his eyes, knowing then she'd never make Alex understand. Everything that was good and beautiful about her love for him wasn't enough to keep her with a man who couldn't love her.

"Where are you going?" he demanded.

"Home." She walked over to the chair and collected her handbag, then turned to face him across the expanse of carpet.

He looked at her, his expression impassive to the point of blandness. "Are we still engaged to be married?" he asked.

She flinched, then shook her head slowly. "I don't know, Alex. That is, I believe, something for you to decide."

Jack left him standing at the window and knew she would carry in her memory forever the image of Alex at his most unreachable.

It was dark when Alex turned the key in his front door and slammed it shut behind him. He threw down his coat and briefcase, flipped on the hall lights, and strode into the study, where he reached for the bottle of Scotch. His fingers had just closed around the neck when he smelled it —rainbows and lilacs, the scent of Jacqueline.

She was here!

An afternoon glutted with regrets and anger was instantly forgotten as he hurried across the hall to the lounge, where he knew she would be waiting. The scent was stronger there, and as he paused at the door of the dark room, he took a deep, soothing breath, silently rejoicing in her presence. Then, unable to wait another moment, he reached for the wall switch.

It only took a moment to discover the room was empty, then several more to convince himself his eyes weren't lying. Without moving from the door Alex swept his gaze repeatedly across the room, but to no avail.

Jacqueline failed to materialize.

His disappointment was so intense, it took a while

longer before he noticed the snooker table. It stood precisely where the piano had been only that morning, looking for all the world as though it belonged there.

It didn't. The piano should be there, Alex thought as he walked slowly toward the island of green baize with its balls racked and waiting. The piano was what he wanted in this room, not this toy that could only manage brittle, clacking noises when played. He circled the table, staring at the cushioned rims and seeing delicate fingers as they caressed the ivory keys, the reflection of her breasts in his hands . . . the teasing look in her eyes as she swirled the carrot into the runny yolk of her egg.

Jacqueline had been wrong about one thing, he decided. He didn't need the piano to recall the bits of life they'd shared around it. That would happen, he suspected, with or without physical reminders. The piano was no more important to him than the sofa where he'd laid her down and thrust for the first time deep inside her. He glanced at the velvet cushions, then back at the snooker table where the piano should be.

No, he didn't need the piano, but that was irrelevant. He had liked the damned thing. It suited him. The snooker table didn't.

She'd filched his money clip, and he hadn't minded.

She'd stolen his horse, and he'd made allowances for her determination.

But in taking his piano she had gone too far.

The anger that had ridden him all afternoon resurfaced in an explosion of language that was explicit and obscene. When that didn't help, Alex turned his back on the table and strode down the hall to his study. Picking up the phone, he punched in Bobby's number and listened for the first ring.

He would get his piano back if he had to take it from Jacqueline one key at a time.

SIXTEEN

Jack huddled beneath a horse blanket in the corner of the stall and stared through the dark at the huge crate that represented all that was left of her hope. It didn't even look like a piano anymore, which was, she supposed, a blessing in case Alex decided to come looking for it.

She didn't want him to see it like that.

The movers had known what they were doing, although Hillary had nearly fainted when they'd lowered the instrument onto its side and begun to unscrew the legs. The piano still rested on its side, supported by a specially designed pallet and enclosed within the well-padded crate the movers had built around it. It hadn't mattered to them whether the instrument was being moved a few miles or a thousand. It still had to be properly crated, or they wouldn't be responsible.

If the men who'd delivered the snooker table hadn't seemed as conscientious as they'd stuck on the legs, they'd made up for it by spending an hour ensuring the table was absolutely level. Their devotion to perfection had been a waste of time, but how could she tell them the table wouldn't last in that spot for any longer than it took Alex to put things back to normal?

She'd never once imagined he would accept the substitution. Any moment now her fiancé would arrive for a confrontation. He would also, she imagined, answer the question she'd left with him earlier that afternoon. Whichever way it turned out, she'd already scheduled the movers to return the piano to where it belonged.

Jack fingered the ring on her left hand and wondered how many times she'd be able to call Alex her fiancé before it wasn't true anymore.

After leaving his office that afternoon she had come back to Hillary's to discover Alex had called Bobby with his good news. He hadn't, she surmised, told Bobby anything else. In kind, Jack hadn't offered any information, not even when Hillary descended a bit from her excited high and realized Jack wasn't up in the clouds with her. Hillary's unembarrassed probing got her nowhere, either, and Jack had hidden in her room to avoid more.

She'd decided to wait until the next day to tell her best friend she'd probably be leaving for home a week early. Nothing was settled yet, although with every hour that passed, Alex's answer became more clear. In the meantime she couldn't bear to talk about it.

She could hardly stand to think about it . . . and had thought of nothing else all afternoon long.

Bobby and Hillary had decided to celebrate Golden Legs' reinstatement at the Red Lion, but Jack had pleaded a headache and asked to stay at home. She'd gone downstairs when she'd heard them getting ready to leave, and though the smile on her face had reassured Bobby, it hadn't fooled Hillary at all.

It was during some good-natured teasing from Bobby that she'd been reminded about the snooker table–piano switch. Jack had run straight to the stables, supposedly to check that the piano was where she'd left it. In reality she needed to be near the thing that she'd pinned her hopes on not twelve hours earlier.

Those hopes had been much higher that morning. Now, though, they were nearly absent from her thoughts. In their place was a sense of futility and utter depression, as well as the frustration that she hadn't done enough to make him understand . . . and that she'd done too much to ever go back.

With a suddenness that drew a startled whinny from the horse in the next stall, Jack threw off the blanket, jumped to her feet, and headed back up to the house. Brooding in front of the crate wasn't getting her anywhere, she realized as she slipped inside the back door. With Bobby and Hillary out of the house, now was as good a time as any to call the airline and reschedule her flight.

If Alex was coming to take back his ring, she might as well be there to answer the door.

She had her hand on the phone when it rang. By the time her heart slowed from the unnatural gallop and the phone rang a second time, she calculated the scare had taken ten years off her life. When it rang a third time, she picked it up and said hello as she reached for the notepad Hillary used for messages.

Alex's deep voice stilled her hand as her heart surged ahead at full gallop. "Jacqueline? Is that you?"

"Mmmph." She couldn't seem to catch her breath, but Alex didn't allow for such inconveniences.

"Use real words, dammit!" he said roughly. "I know you know some. You were certainly eloquent enough this afternoon."

The tone of his voice told her more clearly than words that her hopes had indeed been in vain. Deep inside she felt an unfamiliar lethargy smother the last flickers of any expectations she'd had for sharing her life with the man of her dreams.

Damn his stubborn hide! she swore silently, clenching her teeth to fight the angry response she didn't have the energy for.

"Get to the point, Alex. I need this phone for something useful." There was a pause, and she could hear the deep breaths that he seemed to be having trouble controlling.

Finally he said, "I want my piano back."

She'd expected that. "Why?"

"Because it's mine," he returned sharply.

"Wrong answer. Try again."

"There isn't another answer, Jacqueline. If I'd wanted a snooker table in my lounge, I would have bought one."

"Think of it as a present, Alex," she said, too weak now to fight the anger. "God knows you understand the concept."

Before he could frame a response to her remark, she added, "I assume by what you haven't said that you want me to send the engagement ring back with the piano."

"You assume wrong. That's a different matter altogether."

It wasn't over! Her fingers curled painfully around the receiver as she waited breathlessly for him to continue.

"I'm going to Paris for two days," he said. "When I return, we'll discuss this again. Understand, though, that the conditions of my proposal are unchanged."

Her shoulders slumped, and it was all she could do not to verbalize the agony his words inflicted.

"Jacqueline, did you hear me?"

"I heard you," she said in a near whisper.

A silence fell between them that was so uncomfortable, she nearly put down the phone. He spoke before she could do so.

"Please remember, Jacqueline," he said softly, "that my expectations have not changed either. If we just give it a chance, I know we could have a good life together."

Sure they could. She'd taken on the giant and lost. He just didn't know it yet. Gathering her strength, she mumbled a few words of acknowledgment, then said good-bye.

He wasn't finished with her yet. "The piano, Jacqueline. Please put it back where it belongs before I return."

No way. With a flick of her finger she disconnected the line. Moments later she was negotiating with the airline agent for a seat in the nonsmoking section of the following evening's flight to California.

The midafternoon sun slanted into Alex's eyes as he pulled the Jaguar to a stop at his front door. He rubbed his eyes with one hand and set the brake with the other, then got out and went up the steps before he gave in to impulse and went straight over to see Jacqueline. She wasn't expecting him this early, and he knew he should attempt to shower away the effects of two nearly sleepless nights.

He didn't want her to see him looking as insecure as he felt. The word annoyed him, but he'd gotten used to being annoyed with himself. It seemed Jacqueline had changed things in him she likely hadn't intended. With her stubborn refusal to think rationally about their marriage, she'd managed to make him question things in himself he'd never questioned . . . to doubt things he'd never imagined merited doubt.

He would be glad when they could put this episode behind them and he could get his psyche back to normal.

Alex put his key into the lock, then remembered he'd left his suitcase in the boot. He almost went back for it, but the urge to go inside was too strong. He wasn't even

sure now what he wanted to see when he entered the
lounge.

If the piano was back where it belonged, he should be
pleased that Jacqueline had done what he'd asked . . . or
should he? The key remained in the lock as Alex rested
his forehead against the door behind which his future lay
waiting for him. What if Jacqueline had returned the piano but stayed away herself because she'd lost her crusade? Was it so important that he win the battle only to
lose the reason behind it? Did she mean so little to him
that he couldn't be bothered to look inside himself for the
emotions she swore were there?

Or was he afraid to look, for fear of not finding anything at all?

A sudden fury rose inside him as he saw himself as
he'd been as a young man—defiant in the face of emotional disillusion, arrogant in the face of reason. One bad
experience, and he'd rashly thrown away any chance of
love again. His original intent to protect his heart from
further mauling had evolved into a denial of the very
concept of love.

Arrogance abetted by an acknowledged stubborn nature had served him well in business, but not so well in
life. He could see that now. Lifting his head, he turned
the key and opened the door. Jacqueline was a stubborn
woman, he knew, and prayed she was stubborn enough to
fight even though he'd already claimed the victory.

Slowly Alex walked into his home and stood very still
in the hallway. He could smell her, rainbows and lilacs,
the scent of a woman who had risked everything to make
him feel again. He shut his eyes and inhaled deeply, taking strength from her as though she were there with him.

Even though he knew she wasn't. The scent was too
weak to be recent, and he hurried into the lounge to face
the truth.

The snooker table stood proudly where the piano belonged, and Alex rejoiced. She hadn't given up on him after all. Deep, reviving breaths helped his heart regain a regular beat, and he was turning to race over to Bobby's when he noticed something flash and sparkle at the prodding of the sun's rays. Only then did he realize there was an odd assortment of things scattered across the green baize.

Suddenly he knew he wouldn't find her at Bobby's or anywhere else nearby. Jacqueline had fled before his return, leaving behind that which she didn't want in her life.

He walked slowly to the table where everything he'd ever given her was displayed. The Steuben vase, the watercolor, the diamond necklace, the golden horse and, in the exact center of the table, her ring. It was all there, everything except the bracelet and the vase she'd destroyed. A scrap of paper caught his eye, and he knew the moment he picked it up that it was the pawn ticket from the Innsbruck shop where she'd hocked her bracelet.

Jacqueline had left meaningless gifts and taken the one thing that meant anything to Alex. She'd taken her love to a far-off place where, perhaps, she'd someday give it to a man who knew it for the treasure it was.

With a start he reminded himself she'd taken something else. She'd taken the piano. A slow smile curved his lips, and he knew she was giving him one more chance.

If he wanted the piano, it appeared he would have to go get it . . . even if he had to cross an ocean to do so.

If she still wanted his love, it was there in his heart for her to take.

Jack's flight was delayed in Chicago by weather and in San Francisco by fog. By the time she dragged her suitcases up to the loft, she was exhausted and in no mood to talk to anyone about anything. She didn't therefore call her mother to let her know she was back. She didn't even call the milkman to start delivery again. Instead she went to the grocery store, picked up what she would need for a few days, then went home and watched videos until her eyelids refused to stay open any longer.

If her sleep was bedeviled by jet lag, then her dreams were plagued by a certain giant a full continent and ocean away. When she awakened, it was with less energy and considerably less humor than before.

When a shower and breakfast didn't lift her spirits, she succumbed to impulse and drove down to the antique dealer who had purchased Seymour Jenkins's porcelain cow. Two years and a thousand emotions later it was still there, gathering dust in the corner of a shelf it shared with assorted farm animals, unnaturally painted frogs, and hand-blown crystal unicorns. The dealer was so happy to get rid of it that Jack was able to take it away for barely half what he'd paid her in the first place.

She knew exactly what she was going to do with it when she got it home, and the anticipation brought the first smile to her face in days. She raced up the stairs to her loft with her keys in one hand and the cow in the other, too intent on her mission to notice the man hovering in the shadows until he spoke.

"Jacqueline, love, I want my piano back."

She screamed, launched the cow into the air, and jumped back against the wall. Almost as though it were happening in slow motion, she saw Alex reach out a long arm and catch the black-and-white cow an instant before it would have shattered on the landing. He straightened, lifted the cow to eye level, and quirked a brow at her.

"Is this something you're going to want to bring to England with you?" he asked quietly.

Jack decided it was safer discussing the cow than to ask

if he'd meant what he'd said before she screamed. His use of that four-letter word could be analyzed later, perhaps when her heart stopped doing its best imitation of the French can-can.

She cleared her throat and said in her calmest voice, "That cow has a date with destiny. You've only delayed its demise by a few minutes." She reached out a hand that was remarkably steady, but Alex didn't accommodate her by returning her property.

"You're going to smash it?" he said, and Jack noticed then how deep his voice sounded, how husky it was compared with what she remembered.

"What's wrong with your voice?" she demanded.

He shook his head. "Nothing, love. I'm just a little weary. I don't suppose you'd invite me inside for a coffee?"

There was that word again. She ducked her head so that he couldn't see the hope and despair that warred within her, and opened the door. He waved her ahead of him, then followed without trying to touch her as she passed. Jack led the way into the sun-filled room and waited until she heard Alex shut the door before turning to face him. He stood at the door, suffering her scrutiny as he surveyed her home, the cow clenched in his big fist. His suit was wrinkled, his tie askew, and there was at least a day's growth of beard on his face that nicely complemented the dark circles under his eyes.

"You look horrible, Alex."

He brushed her comment aside with a tired wave of his hand. "You can skip the flattery, Jacqueline. I've only got a few minutes left before I fall dead asleep at your feet. Let's try to spend them productively."

"Define *productively*." She crossed her arms under her breasts and glared at him in a defiance reminiscent of their first battle. Then only the fate of a diamond bracelet had hung in the balance.

Today it was their future that would be decided.

"Must you turn this into an argument?" he asked wearily. When she didn't reply, he thrust his fingers through his hair, then looked up to capture her gaze in his. "I came to give you something you left behind. I'm just not sure if you still want it."

"What?" Oh, please, God, she prayed. Please don't let him try to return any of those horribly expensive things she'd decided didn't belong to her. She didn't think she could take it.

"My heart."

Her own heart crowded her throat, making it impossible to speak as he began to walk toward her. He didn't lift his gaze from hers, not even when he dropped the cow onto the sofa as he walked past it.

"I didn't admit until you left that I'd not given you the only thing that mattered to you," he said softly as he stopped with just inches remaining between them. "I didn't even know I could. All you wanted was love, and I was so damned convinced you were asking for something that didn't exist." He lifted a hand and cupped the side of her face. "I was wrong."

"How wrong?" she whispered.

"All the way wrong." He bent to touch his lips to her forehead, then straightened when she showed she would rather he didn't. "I love you, Jacqueline. It's not an empty phrase that I'm saying because I know it's the only way I can get you back. I love you with my heart and soul, and if you don't believe me now, then at least give me time to prove it to you."

"Time is something we haven't had much of," she said, then reached up to twine her hands around his neck. "I shouldn't have rushed you."

"*I'm* not the one who had trouble keeping up. Now that you have, though, I have to admit you've swept me off my feet." Before he could say anything, she added, "Perhaps we can approach the rest of our lives together at a somewhat slower pace."

A worried look crossed his brow. "You want to wait longer than July to get married?"

"Heavens no!" she exclaimed. "I would, however, like to have you all to myself for a while before we have our first child."

His shudder pulsed through her fingertips all the way to her heart. She felt his arm slip around her back and sighed as he pulled her against him.

"That's something we've not exactly discussed," he said.

"Children?"

"Mmm." He nibbled at her ear, then soothed the delicate skin with his tongue. "I don't know whether you noticed, but there were a couple of times when I failed to take precautions."

Jack nudged his head down until his lips were next to hers. "You may have swept me off my feet, darling, but my head wasn't in the clouds. I didn't worry about it because I had that base covered all along."

His laugh was deep and full of pleasure. "You could have told me that sooner, Jacqueline. It would have saved a certain amount of—"

"Delay?" she asked, then shrieked as he pinched her bottom. "I didn't say anything because I liked the challenge of seeing if I could get you to forget."

"You're a wicked woman, my love." He brushed his lips across hers, then did it a bit harder. "Do you have any more surprises for me that I should know about?"

She gave herself two seconds to think about it. "Nothing a man like you can't handle, Alex. Now, kiss me before I go mad from waiting."

He did just that, throwing all the passion and love he felt for her into a mating of their mouths that went beyond a mere kiss. His hunger for her was great, as was his need to say and hear the words that were so new and precious to him. He loved her, she loved him, and their world was complete.

Well, nearly complete. Jacqueline was trembling in his arms several minutes later when he lifted his head and said, "So where's the piano?"

"On a boat." She rested her cheek against his chest, her palm flat against his heart. "They wouldn't let me bring it on the plane. What did you do with the snooker table?"

"I didn't have time to do anything with it. There were more important things to do before I chased after you." Thus reminded, he reached into his pocket and pulled out her bracelet and ring. The latter he slipped onto her finger, but it was the string of diamonds that caught her attention.

She stared at it without touching, and he knew the moment she'd found the flaw because her eyes filled with tears and her mouth trembled with emotion. "You went to Innsbruck."

"I would have been here six hours earlier if I hadn't," he said as he fastened it around her wrist. "But I decided there were some things that were more important than time."

"But I thought you didn't mind when I hocked it."

"I didn't," he said gently, "but that was only because doing so kept you safe. I'd always planned to go back for it, though I told myself it was because that would be cheaper than buying you a new one."

She leaned back in his arms and cocked her head to

the side. "So what was the real reason you went back for it?"

"Because not only did I finally admit to loving you, I realized that I'd loved you ever since that night when I didn't know if you were stranded or hurt or too furious with me ever to speak to me again." He brushed the hair from her eyes and kissed her again before adding, "I fell in love with you that night, and didn't know it."

Her voice was shaky as she said, "If you weren't so tired, I'd say now is an excellent time to make love."

He grinned. "Tired has nothing to do with it."

EPILOGUE

Her scent was light and elusive, rainbows and lilacs, filtering into his awareness with the delicacy of a gentle summer's rain. Alex looked up from the race card and glanced around him, the fragrance fading a little as he studied the shifting crowd.

Where was she?

Beneath a brilliant September sun that seemed more Mediterranean than English, racegoers both familiar and unknown to him drifted past, their attention on the horses at the far side of the track where they were lining up for the start. He was beginning to think he'd imagined her scent when a delicate feminine hand snatched his race card and tossed it aside.

"You don't need that, Alex. There are eight horses in this race, and the only one that counts is Golden Legs." Jacqueline looked up at him, her laughing eyes daring him to disagree.

He couldn't. Sliding his arm around her shoulders, he pulled her close to his side and kissed the top of her head. "Where have you been, love? I thought you knew you were expected to make an appearance in the parade ring."

"It's the winner's circle that's really important," she retorted. "Besides, Hillary wanted to put a bet on Golden Legs, and it was the only time she could do it without Bobby catching her. I went with her."

"I thought she and Bobby put their bets down when we arrived," he said.

"She wants to win a little extra so that she can take Bobby to Le Manoir next week."

There was a clamor around them that probably meant the race had begun, but Alex decided he'd rather look at Jacqueline than watch a race that was of no real importance. "I'll have to take them myself if Golden Legs loses. I'd hate for her to miss out on Le Manoir because of a horserace."

Jacqueline's grin widened. "I've already told her you'll take us tonight, win or no win."

Alex snorted. "We should make Sam Beckett do the honors."

"I thought you agreed it wasn't his fault Golden Legs didn't like his aftershave." She rubbed her cheek against his arm in a way that always reminded him of a contented cat. "Besides, who'd have thought a horse was so sensitive to smell?"

Alex didn't comment. He was still a bit nonplussed by a solution that had presented itself in the form of a brainstorm by Bobby's lovely wife.

"If Hillary hadn't been with Laura when she bought Sam that aftershave, none of us would have thought of it." Jacqueline raised herself up on her toes to catch a glimpse of the horses as they thundered past on the first circuit. "I still think you should have thought of it first."

"Why me?" He glanced toward a far hurdle where one of the horses had thrown his jockey rather than take the jump. It wasn't Sam, but then, he hadn't expected it to be. Golden Legs had been so eager in his schooling jumps that week that it was unimaginable he would falter now.

She turned in his arm until she was facing him, totally ignoring the race as she gave Alex her full attention. "You're the one who smells rainbows, my love. With a nose like that, you should have sniffed out Golden Legs' problem long ago."

"You're too sassy for your own good." Alex clasped his hands around her waist and lifted her clean off her feet so that when their mouths met, he didn't have to take his eyes off the race.

Jacqueline was the most important thing in his life, but not even love could keep his gaze from the finish line. Unfortunately his wife had other ideas.

She wanted to watch the race too. Twisting in his grasp so that he ended up kissing the back of her head, Jacqueline hung onto his shoulder and cheered as Alex's wedding gift to her led the field past the stands in an indisputable win.

Alex turned Jacqueline in his arms and gave Golden Legs' new owner a thorough kiss before taking her hand to lead her into the winner's circle.

It was some time later that his wife slid a stack of betting tickets into his hand and said, "Tonight Le Manoir is on me."

YOU'VE READ THE BOOK.
NOW DOUBLE YOUR FUN BY ENTERING
LOVESWEPT'S TREASURED TALES III CONTEST!

Everybody loves a good romance, especially when that romance is inspired by a beloved fairy tale, legend, even a Shakespearean play. It's an entertaining challenge for the writer to create a contemporary retelling of a classic story—and for you, the reader, to find the similarities between the retold story and the classic.

For example:

- While reading STALKING THE GIANT by Victoria Leigh, did you notice that the heroine's nickname is exactly the same as the giant-slayer's in "Jack and the Beanstalk"?
- How about the fact that, like Adam and Eve, the hero and heroine in Glenna McReynold's DRAGON'S EDEN are alone in a paradise setting?
- Surely the heroine's red cape in HOT SOUTHERN NIGHTS by Patt Bucheister reminded you of the one Little Red Riding Hood wears on the way to her grandma's house.
- You couldn't have missed the heroine's rebuffing of the hero in Peggy Webb's CAN'T STOP LOVING YOU. Kate, in Shakespeare's *Taming of the Shrew*, displays the same steeliness when dealing with Petruchio.

The four TREASURED TALES III romances this month contain many, many more wonderful similarities to the classic stories they're based on. And with LOVESWEPT'S TREASURED TALES III CONTEST, you have a once-in-a-lifetime opportunity to let us know how many of these similarities you found. Even better, because this is LOVESWEPT's third year of publishing TREASURED TALES, this contest will have **three winners!**

Read the Official Rules to find out what you need to do to enter LOVESWEPT'S TREASURED TALES III CONTEST.

Now, indulge in the magic of TREASURED TALES III —and grab a chance to win some treasures of your own!

LOVESWEPT'S TREASURED TALES III CONTEST

OFFICIAL RULES:

1. *No purchase is necessary.* Enter by printing or typing your name, address, and telephone number at the top of one (or more, if necessary) piece(s) of 8½" X 11" plain white paper, if typed, or lined paper, if handwritten. Then list each of the similarities you found in one or more of the TREASURED TALES III romances to the classic story each is based on. The romances are STALKING THE GIANT by Victoria Leigh (based on "Jack and the Beanstalk"), DRAGON'S EDEN by Glenna McReynolds (based on "Adam and Eve"), HOT SOUTHERN NIGHTS by Patt Bucheister (based on "Little Red Riding Hood"), and CAN'T STOP LOVING YOU by Peggy Webb (based on *Taming of the Shrew*). Each book is available in libraries. Please be sure to list the similarities found below the title of the romance(s) read. Also, for use by the judges in case of a tie, write an essay of 150 words or less stating why you like to read LOVESWEPT romances. Once you've finished your list and your essay, mail your entry to: LOVESWEPT'S TREASURED TALES III CONTEST, Dept. BdG, Bantam Books, 1540 Broadway, New York, NY 10036.

2. PRIZES (3): All three (3) winners will receive a six (6) months' subscription to the LOVESWEPT Book Club and twenty-one (21) autographed books. Each winner will also be featured in a one-page profile that will appear in the back of Bantam Books' LOVESWEPT'S TREASURED TALES IV romances, scheduled for publication in February 1996. (Approximate retail value: $200.00)

3. Contest entries must be postmarked and received by March 31, 1995, and all entrants must be 21 or older on the date of entry. The author of each romance featured in LOVESWEPT'S TREASURED TALES III has provided a list of the similarities between her romance and the classic story it is based on. Entrants need not read all four TREASURED TALES III romances to enter, but the more they read, the more similarities they are likely to find. The entries submitted will be judged by members of the LOVESWEPT Editorial Staff, who will first count up the number of similarities each entrant identified, then compare the similarities found by the entrants who identified the most with the similarities listed by the author of the romance or romances read by those entrants and select the three entrants who correctly identified the greatest number of similarities. If more than three entrants correctly identify the greatest number, the judges will read the essays submitted by each potential winner in order to break the tie and select the entrants who submitted the best essays as the prize winners. The essays will be judged on the basis of the originality, creativity, thoughtfulness, and writing ability shown. All of the judges' decisions are final and binding. All essays must be original. Entries become the property of Bantam Books and will not be returned. Bantam Books is not responsible for incomplete or lost or misdirected entries.

4. Winners will be notified by mail on or about June 15, 1995. Winners have 30 days from the date of notice in which to claim their prize or an alternate winner will be chosen. Odds of winning are dependent on the number of entries received. Prizes are non-transferable and no substitutions are allowed. Winners may be required to execute an Affidavit Of Eligibility And Promotional Release supplied by Bantam Books and will need to supply a photograph of themselves for inclusion in the one-page profile of each winner. Entering the Contest constitutes permission for use of the winner's name, address (city and state), photograph, biographical profile, and Contest essay for publicity and promotional purposes, with no additional compensation.

5. Employees of Bantam Books, Bantam Doubleday Dell Publishing Group, Inc., their subsidiaries and affiliates, and their immediate family members are not eligible to enter. This Contest is open to residents of the U.S. and Canada, excluding the Province of Quebec, and is void wherever prohibited or restricted by law. Taxes, if any, are the winner's sole responsibility.

6. For a list of the winners, send a self-addressed, stamped envelope entirely separate from your entry to LOVESWEPT'S TREASURED TALES III CONTEST WINNERS LIST, Dept. BdG, Bantam Books, 1540 Broadway, New York, NY 10036. The list will be available after August 1, 1995.

THE EDITOR'S CORNER

With March comes gray, rainy days and long, cold nights, but here at LOVESWEPT things are really heating up! The four terrific romances we have in store for you are full of emotion, humor, and passion, with sexy heroes and dazzling heroines you'll never forget. So get ready to treat yourself with next month's LOVESWEPTS—they'll definitely put you in the mood for spring.

Starting things off is the delightfully unique Olivia Rupprecht with **PISTOL IN HIS POCKET**, LOVESWEPT #730. Lori Morgan might dare to believe in a miracle, that a man trapped for decades in a glacier can be revived, but she knows she has no business falling in love with the rough-hewn hunk! Yet when Noble Zhivago draws a breath in her bathtub, she feels reckless enough to respond to the dark stranger who seizes her lips and pulls her into the water. Wooed with passion and purpose by a magnificent warrior who tantalizes her senses, Lori must admit to adoring a man with a dangerous past. Olivia delivers both sizzling sensuality and heartbreaking emotion in this uninhibited romp.

The wonderfully talented Janis Reams Hudson's hero is **CAUGHT IN THE ACT**, LOVESWEPT #731. Betrayed, bleeding, and on the run, Trace Youngblood needs a hiding place—but will Lillian Roberts be his downfall, or his deliverance? The feisty teacher probably believes he is guilty as sin, but he needs her help to clear his name. Drawn to the rugged agent who embodies her secret yearnings, Lillian trusts him with her life, but is afraid she won't escape with her heart. Funny and wild, playful and explosive, smart and sexy, this is definitely another winner from Janis.

Rising star Donna Kauffman offers a captivating heart-stopper with **WILD RAIN**, LOVESWEPT #732. Jillian Bonner insists she isn't leaving, no matter how fierce the tempest headed her way, but Reese Braedon has a job to do—even if it means tossing the sweet spitfire over his shoulder and carrying her off! When the storm traps them together, the sparks that flash between them threaten spontaneous combustion. But once he brands her with the fire of his deepest need, she might never let him go. With a hero as wild and unpredictable as a hurricane, and a heroine who matches him in courage, will, and humor, Donna delivers a tale of outlaws who'd risk anything for passion—and each other.

Last, but never least, is the ever-popular Judy Gill with **SIREN SONG**, LOVESWEPT #733. Returning after fifteen years to the isolated beach where orca whales come to play, Don Jacobs once more feels seduced—by the place, and by memories of a young girl who'd offered him her innocence, a gift he'd hungered for but had to refuse. Tracy Maxwell still bewitches him, but is this beguiling woman of secrets finally free to surrender her heart? This evocative story explores the sweet mystery of longing and passion as only Judy Gill can.

Happy reading!

With warmest wishes,

Beth de Guzman

Senior Editor

P.S. Don't miss the women's novels coming your way in March: **NIGHT SINS**, the first Bantam hardcover by bestselling author Tami Hoag is an electrifying, heart-pounding tale of romantic suspense; **THE FOREVER TREE** by Rosanne Bittner is an epic, romantic saga of California and the courageous men and women who built their dreams out of redwood timber in the bestselling western tradition of Louis L'Amour; **MY GUARDIAN ANGEL** is an enchanting collection of romantic stories featuring a "guardian angel" theme from some of Bantam's finest romance authors, including Kay Hooper, Elizabeth Thornton, Susan Krinard, and Sandra Chastain; **PAGAN BRIDE** by Tamara Leigh is a wonderful historical romance in the bestselling tradition of Julie Garwood and Teresa Medeiros. We'll be giving you a sneak peek at these terrific books in next month's LOVESWEPTs. And immediately following this page, look for a preview of the exciting romances from Bantam that are *available now!*

Don't miss these irresistible books by
your favorite Bantam authors

On sale in January:

VALENTINE
by Jane Feather

*PRINCE OF
DREAMS*
by Susan Krinard

FIRST LOVES
by Jean Stone

From the beguiling, bestselling author of *Vixen* and *Velvet* comes a tale brimming with intrigue and passion

VALENTINE
BY
Jane Feather

"An author to treasure."
—*Romantic Times*

A quirk of fate has made Sylvester Gilbraith the heir of his sworn enemy, the earl of Stoneridge. But there's a catch: to claim his inheritance he has to marry one of the earl's four granddaughters. The magnetically handsome nobleman has no choice but to comply with the terms of the will, yet when he descends on Stoneridge Manor prepared to charm his way into a fortune, he finds that the lady who intrigues him most has no intention of becoming his bride. Maddeningly beautiful and utterly impossible, Theodora Belmont refuses to admit to the chemistry between them, even when she's passionately locked in his embrace. Yet soon the day will come when the raven-haired vixen will give anything to be Sylvester's bride and risk everything to defend his honor . . . and his life.

"You take one step closer, my lord, and you'll go down those stairs on your back," Theo said. "And with any luck you'll break your neck in the process."

Sylvester shook his head. "I don't deny your skill, but mine is as good, and I have the advantage of size and strength." He saw the acknowledgment leap into her eyes, but her position didn't change.

"Let's have done with this," he said sharply. "I'm prepared to forget that silly business by the stream."

"Oh, are you, my lord? How very generous of you. As I recall, you were not the one insulted."

"As I recall, you, cousin, were making game of me. Now, come downstairs. I wish you to ride around the estate with me."

"You wish me to do *what*?" Theo stared at him, her eyes incredulous.

"I understand from your mother that you've had the management of the estate for the last three years," he said impatiently, as if his request were the most natural imaginable. "You're the obvious person to show me around."

"You have windmills in your head, sir. I wouldn't give you the time of day!" Theo swung on her heel and made to continue up the stairs.

"You rag-mannered hoyden!" Sylvester exclaimed. "We may have started on the wrong foot, but there's no excuse for such incivility." He sprang after her, catching her around the waist.

She spun, one leg flashing in a high kick aimed at his chest, but as he'd warned her, this time he was ready for her. Twisting, he caught her body across his thighs, swinging a leg over hers, clamping them in a scissors grip between his knees.

"Now, yield!" he gritted through his teeth, adjusting his grip against the sinuous working of her muscles as she fought to free herself.

Theo went suddenly still, her body limp against him. Instinctively he relaxed his grip and the next instant she was free, bounding up the next flight of stairs.

Sylvester went after her, no longer capable of cool

reasoning. A primitive battle was raging and he knew only that he wasn't going to lose it. No matter that it was undignified and totally inappropriate.

Theo raced down the long corridor, hearing his booted feet pounding behind her in time with her thundering heart. She didn't know whether her heart was speeding with fear or exhilaration; she didn't seem capable of rational, coherent thought.

His breath was on the back of her neck as she wrenched open the door of her bedroom and leaped inside, but his foot went in the gap as she tried to slam the door shut. She leaned on the door with all her weight, but Sylvester put his shoulder against the outside and heaved. Theo went reeling into the room and the door swung wide.

Sylvester stepped inside, kicking the door shut behind him.

"Very well," Theo said breathlessly. "If you wish it, I'll apologize for being uncivil. I shouldn't have said what I did just now."

"For once we're in agreement," he remarked, coming toward her. Theo cast a wild look around the room. In a minute she was going to be backed up against the armoire and she didn't have too many tricks left.

Sylvester reached out and seized the long, thick rope of hair hanging down her back. He twisted it around his wrist, reeling her in like a fish until her face was on a level with his shoulder.

He examined her countenance as if he was seeing it for the first time. Her eyes had darkened and he could read the sparking challenge in their depths; a flush of exertion and emotion lay beneath the golden brown of her complexion and her lips were slightly parted, as if she was about to launch into another of her tirades.

To prevent such a thing, he tightened his grip on her plait, bringing her face hard against his shoulder, and kissed her.

Theo was so startled that she forgot about resistance for a split second, and in that second discovered that she was enjoying the sensation. Her lips parted beneath the probing thrust of his tongue and her own tongue touched his, at first tentatively, then with increasing confidence. She inhaled the scent of his skin, a sun-warmed earthy smell that was new to her. His mouth tasted of wine. His body was hard-muscled against her own, and when she stirred slightly she became startlingly aware of a stiffness in his loins. Instinctively she pressed her lower body against his.

Sylvester drew back abruptly, his eyes hooded as he looked down into her intent face. "I'll be damned," he muttered. "How many men have you kissed?"

"None," she said truthfully. Her anger had vanished completely, surprise and curiosity in its place. She wasn't even sure whether she still disliked him.

"I'll be damned," he said again, a slight smile tugging at the corners of his mouth, little glints of amusement sparking in the gray eyes. "I doubt you'll be a restful wife, cousin, but I'll lay odds you'll be full of surprises."

Theo remembered that she *did* dislike him . . . intensely. She twitched her plait out of his slackened grip and stepped back. "I fail to see what business that is of yours, Lord Stoneridge."

"Ah, yes, I was forgetting we haven't discussed this as yet," he said, folding his arms, regarding her with deepening amusement. "We're going to be married, you and I."

PRINCE OF DREAMS
BY
Susan Krinard

San Francisco psychologist Diana Ransom can't take her eyes off the gorgeous, green-eyed stranger. But when she finally approaches him across the smoke-filled room, her reasons have little to do with the treacherous feelings he inspires. Diana suspects that this brooding, enigmatic man is responsible for the disappearance of her young cousin. Desperate to find her, and determined to plumb the mystery behind Nicholas Gale's hypnotic charm, Diana will follow him into the velvety darkness . . . and awake to a haunting passion. For Nicholas is no mere human, but a vampire with the power to steal into a woman's dreams and fill her nights with untold rapture. And soon, blinded by an ecstasy sweeter than any she's ever known, Diana will find herself risking her eternal soul for a love that promises to be forever. . . .

For a moment the woman across the table was no more than a jumble of colors and heat and flaring life force. Nicholas struggled to focus on her face, on her stubborn, intelligent eyes.

He said the first thing that came into his head. "Do you have a first name, Dr. Ransom?"

She blinked at him, caught off guard and resentful of it. "I don't see what that has to do with Keely or where she is, Mr. Gale. That's all I'm interested in at the moment. If you—"

"Then we're back to where we started, Dr. Ransom. As it happens, I share your concern for Keely." He lost his train of thought for a moment, looking at the woman with her brittle control and overwhelming aura. He could almost hear the singing of her life force in the three feet of space between them.

He nearly reached out to touch her. Just to see what she would feel like, if that psychic energy would flow into him with so simple a joining.

He stopped his hand halfway across the table and clenched it carefully. She had never seen him move.

"What *is* your business, Mr. Gale?" she asked. The antagonism in her voice had grown muted, and there was a flicker of uncertainty in her eyes.

"I have many varied . . . interests," he said honestly. He smiled, and for a moment he loosed a tiny part of his hunter's power.

She stared at him and lifted a small hand to run her fingers through her short brown hair, effectively disordering the loose curls. That simple act affected Nicholas with unexpected power. He felt his groin tighten, a physical response he had learned to control and ignore long ago.

When was the last time? he asked himself. The last time he had lain with a woman, joined with her physically, taken some part of what he needed in the act of love?

Before he could blunt the thought, his imagination slipped its bonds, conjuring up an image of this woman, her aura ablaze, naked and willing and fully conscious beneath him. Knowing what he was, giving and receiving without fear. . . .

"Diana."

"What?" Reality ripped through Nicholas, dispelling the erotic, impossible vision.

"My first name is Diana," she murmured.

Her face was flushed, as if she had seen the lust in his eyes. She was an attractive woman. Mortal men would pursue her, even blind to her aura as they must be. Did she look at him and observe only another predictable male response to be dissected with an analyst's detachment?

His hungers were not so simple. He would have given the world to make them so.

"Diana," he repeated softly. "Huntress, and goddess of the moon."

She wet her lips. "It's getting late, Mr. Gale—"

"*My* first name is Nicholas."

"Nicholas," she echoed, as if by rote. "I'll be making a few more inquiries about Keely. If you were serious about being concerned for her—"

"I was."

Diana twisted around in her chair and lifted a small, neat purse. "Here," she said, slipping a card from a silver case. "This is where you can reach me if you should hear from her."

Nicholas took the card and examined the utilitarian printing. *Diana Ransom, Ph.D. Licensed Psychologist. Individual psychotherapy. Treatment of depression, anxiety, phobias, and related sleep disorders.*

Sleep disorders. Nicholas almost smiled at the irony of it. She could never cure his particular disorder. He looked up at her. "If you need to talk to me again, I'm here most nights."

"Then you don't plan to leave town in the next few days?" she asked with a touch of her former hostility.

His gaze was steady. "No, Diana. I'll make a few inquiries of my own."

They stared at each other. *Diana.* Was she a child of the night, as her name implied? Did she dream vivid dreams that he could enter as he could never enter her body? Or was she part of the sane and solid world of daylight, oblivious to the untapped power that sang in her aura like a beacon in darkness?

She was the first to look away. Hitching the strap of her purse higher on her shoulder, she rose. "Then I'll be going." She hesitated, slanting a look back at him with narrowed blue eyes. "Perhaps we'll see each other again . . . Nicholas."

He watched her walk away and up the stairs. Her words had held a warning. No promise, no hint of flirtation. With even a little effort he could have won her over. He could have learned more about her, perhaps enough to determine if she would be a suitable candidate to serve his needs. One glimpse of her aura was enough to tempt him almost beyond reason.

But she had affected him too deeply. He could not afford even the slightest loss of control with his dreamers. Emotional detachment was a matter of survival—his and that of the women he touched by night.

Diana Ransom was something almost beyond his experience—.

Although he would never sample the promise behind Diana Ransom's unremarkable façade, would never slip into her dreams and skim the abundance of energy that burned beneath her skin. . . .

As he had done a thousand times before, Nicholas schooled himself to detachment and consigned hope and memory to their familiar prisons. If he arranged matters correctly, he need never see Diana Ransom again.

What if you could go back and rediscover
the magic . . . ?

FIRST LOVES
BY
Jean Stone

*For every woman there is a first love, the love she never
forgets. You always wonder what would have happened,
what might have been. Here is a novel of three women
with the courage to go back . . . but could they recover
the magic they left behind?*

"Men," Alissa said. "They really are scum, you
know."

"Maybe it's partly our fault," Meg replied quietly.

"Are you nuts?" Alissa asked. "Besides, how
would you know? You're not even married." She took
a sip of wine. "Bet you have a boyfriend, though.
Some equally successful power attorney, perhaps? Or
maybe that private investigator? What was his
name?"

"His name is Danny. And no, he's only a friend. A
good friend. But right now, there's no one special in
my life."

Alissa set down her glass. "See? If someone as
beautiful and clever and smart as you doesn't have a
boyfriend, it proves they're all scum. I rest my case."

Though she knew Alissa's words could be considered a compliment, Meg suddenly found old feelings
resurfacing, the feelings of being the kid with no fa-

ther, the one who was different, inadequate. "I've had a lot of boyfriends—men friends," she stuttered.

"But how about relationships?" Alissa pressed. "*Real* relationships?"

In her mind Meg saw his face, his eyes, his lips. She felt his touch. "Once," she replied quietly, "a long time ago."

Alissa leaned back in her chair. "Yeah, I guess you could say I had one once, too. But it sure as shit wasn't with my husband. It was before him." She drained her glass and poured another. "God, it was good."

Meg was relieved to have the focus of the conversation off herself. "What happened?"

"His name was Jay. Jay Stockwell. Our parents had summer homes next to each other."

"You were childhood sweethearts?" Zoe asked, then added wistfully, "I think they're the best. Everyone involved is so innocent."

Alissa shook her head. "This wasn't innocence. It was love. Real love."

They grew quiet. Meg thought of Steven Riley, about their affair. That was love. Real love. But it was years ago. A lifetime ago.

The waiter arrived and set their dinners on the red paper placemats. Meg stared at the cheeseburger. Suddenly she had no appetite.

After he left, Zoe spoke. "What is real love, anyway? How do you know? William took good care of me and of Scott. But I can't honestly say I loved him. Not like I'd loved the boy back home."

"Ah," Alissa said, "the boy back home. For me, that was Jay. The trouble was, he didn't want to stay home. He had things to do, a world to save."

"Where did he go?"

Meg was glad Zoe was keeping Alissa talking. She

could feel herself sliding into the lonely depression of thoughts of Steven. She could feel her walls closing around her, her need to escape into herself. For some reason she thought about the cat she'd had then—a gray tiger named Socrates. For the longest time after Steven was gone she'd closed Socrates out of her bedroom. She'd not been able to stand hearing him purr; the sound was too close to the soft snores of Steven beside her, at peace in his slumber after their love-making.

"First, Jay went to San Francisco," Alissa was saying, and Meg snapped back to the present. "It was in the early seventies. He'd been deferred from the draft. From Vietnam."

"Was he sick?" Zoe asked.

"No," Alissa said. "He was rich. Rich boys didn't have to go. Jay's family owned—and still do—a mega-broadcast conglomerate. TV stations. Radio stations. All over the country. Jay loved broadcasting, but not business. He was a born journalist." She pushed the plate with her untouched cheeseburger and fries aside. "When he went to San Francisco, he gave his family the finger."

"And you never saw him again?" Zoe asked.

Alissa laughed. "Never saw him again? Darling," she said, as she took another sip of wine, "I went with him."

"You went with him?" Even Meg was surprised at this. She couldn't picture Alissa following anyone, anywhere.

"I was eighteen. Love seemed more important than trust funds or appearances or social standing."

"So what happened?" Zoe asked.

She shrugged. "I realized I was wrong."

The women were quiet. Meg felt sorry for Alissa. Something in the eyes of this tiny, busy, aggressive little blonde now spelled sorrow. Sorrow for a life gone by. Sorrow for love relinquished. She knew the feeling only too well.

"God, he was handsome," Alissa said. "He still is."

"Still is?" Zoe asked. "You mean you still see him?"

Alissa shook her head. "I left him standing at the corner of Haight and Ashbury. It seemed appropriate at the time. He was working for one of those liberal underground newspapers. I went home to Atlanta, married Robert, had the kids. Then one day I turned on the TV and there he was. Reporting from Cairo."

"So he went back into broadcasting," Zoe said.

"Full steam ahead, apparently. Delivering stories on the oppressed peoples of the world. Over the years I've seen him standing against backdrops in Lebanon, Ethiopia, Iraq, you name it. He was on the air for days during that Tiananmen Square thing in China or wherever that is."

"Oh," Zoe said, "Jay Stockwell. Sure. I've seen him, too. His stories have real sensitivity."

Alissa shrugged. "I never paid much attention to his stories. I was too busy looking at him. Wondering."

Zoe picked at her scallops, then set down her fork. "Wondering what would have happened if you'd stayed together?"

"Sure. Haven't you ever done that? Wondered about your boy back home?"

"You mean, the man I could have married?" Zoe asked.

"Or should have," Alissa said.

Should have, Meg thought. Should I have? Could I have?

"Sure I've wondered about him," Zoe said. "All the time."

"What about you, Meg? What about your one and only? Don't you ever wonder how your life would have been different. How it would have been better?"

Meg silently wished she could say, "No. My life wouldn't have been better. It would have been worse. And besides, my life is just fine the way it is." But she couldn't seem to say anything. She couldn't seem to lie.

There was silence around the table. Meg looked at Zoe, who was watching Alissa. Meg turned to Alissa, just in time to see her quickly wipe a lone tear from her cheek. Alissa caught Meg's eye and quickly cleared her throat. Then she raised her glass toward them both. "I think we should find them," Alissa said. "I think we should find the men we once loved, and show them what they've missed."